The Winds of

2025

The Winds of Change

JOAN FALLON

THE WINDS OF CHANGE

SCOTT PUBLISHING
(ESPAÑA)

To David and Sarah

Joan Fallon

with best wishes

The Scottish novelist Joan Fallon, currently lives and works in the south of Spain. She writes contemporary, historical and crime fiction and almost all her books have a strong female protagonist. She is the author of:

FICTION:
Spanish Lavender
The House on the Beach
Loving Harry
Santiago Tales
The Only Blue Door
Palette of Secrets
The Thread That Binds Us
Love Is All
The al-Andalus series:
The Shining City (Book 1)
The Eye of the Falcon (Book 2)
The Ring of Flames (Book 3)
The City of Dreams series:
The Apothecary (Book 1)
The Pirate (Book 2)
The Prisoner (Book 3)
The Jacaranda Dunne Mysteries:
Sophie is Still Missing
Dark Heart
Strawberry Moon

NON-FICTION:
Daughters of Spain

(Available in paperback, audiobooks and as ebooks)

THE WINDS OF CHANGE

Joan Fallon

ISBN 978-84-09-52121-0
First published in 2023
Scott Publishing
España

ACKNOWLEDGMENTS

My sincere thanks to my editor Sara Starbuck for editing this book, to Angela Hagenow for proof reading the manuscript and to Rachel Lawston for the stunning cover. Their advice and support have, as always, been invaluable.

"Ms Fallon has the talented ability to bring her fictional characters to life; you are there with them, discretely observing what they do and say - wishing you could join in with their conversations, and become an integrated part of this vigorous story."
Helen Hollick author https://helenhollick.net/

Joan Fallon brings us a revealing portrayal of life in pre-civil war Spain. This is an evocative tale of the hardships endured by the very poorest and the injustices they suffered at the hands of those in positions of power and influence. Susan Carew author https://susancarew.com/

THE WINDS OF CHANGE

SOUTHERN SPAIN AUTUMN 1935

CHAPTER 1

Hugo is bored. He stands by the open windows of the lounge which overlook the grounds of the *cortijo*. It is the perfect evening for a ride.

'Things have to change,' his friend declares, following his gaze out of the window. 'Do you know how the land in our country is divided up?' Cristóbal does not wait for an answer, but continues, 'Well I'll tell you.'

Hugo continues to stare at the view; the sun is sinking lower and casting long shadows across the immaculate lawns. Beyond, and stretching as far as the horizon, rows and rows of perfectly straight vines are tinged a reddish brown by the sun's dying rays. It is a familiar sight; Hugo was born here, in this house. He has never lived anywhere else and would never want to; this is his home. Cristóbal knows full well that Hugo is not interested in politics, but it makes no difference; he will have his say no matter what. He seems to think it is his duty, as his oldest friend, to educate him in these things. Hugo listens with half an ear as Cristóbal continues, 'One per cent of the population of Andalusia owns more than forty per cent of all the fertile land. One per cent and they don't even cultivate half of it. Much is just left for hunting and produces nothing of value. Good fertile soil going to waste. That's a crime.'

'Pleasure is valuable too,' mutters Hugo, but his friend does not respond; he is too caught up in his own train of thought.

'One day that will change,' he announces as though Hugo has not spoken. 'It has to. One day people will wake up and ask themselves why? Why are they condemned to poverty in a land as rich and fertile as ours? Why can't a man earn an honest living in the country where he was born? Why do his children have to die from malnutrition and sickness?'

Cristóbal's head is full of lofty thoughts and ideals. He is training to be a doctor, and Hugo knows that some of the cases he has seen have been distressful, but pontificating on his political ideals is not going to change anything. Things are as they are.

His friend continues, 'Tell me Hugo, why is there so much hatred in the world?' He turns and looks at him. 'I'm warning you my friend, the wind of change is blowing and very soon it will become a hurricane. You and your rich friends need to wake up.'

Hugo says nothing, just smiles at him. Cristóbal's face is flushed with passion and he pulls at the neck of his immaculate white shirt as if it were strangling him. A gold ring on his left hand glints in the sun. 'I hope you include yourself among my rich friends,' Hugo says with more than a hint of sarcasm. 'Anyway, in my opinion, we have already had too many changes since the king was deposed; first we had two years of radical social change from the centre-left party, now the centre-right party is in power and has immediately overturned the previous legislation. What we need is not change, but stability.' Personally, he cannot care less. He is not interested in politics; there always seems to be too much talking and too little action from the politicians he has come across. Nobody wants to do anything except spout their own opinions, but he is not going to say that to Cristóbal because it will only encourage him to continue doing just that. He is the same as the rest of them; he gets excited over the injustice, as he sees it, but what does he do to rectify things for the workers? Nothing. When he is not studying, he is always too busy with his real passions, horses and hunting.

'And now we have members of this Falange party strutting about in their blue shirts and waving their manifestos like fans,' Cristóbal continues in the same vein; he is warming to his subject. Hugo yawns. It is possible he will go on like this until dinner time.

'How about a walk around the stables? Father bought a new mare last month. She really is a beauty, a Retuerta. I've been looking for a chance to take her out.'

At last his friend stops pontificating and turns to look at him. Finally he has Cristóbal's attention. 'A Retuerta? You don't say. From Doñana?' he asks.

'Yes. Where else?'

'What a good idea. I could do with some fresh air, and it's a beautiful evening for a ride.' Politics forgotten, Cristóbal stands up and puts on his jacket.

'Enrique says there's a lynx in the woods with some kittens. If we're lucky we might flush her out and get the chance to take a pop at her.'

Cristóbal follows Hugo out onto the patio, a wide paved area encircled by marble pillars and potted palms, and shaded by a semi-circle of cypress trees. They take a shortcut to the stables across the beautifully manicured lawns. 'You are so lucky to live here,' he tells Hugo, breathing in the evening air, heavy with the scent of the many plants that border the garden. This is a working vineyard, but Hugo's mother loves her garden so insists that all the land immediately around the house is taken over with ornamental trees and plants. Beyond the acres of chalky white soil that is the life blood of the vineyard lie kilometres of woods and scrubland. That is just what he was talking about earlier; if Don Luis was so inclined he could cultivate the land and produce more wine, but he prefers to leave it wild and use it for hunting. All the landowners are the same; it is a question of status for them to have extensive woods for hunting. Cristóbal has heard his father, who is Don Luis's lawyer and knows everything about the estate, tell his secretary that there is as much land lying idle on the Butler & Rodriquez estate as there is cultivated.

'Why so serious?' asks Hugo. 'I thought you wanted to relax?'

'It's nothing. Just a twinge of conscience. I have exams next week.' He knows that if he mentions the hunting land, Hugo will be offended and he does not want to ruin what promises to be an enjoyable evening.

'Look there's Pablo now.' The chief groom walks towards them, leading a rather lively mare. '*Buenas tardes*, Pablo,' Hugo shouts. 'Thought we'd take out the new mare. How's she settling in?'

'She's a real beauty and as gentle as a lamb. Mind you, once she gets going, she can really go. I'll get her for you. And for Señor Cristóbal?'

'Yes, one with some high spirits, I think. We thought we'd have a look for the lynx while we're out there.'

'Oh aye.' He looks at the sky. 'You're a bit early for that, *Señor*. She's a wary creature, the lynx; she likes to wait until it's dark.'

'Is that her, your new mare?' asks Cristóbal, who is looking nervously at the horse that Pablo is trying to encourage into its stable.

'No, of course not. That's a mare that Pablo is training for Mama. She's a nice enough filly but she's not a Retuerta. You'll see the difference in a minute.' They wait and watch as the grooms move around the stables completing their evening duties. 'As you are so fond of horses, why don't you have any of your own?' Hugo asks.

'I'd love to but as you know we live in the city. It's not really possible. My father keeps an old mare in the stable attached to his offices, but only people with very large houses can manage to stable horses in Seville these days.' He casts a wistful look at the extensive row of stables before him; there is a horse in every one of them and at the moment they all have their heads out and are watching the two men. 'But I have thought about it. Maybe I'll have another word with Papa; he may know someone who would let me stable it with theirs.'

'You should. A man needs to get some exercise. I'm sure one of his wealthy clients would find room for such a magnificent horse as a Retuerta.' Hugo begins to pace up and down the yard. 'What's keeping that man? Doesn't he realise we need to get back in time for dinner?'

'I think that's him, now,' says Cristóbal, as Pablo reappears, leading two horses by the reins. It is instantly apparent which is the Retuerta; her glossy brown coat gleams in the sunlight and she looks straight at them and shakes her long black mane, very assure of her position. 'She's beautiful,' Hugo murmurs, going straight up to her and stroking her prominent Roman nose. 'That's what I will name her, Beauty.'

'She is indeed a beauty,' says Pablo. 'She's fiery but manageable. I've seen some Retuertas before, impossible to tame, but this one is different. Someone has done a good job with her.' He hands the reins to Hugo. 'Take it easy at first, *Señor*. Let her get used to you.'

13

'I take it this one's for me, is it?' asks Cristóbal, looking at the rather docile mare standing next to the Retuerta. He feels disappointed.

'Like I said, you should buy your own horse,' says Hugo, leaping into the saddle and heading for the gate. 'Come on. I'll race you.'

Dinner is a leisurely meal and they are joined in the dining room by Hugo's father, Don Luis, his mother, Doña Isabel, his brother Felipe and his sister-in-law Beatrice.

'Cristóbal, how nice to see you again,' says Don Luis. 'How is your father? Well, I hope. Seeing you has reminded me that I must talk to him soon. I have some urgent business that has to be taken care of and before I do anything about it, I want his advice.'

Before Cristóbal can reply, Felipe interrupts. 'What sort of business, Papa? You haven't mentioned anything to me?' He scowls at his father.

'It's nothing for you to worry about. Just something I want to speak to Benito about.'

'But you just said it was urgent.'

'Leave it, Felipe. I told you it's nothing to do with you.'

It looks as though Felipe is about to get up and leave the table, but just then the soup arrives, and good manners or hunger dissuades him.

'I'll let him know, *Señor*,' says Cristóbal, avoiding Felipe's angry eyes. 'Will you come to his office?'

'What a good idea,' Doña Isabel breaks in. 'I'm dying to go to Seville. It's ages since I did any shopping. There are so many things I need to buy and I can go to the shops while you and Benito discuss business. Then you can buy us all a lovely lunch at Mario's.'

Cristóbal can see that she has caught her husband off guard. At first he looks annoyed but then he musters up a smile and says, 'Of course, my dear. If that's what you would like to do, then we will do it.' He turns to Cristóbal. 'My wife seems to think I have unlimited time and unlimited money. Mario's indeed. Please tell your father I will be at his office on Friday at twelve midday. I hope that is convenient for him,' he adds.

'I would think so. He never has any appointments in court on a Friday and I'm sure he would make time for you anyway, Don Luis.' He knows his father will kill him if he says anything to upset one of his most important clients. 'I will ring him this evening.'

'So, Hugo, has that latest shipment gone to the docks, yet?' Don Luis asks, turning his attention to his youngest son.

'Tomorrow morning, Papa.'

'Why the delay? The order was completed yesterday,' snaps Felipe. 'If you would get on with your work instead of spending all day down at the stables, this place might not be losing money.'

'In case you haven't noticed, we have a guest staying with us. What would you have me do, leave him to sit twiddling his thumbs while I complete order forms?' says Hugo, only slightly irritated. He is used to his brother finding fault with everything he does and most of the time he just ignores him.

'What about the new distributer you found in Bristol?' asks his father.

'I'm going to England to talk to him next week.'

'Good. Very good. Well, Cristóbal, did you see our new acquisition when you were looking around the stables?' asks Don Luis.

'The new mare? Yes, she is stunning. I have to admit that I am very envious,' says Cristóbal.

'You should see them in the wild; they are spectacular.' Don Luis pauses while the servants clear away the soup plates. 'Get Hugo to take you down to Doñana to see for yourself. I guarantee you won't want any other horse after you've ridden one of them.'

'Now you're exaggerating, Papa,' says Felipe. 'They're nice enough horses but in my mind nothing can beat the Arabian.'

The talk turns to horse breeding until the servants return with roast duck and a platter of mixed vegetables.

'Yes, get Hugo to take you down there,' Don Luis repeats. 'He knows the place well. When he was a boy he often went there with our old groom, Felix, Loved it down there.'

'Where is that exactly, *Señor*?' Cristóbal asks.

'The Coto de Doñana. Brilliant hunting reserve. They've got everything there: wild pigs, foxes, deer and every kind of bird imaginable. Used to belong to the Duke of Medina Sidonia in the old days but then it was bought by William Garvey, a good friend of mine. He was in the same business as us. Mind you, his sherry was not as good as ours, but he did all right from it.' He lifts his glass and studies the golden liquid before drinking it down slowly.

'He must have done, Papa, if he could afford to buy the hunting reserve. Anyway, it's been sold again. They say his business was not doing as well as he'd hoped, so he sold the hunting land to the Marchioness of Borghetto, so that he could reinvest the money in his sherry company. I expect you know the new owner as well,' says Felipe, sarcastically.

'Not personally, but I do know her husband.' Don Luis ignores his elder son and motions for the servant to pour him some sherry, then adds, 'She is, of course, William Garvey's niece.'

'So it's still in the family,' Cristóbal comments politely as he helps himself to some more roast duck. These names mean little to him. He looks across at Hugo; he can't stop thinking about how lucky his friend is to have his own horse. 'What about it then? Shall we go down there next week, before you disappear off to England for months?'

'You mean to buy one?'

'It's worth having a look, isn't it?'

'Well, I suppose we ought to if you're that keen. But where are you going to stable it?'

'He can stable it here, with ours, at least until he qualifies and knows where he is going to have his doctor's practice. We have plenty of room,' says Don Luis, deliberately avoiding his elder son's angry gaze.

'When do you complete your training, Cristóbal?' asks Hugo's mother. 'It must be soon, I would think.' She smiles at him as she delicately puts a grape in her mouth.

Doña Isabel is a very elegant woman, slim and beautifully dressed in the latest fashion; she is quite unlike his own mother who is what his father refers to as a comfortable shape. 'Next year,' he replies. 'But I may go to America for a year when I finish. I have been invited to stay with an old friend of my father's; he's a doctor in New York.' He can feel Hugo's eyes on him.

'You never said anything about America,' says Hugo. He looks surprised and maybe even a little disappointed.

'Well, I haven't decided yet. It may never happen. I have to pass my exams first.'

'Lucky boy. How lovely to travel. I have never even been to England, although as you know, we have business interests in that country,' says Doña Isabel, casting a discontented look at her husband.

'I never imagined you would want to go there, *Cariño*,' says her husband. 'It's a cold, wet place. I'm not sure you would enjoy it, but if you insist, you can accompany Hugo when he goes to talk to our new distributor next week.'

'Papa.' Hugo looks horrified at this suggestion and both his mother and father burst out laughing. 'I don't find that very funny,' he adds when he realises that it is a joke.

'Frightened you might have to actually do some work?' whispers Felipe so his father cannot hear him.

'Leave me alone. What I do is nothing to do with you,' Hugo hisses back.

'What about going to Doñana tomorrow, Hugo? I can manage another day before Papa notices that I'm not at home studying,' Cristóbal says. He cannot get the image of the Retuerta out of his head even though he knows it is an extravagance. With the country in such disarray, now is not really the moment to be buying an expensive horse, even if he can keep it in the stables at the vineyard. If he waits until Hugo gets back from England he may have changed his mind, and he doesn't want to do that. He is consumed with the desire to own such a lovely creature, and as Hugo often tells him, every gentleman should have a good horse for hunting.

'Well it would make sense. You're staying tonight, aren't you?'

Cristóbal nods. 'If that's all right with everyone?' he asks, looking at Doña Isabel.

'Of course. Sounds an excellent idea,' says Don Luis. 'And as you're going there anyway, you can take something for me. I still owe Vano for that colt we have. You can pay him.'

'But you bought him months ago, Papa.'

'I know, but Vano doesn't mind. He knows I will pay him in the end.'

'Well, in that case, I think we should make an early start tomorrow morning,' says Hugo. He smirks at his brother. 'You can manage without me for a few hours, Felipe?' His brother scowls at him in return and looks as though he will choke on the brandy he is drinking.

CHAPTER 2

Vano is a proud man and he knows it, although the only one who dares say this to his face is Father Sanchez, and only then in the privacy of the confessional. Pride is a mortal sin. How many times has he heard that, but he does not agree. He is respected within his clan; he is the brother of the patriarch, after all. If they show him disrespect it is the same as being disrespectful to the patriarch, he tells himself. Even the *payos* show him respect because they admire him for the skill he has with the wild horses that roam the pine forests and graze on the waterlogged fields. He has good reason to feel proud.

Vano works hard for his family. He is the father of eight children who fear and respect him as any good child should— and there would be more if God had not taken them before they could even crawl and made his wife infertile in the process. The priest has tried to tell him that this was God's punishment for his pride, but he refuses to believe it. His wife is a very religious woman so naturally she believes every word the priest says; he can read it in her eyes but she would never dare to put her thoughts into words.

Of course he is proud. He has every right to be proud. His kinsfolk go back a long way; they were the first of the *gitanos* to settle here in the south, in the dense woodlands of Doñana. They had travelled the length and breadth of Spain before making this their home, and before that his ancestors had journeyed across continents, crossing rivers and climbing through

mountain passes until they eventually reached the Iberian penin-
sula. Yes, he has reasons to be proud; he has the blood of brave
and resourceful men in his veins, travellers who never bowed to
tyranny and whose strength lay in their loyalty to each other.
The priest will never understand that. Never.

He strokes the long nose of the Marsh mare and whispers
softly in her ear. He has worked with horses all his life. It is a
gift he has inherited from his father and one he hopes to pass on
to his sons, two of whom work with him each day rounding up
the horses. He coughs and spits angrily on the ground as he
thinks of them. Not one of them has the patience to train a wild
horse. He doubts if they could train a mule never mind the magnificent Retuerta horses who roam through the pine forests. The
mare whinnies restlessly. 'All right, my lovely. Off you go and
join the others.' He watches as the Marsh mare trots across to
join the herd that is wading through the shallow lagoon. He
knows them all, each and every one of them; most of the herd
are still wild but one or two, like the mare, have already been
domesticated. They are such intelligent animals that it is a treat
to train them and they make excellent work horses. A land agent
for a big estate to the north of Huelva has asked him to catch
and train six of them in total. It is a big order and he has told the
agent that he is not going to rush it. If he wants horses that he
can rely on then he will have to be patient. He could see the
agent did not like him speaking to him like that, but he bit his
lip and nodded in agreement. They all know that a well trained
Marsh horse is worth waiting for. Vano whistles and the mare
returns, closely followed by two others, a grey one and a chest-
nut, both of which he has already tamed. He opens the stockade
and they trot inside as docile as lambs. They are the perfect
work horses for this kind of terrain, with their wide hooves and

their sturdy legs they are capable of doing most jobs on the marshy land.

'Álvaro,' he shouts. 'Get your lazy butt over here and help me catch one of those mares.'

A gangly lad of sixteen comes out from the thatched hut which is their home; a spiral of wood smoke twists its way through the hole on the roof and floats into the cold morning air. 'What is it, father?'

'Get the rope. We're going to catch one of the horses.' He puts a makeshift halter on to the mare and leads her out of the stockade.

'I haven't had any breakfast yet,' the boy complains. His shirt flaps open and exposes his boney ribs.

Vano ignores him and strides off in the direction of the horses. Already they have edged closer to the shelter of the pine forest and if he moves too quickly they will scatter and then it will take him forever to catch the one he has his eye on. Earlier he had been watching the mare; she favours a dark brown horse with a black mane. He likes to be selective about the horses he chooses and this one seems to be a placid creature, with no defects. The agent would not know any different, but Vano wants them to be a cohesive group; he does not want any renegades. The mare knows instinctively that they are heading for the dark brown horse and whinnies in greeting, but the horse is not fooled and edges away.

'Papa. Papa,' a girl's voice calls to him. It is Clementina; she is running across the field waving at him. Instantly the horses are on the move, galloping towards the pine forest.

'*Mierda*,' he swears, glowering at his son. There is no point trying to catch them now; they are too spooked. He will come out later in the evening, before it gets dark. He turns and walks back towards his daughter. 'What is it child?' he asks, smiling at her despite his annoyance. He cannot help it; the sight of her beauty always brings a smile to his face. She is the most lovely thing in his life; more precious even than his horses.

'They have sold Doñana,' she cries, as the tears run down her honey coloured cheeks.

'What do you mean, child? Who has sold Doñana?' He looks around him at the sun gleaming on the lagoon and the wading birds foraging in the shallow water for food. The horses are calm now and quietly grazing on the far side of the lagoon. He feels bemused. How can anyone sell this wild place? It is not a field of rice or a house to be bought and sold. It is God's own land.

'The Duke has sold it to his wife's sister, the Marchioness. It's hers now. What will she do with it? What will happen to us? Oh, Papa, what will become of us?'

'Hush child. Nothing will change. The Marchioness and her husband will use it in much the same way as the Duke and Duchess did; they will come here from time to time to hunt and entertain their rich friends and then they will leave again. Nothing will change for us. Now wipe those tears and forget your foolishness.' He puts his arm around her and hugs her to him, but he does not wholly believe his own words. You can never rely on the aristocracy. Up until now, he has almost convinced himself that these beautiful horses are free, that they belong to no-one and he can do as he pleases with them, but his daughter has just given him a harsh reminder that this is not the case; Doñana and everything that lives there belongs to someone. Since the time of the Duke of Medina Sidonia, the *gitanos* have lived there in peace; but each time the land passes to a new owner he is filled with dread.

'Are you sure, Papa?' She looks at him so trustingly that he feels a wave of tenderness towards her and wants to sweep her into his arms and protect her from all life's hardship.

'What do you want me to do now, Father?' asks Álvaro. He is standing there with the rope dangling from his hand.

'Put that damn rope away for a start, you useless streak of lard, and then start mucking out the stables,' his father snarls.

'But...' the boy begins but then stops.

Vano is not interested in what his son is about to say; he is thinking about the Marsh horses he must get ready for the agent. He strides across to the corral where the three mares are held. Two of them are still a little nervous and shy away from him when he enters. These Marsh horses—Marismeño is their proper name but the local people prefer to say Marsh—are as ancient a breed as time itself. They are plucky little animals and ideally suited for working in the waterlogged soil that stretches along the coast. He stands and watches them. In the next pen a grey stallion has his ears flattened against his head. This is not a good sign; what is going through his mind, he asks himself. Is he planning on making a bolt for it? Quietly he walks towards the stallion, and begins to hum a *gitano* melody; it is the same song his wife sings to the babies and he has found it works just as well at calming the horses. 'Gently now,' he says and inches his way closer to him. He continues talking to the grey stallion in a sing-song way until, gradually, the horse begins to realise he means him no harm and his ears relax. Vano moves around him, carefully, encouraging the stallion to look at him and taking care to avoid his back legs; like the other Marsh horses, he is small and compact, similar to an Arabian horse, but sturdier and stronger. If it lashes out at him it could land him a severe blow. Vano has received many a kick over the years and is not keen to receive another one today. He reaches out and strokes the horse's muzzle. 'Well, my boy. How about we go for a ride to-day?' He knots a rope to the ring on the stallion's halter. The horse knows what this means and pulls its head away but Vano does not scold him; instead he continues to stroke the animal's muzzle and whispers, 'Easy now, boy. Nobody is going to hurt you. Easy does it.' He decides not to bother with a saddle yet and grasping the lead rope and a hunk of the stallion's mane in his left hand, leaps onto its back before it can move away. The horse makes a half-hearted attempt to rear up but changes its mind. 'Good boy,' Vano whispers, patting its neck and continuing to hum the lullaby. 'Well done.' Gently he directs the horse towards the gate.

'I'll get it, Father,' shouts Álvaro and runs to open the gate for them.

Vano allows the stallion just enough rope to make it feel comfortable and once they are away from the clearing he urges it into a trot. It is a beautiful horse. He has decided he will ask the top price for it and if the agent does not want to pay then he will keep it for himself. It will sire some fine colts. Vano chuckles; he always plans to do this, but in the end he sells it for what he can get. He strokes the stallion's neck and encourages it into a gentle gallop. Even without a saddle Vano feels as secure on this mount as on any he has ever ridden. Maybe he should make an exception this time and keep it for himself. He shifts his weight more to the back and the stallion begins to slow down, then with the slightest of pressure from his knees he turns it towards home.

He can understand why Clementina is so upset. There has been talk of moving them on before now but then it goes quiet and they hear no more about it. He thinks that maybe the Duke spoke out against it because he knows that while the *gitanos* are there the local herds of wild horses will be safe. At least that is what Vano had thought at the time but now he realises that the Duke was not really interested in them; he had planned to sell the estate anyway. Maybe Clementina does have cause to be worried. He sighs. It will break him if he has to leave Doñana after all these years. Their clan is small enough as it is; some twenty families now. There just is not enough work in the woods for even that many. In order for most *gitanos* to earn a living they need to be around other people, especially *payos,* so most of the men travel to the towns to make what money they can. Some sell pots and pans in the local markets, others tour the streets sharpening knives. Many earn money by playing their guitars in the squares or singing in bars. Others, mostly old men or women, sit begging while the younger ones pick the pockets of the rich. Those who remain in Doñana are people like him, who are able to make a living from the forest and the marshes. His mother, for example, weaves bulrushes into baskets and mats which his sister and her husband then sell in the market.

There used to be nearly a hundred people in their clan but over time it has split into two separate parts; now the larger group live in Osuna with the patriarch while he, as the brother of the patriarch, remains in Doñana with the rest.

The stallion has behaved well; it is almost ready to be sold. Although Vano clings to the idea that he might be able to breed from it, reason tells him that it is unlikely to happen. By all rights he should be a rich man; he has the reputation of being the best trainer in Andalusia with some of the most desired horses in the area, yet his children still go hungry. It would help if those who complement and praise him were to actually pay him on time. But, as his father always says, the rich are rich because they don't like to part with their money. And what can he do about it when they are all aware of who really owns the horses. A word from them and the Guardia Civil would lock him up and chase all the *gitanos* out of the forest.

As he leads the stallion into its stable, he notices his daughter is sitting on an old log outside their hut; a small fire is burning in the pit and the flames light up her face. She is sewing something; he cannot see what it is, but the colours are bright in the light of the fire. The dog lies on the ground next to her, snoring quietly.

'Everything all right now, child?' he asks.

She nods. Her lovely face is still stained with tears and there is smut from the fire on her cheek.

'Where's your mother?'

'She's helping Zita give birth. It's her time.'

He grunts. So that is what all the commotion is about. He does not ask any questions; even though Zita is one of his daughters he is not interested in any details. When the baby is born they will tell him. If God is willing, the child will be healthy. If not, what can he do about it. That is women's work and he leaves that to his wife.

Clementina gives a quiet sob. Her shoulders are shaking and now he notices that the material she has been sewing is wet with her tears.

'Surely you're not still crying about the sale? I told you, nothing will change. It won't affect us.' It is ridiculous that she should be so upset, but then maybe she is not as foolish as he is. Maybe he only sees what he wants to see.

'It's not just that. Mama says I am to get married,' his daughter sobs. 'She says she wants her next grandchild to be my son. But I don't want to, Papa. I don't want to get married. I want to stay at home.'

He kneels down beside her and puts his arms around her. 'Don't cry my sweet child. You will have to marry one day, you know. That's what happens. It's the way of the world.'

'But not yet, Papa. It's too soon.'

'Hush, my dear. I'll speak to your mother. I'm sure she doesn't mean right away. You are still a child and you are making yourself upset for nothing. Now dry your tears and go and see if you have a new niece or nephew yet. It's gone very quiet over there.'

He watches as she carefully folds the tear-stained sewing and wanders over to a hut identical to theirs but on the other side of the clearing. His son-in-law is squatting outside the hut with some of his own family and looks up as Clementina approaches. Vano is too far away to see his expression, but he assumes everything is all right as none of the women are having hysterics. He wanders over to the well and draws himself some water. Poor Clementina, he does not have the heart to tell her that as soon as she is sixteen she will be married; he and Lavinia have already selected a husband for her although nothing has been settled.

'It's a boy, Papa,' calls Clementina, coming out of the hut and waving to him. 'It's a boy.' She disappears back inside the hut.

So Zita has had a son. That's a good omen. It is her first child and now, God willing, she will give her husband more sons.

'Papa, someone is coming,' says Álvaro.

'It's probably the agent, wanting to hurry me up. Well coming all the way out here isn't going to help him. I do things in my own time.'

'No, Papa. It's Don Luis's son. The young one. And there's another man with him.' The boy's eyes are wide with surprise, as if the Holy Father himself has arrived.

'Don't stand there like a startled doe, you idiot. Go and take his horse for him.' *Dios mio*, when is that lad going to use some initiative. Vano bends down and splashes some water on his face and gives it a wipe with his neckerchief, then replaces the sodden rag around his neck. He dries his hands on the seat of his trousers and walks over to greet his guests. He hopes Don Luis has not sent his son to complain about the colt he bought from him last time. Maybe he has sent him to pay for it. Now that would be good.

'Don Hugo, what a pleasure to see you. Is your father not with you?' Don Luis never comes here in person, but he always asks the same question; it is years since Vano has seen him. He holds out his hand in greeting but the young man ignores it.

'*Buenos días,* Vano. No, my father is busy this morning. I have come to see if you can find a suitable horse for my friend, here, Don Cristóbal Herrera de Vega.'

'*Buenos días* Señor Herrera. How can I help you?' So here is another spoiled, rich bastard wanting to spend his father's money. Well that is good news for him. But the young man is not looking at him, he is staring past Vano at something in the distance. Vano turns to see what he finds so interesting. Of course, he should have known. Clementina has emerged from her sister's hut and is walking towards them. The sun is shining on her glossy black hair and she is smiling; her face, flushed from the heat inside the hut, is more beautiful than ever. She is like an angel descended from heaven. Normally Vano knows beforehand if buyers are coming to see him and he always makes a point of telling his daughters to keep out of sight until his visitors have gone. Today he has been taken unawares. He looks at Hugo's friend. 'Señor Herrera?' he repeats.

'Ah, yes. Forgive me Vano. Yes, I am in need of a horse and my friend has told me that you can provide the best horses in all of Spain,' Cristóbal at last manages to say.

Vano turns around again but there is no sign of his daughter now. He breathes a sigh of relief. 'Well I would not dare to contradict Don Hugo,' he says with a grin which exposes a gold tooth where one of his incisors should be. 'Come with me and I will show you what I have in my stables at the moment.'

'Was that your daughter, Vano?' Hugo asks. He too is staring at the place where moments before Clementina had appeared. 'Was that Tina?'

'Yes, Don Hugo. That was Clementina. I am surprised that you remember her.'

Hugo turns to Cristóbal and says, 'When I was a lad, ten or eleven, I often used to come here with our groom. While he talked business, I used to play with Vano's children.'

'You did indeed, *Señor*,' says Vano, struggling with his irritation. 'As I said, I'm surprised you recognised her; she was no more than six-years-old at the time.'

'How could I forget her. She was always a pretty child and I see she has grown into a fine young woman. Does she still ride?' He turns to Cristóbal and says, 'For a girl she was excellent, the best rider amongst us. And fearless, too.'

'No, *Señor*, she doesn't ride any more. It wouldn't be suitable for a young woman who is soon to be married, to ride a horse.'

'Indeed. Why don't you bring her out and see if she remembers me.'

He says it casually but Vano can see it is a command, but it is a command he has no intention of obeying. 'I would, *Señor*, but her sister has just this minute given birth and Clementina is needed. I will tell her you were here.'

A fleeting scowl passes across Hugo's face but all he says is, 'I understand. Maybe I will call in another day. Now, enough of the chatter, show us what you have for my friend.'

Vano expects to take them out into the forest to see the horses in the wild and let Cristóbal choose one for him to catch, but they do not get that far. As they pass the stables Hugo's friend spots the grey stallion.

'What a beauty,' he cries and instantly makes towards it.

'Hang on, Señor Herrera. I haven't finished training that one yet. Mind he doesn't kick you.'

Cristóbal stops and turns to Hugo, 'That's the one I want,' he says.

'It is a beauty,' his friend agrees. 'But it's not a Retuerta. Don't you want to see what else Vano can get for us?'

'Yes, I was looking at the herd only this morning and there are some excellent horses, both Retuerta and Marsh. You shouldn't rush into choosing the first one you see,' interrupts Vano, who had no desire to sell the grey stallion, and especially to this young man who, from the way he was riding, appears to know very little about horses. The stallion would be wasted on him.

'No, that's the one for me. How much do you want for it?' Cristóbal asks, refusing to move.

'I'm sorry, *Señor*, this one is already spoken for. I have an agent coming for him later in the week. I'm sorry, but I know I can find you another horse equally as good if not better.'

'It would be sensible to have a look at what else he can offer,' whispers Hugo.

'No, that's the one I want,' Cristóbal repeats.

'Well before you decide, my friend, you should at least examine him to make sure that he is fit and healthy.' Hugo turns to Vano and says, 'Bring him out so we can get a good look at him.'

Reluctantly Vano walks over to where he has tethered the stallion outside its stable. 'Come on, my lovely,' he whispers in its ear. He strokes the horse's nose gently and slowly leads him towards the watching men.

'Yes, he is so beautiful,' says Cristóbal. 'I must have him.' There is determination in his voice.

'He does look good, but we need to see him go through his paces,' says Hugo.

Cristóbal looks at him, blankly.

'He's still a young horse,' says Vano, leading the stallion gently by the rope and walking him up and down in front of them.

'Show me his teeth,' says Hugo.

Vano stops and pulls back the horse's lips to show a set of perfectly aligned young teeth.

'May I?' asks Hugo, pointing to the stallion's legs. Vano knows he is not asking permission, but ensuring that it is safe for him to examine the animal's legs. He nods. 'Well he looks all right to me. A fine animal, considering,' says Hugo, running his hand expertly up and down the stallion's legs. He lifts one of its hooves and examines it.

Cristóbal looks at him. 'Considering what?' he asks.

'Considering he's a wild horse and we have yet to see how he performs. What about it, Vano, can we try him out?'

'I am afraid not, Don Hugo. Your father would never forgive me if anything happened to you or your friend. As I said, I haven't finished training this one yet and he is already promised to another customer.'

'My father will pay you handsomely for him,' says Cristóbal.

'His father is well-known in Seville,' Hugo adds. 'He is my father's lawyer, and your new landlady is another of his clients, the Marchioness.'

Vano looks at their smug, confident faces and realises he cannot refuse; they know he does not own these horses and for all that he is the best horse trainer in the area, he has no power over these men. 'Very well, but you must leave him with me for a few more days. I would hate him to throw you on your first outing.'

'Is that likely?' Cristóbal asks, suddenly looking nervous.

'Not when I have finished training him, no.'

Cristóbal sticks out his hand, 'So that's a deal then?'

Vano grabs the outstretched hand and shakes it vigorously. 'It's a deal. Come back in three days and he will be yours.' He knows he is making a mistake; the agent will be angry if there is more delay but what can he do. Now he has to find another horse to replace the stallion and train him up as quickly as he can.

Vano watches as they ride away. He should be feeling pleased with himself; Hugo has paid him the money that his father owed him, and his friend Cristóbal has insisted on paying him a deposit for the grey Marsh stallion. Vano has asked an exorbitantly high price for it in the hope of persuading the young man to choose another, but he would not be moved. He declares he is in love with the grey and nothing else will do. It has been a profitable morning, but Vano cannot forget the look on the faces of both young men when they saw Clementina.

'What is it, husband?' Lavinia asks. 'Did everything go all right?' She nods towards the retreating horsemen.

'Yes.' He pauses and adds, 'I think you are right about Clementina, *mujer*. It is time she was married. See what you can do about bringing the wedding forward.'

CHAPTER 3

So far this year Pedro has been lucky and at the beginning of each season there has been work for him. He is even part of the gang who are digging the *asperpia* channels between the rows of vines to collect and store the winter rains. It is back-breaking work—the channels have to be dug from the chalky soil on the hillside—but it is necessary if there is to be enough water for the vines throughout next year's hot dry summer. And he is grateful to the foreman for picking him, even though he never knows from one day to the next whether he will be working again. He cannot explain to anyone, not even his wife, how humiliating it is to stand there, his hat in his hand, silently praying that he will be chosen, how his stomach churns with the fear that there will be no food for them to eat that night. If Enrique takes a dislike to you, that is it; he will give you no more work that season. Pedro has the uncomfortable feeling that it is because of Ana that he is chosen so often. His wife is still an attractive woman despite having borne four children, one of whom was stillborn and another who died at six months. Her hard life is etched on her face, but it does not detract from her beauty. She was beautiful when he met her and to him she is just as lovely as ever. He has seen Enrique staring at her with his rapacious, dark eyes when she has come to the vineyard at midday carrying his meagre lunch. Pedro has told her not to come, that he can wait until nightfall to eat, but she insists. It is not a great distance; they have a house on the edge of the vineyard. A house, he smiles bitterly, a roof over their heads is all it is; he looks around the darkened single room with its mud floor. No matter how hard his wife works she can never keep it clean and now the weather is growing colder it will be worse because they will have to light the fire inside and then the baby will cough and choke like she did last winter. But what can he do. Without the work in the vineyard he does not know how they would survive; there is very little else around here. All the men who work on the Butler & Rodriguez estate are in the same situation; they are *los braceros*, the landless labourers who are the most wretched of all men. For half the year they are employed and for the rest they have to make do on what they can scavenge.

Ana has suggested that he goes to work in the mines at Rio Tinto when there is no work in the vineyard but that is too far away from his family. He wants to stay close to them; if they are to starve then they will starve together.

He steps outside into the cool night air. A shadowy figure is walking towards his home. There is something about his gait that looks familiar. Surely not. It can't be.

'It's only me, brother,' a voice calls out in the darkness.

'Ramon, what the hell? Why are you here?' Pedro has not seen his brother for almost a year, but he has heard about the strikes and the demonstrations in Andalusia and knows that Ramon will be involved in some way; he was sure that he was either dead or in gaol.

'Well that's a nice way to greet your brother after all this time.' He comes right up to him and hugs him. 'I've missed you, Pedro.'

'Really. So where were you when Mama died?' He feels the anger flare up inside him again.

'What? Mama is dead? When did that happen?' Even in the weak flicker of light from the fire he can see that his brother has gone pale.

'Last winter. Not long after you disappeared. I couldn't find any work for months and we had hardly anything to eat. We didn't realise it but Mama was giving her share of the food to the children; she grew so weak that she became ill and died.'

'What did the doctor say?'

'Doctor? Are you mad? We couldn't afford to get a doctor. Anyway it was obvious she wasn't going to make it; she just turned her face to the wall and lay there until she passed away.' He struggles to keep the bitterness out of his voice. It is not Ramon's fault; he knows that but he wants someone to blame. 'Father Sanchez came and gave her the last rites. I didn't want him to but Ana convinced me that it was what Mama wanted.'

'I expect he needed paying,' says Ramon, bitterly.

'Of course. It pained me to do it, but I had no choice.'

'Poor Mama. So she starved to death,' Ramon murmurs, more to himself than to his brother.

'No, don't say that. It wasn't our fault. We gave her what food we could. She just wouldn't eat it. She had not been herself since Papa passed away. I think she was just tired of living.'

'You should have done more to help her,' Ramon says.

'Oh yes, and where were you? For you, it was more important to be marching with your new friends than staying at home and looking for work. It was you who deserted your family. I've been slaving here trying to make ends meet, working for a pittance that hardly stretches to buy food for my wife and two children, while you play at being a revolutionary.' Pedro sits on the ground outside his home and Ramon squats beside him. He picks up a bundle of sticks and begins to add them carefully to the fire, which gives out little heat and a lot of smoke.

'It's not like that, Pedro. This fight is important. Think of your children. Do you want them to have no future? Don't you think they are entitled to a better life than you and I have had?

It's not right that children are undernourished and deprived of education. We have to fight these people.'

'These people? Who are these people that you talk about? Where are they?'

'You know very well. Landowners and business men like your boss, Don Luis Felipe Rodriguez Domingo. That's who. Those who exploit the poor and take advantage of them to make themselves rich; the Church, which controls our education system in order to keep the poor ignorant and fill their heads with religious rubbish; the politicians who want to keep women in their place and by that I mean in the home, with no money of their own and no power to improve their lives. That's who *these people* are.'

'But what good does it do, all this shouting and demonstrating? First one party and then another are in power. Now that the centre-right have taken over the government all they are doing is reversing the improvements that the previous government made.' He laughs bitterly. 'Ana is furious that she can no longer vote. She was so pleased to have the right to vote and be treated like an equal at last, but she never got a chance because they took it away as soon as they could. Not that she would have known which party to vote for; they are all as bad as each other.'

'That's because they are frightened of the women. They don't want them to have any power. They want them where they have always been, in the kitchen and in the bedroom. Haven't you heard about the new Falangists? They and the Church are running courses for newly married women to teach them the duties of being a good wife.' He coughs and spits on the ground. 'It's all about control and they are being very clever about it because they are targeting the families, the wives and the children. Don't you understand, Pedro, it's for women like Ana that we must do this. It is for your children and all the children who never have a chance. It's for Mama.' Ramon's face is flushed with rage.

Pedro knows his brother really believes what he is saying, and well maybe he is right, but all Pedro can think about is the ache in his stomach and whether Ana has managed to find enough food to make them any supper tonight. 'You keep telling yourself that; all I know is that you were not here when we needed you.' He pauses, then says, 'She kept asking for you, Ramon. She thought you had been killed.'

His wife comes out of the hut and smiles at Ramon. 'I thought it was you making such a rumpus. How are you?' She bends down and kisses him. 'Are you staying?'

Ramon looks at his brother. 'Yes, stay with us,' Pedro says. 'You will have to sleep outside, I'm afraid. But you can share our meal.' He looks across at his wife to make sure he has not said the wrong thing. She smiles and nods her head.

'That's all right; I'm not all that hungry anyway. It will be so good to just relax and go to sleep without having to keep one ear open all night for the Guardia Civil.'

'Are they looking for you?' Pedro asks, peering anxiously at his brother's face through the smoke.

'Possibly.'

'Are they?'

'Yes.'

'So what happened? Why do they want you?'

Ramon opens his canvas satchel and takes out a leather bottle. 'How about a drink, brother?' He hands the full *bota* to Pedro who removes the stopper and holds it above his face, then tilts it so a stream of sherry flows into his mouth.

'Delicious,' he says, wiping his mouth with his sleeve. 'What about you Ana?'

'I prefer mine in a mug.' She gets up and goes into the hut and returns with a small pottery beaker. 'This will do.'

'If there's a hole at the top and not at the bottom, then it will do fine,' Ramon says, taking the leather wineskin from his brother and pouring some of the golden liquid into her beaker. 'Jerez's finest,' he adds, giving her a big smile. He drinks from the *bota* and passes it back to Pedro.

Pedro sniffs at the sherry and smiles. 'It's good,' he says and then lifts the *bota* again. 'My, that is nice,' he says, smacking his lips. 'It's a while since I had even a sip of sherry.'

'And there's you working for the best bodega in the area. Don't you ever slip into the warehouse and take a sample out of the barrel?'

'No, I wouldn't risk it. They would have me out on my ear and I'd never work again. Enrique would make sure of that; he'd tell all the other bodegas that I was a thief.'

'Bastard, just for a sip of sherry.'

'So why are the Guardia Civil after you?' Pedro asks, eager to change the subject. 'I thought you were in Seville.'

'I was and I was determined not to get into any trouble but sadly it didn't turn out that way. There was a big demonstration planned about the underuse of farming land, particularly in Seville where seventy-five thousand acres of agricultural land are kept for breeding fighting bulls, and in Osuna where there is another 33,000 acres not cultivated, and more in Jerez de los Caballeros. The list goes on and on. Andalusia could grow enough food to feed the whole country if it wasn't for these selfish bastards. We weren't trying to start a revolution, we just wanted to draw the government's attention to the fact that the land isn't being used properly and that people are starving because they can't grow enough food.'

'So what happened?' asks Ana, who has a flush to her cheeks now from drinking the sherry.

'The Guardia Civil is what happened. They came in wielding their batons and striking out at everyone.'

'But how did you get involved? What did you do?'

'Oh, well, I lost it and lashed out at one of the officers. I didn't intend to lose my temper but I just got so angry. We weren't doing anything; it was a peaceful march until the Guardia Civil turned up. The truth is that I barely touched the guy but unfortunately he slipped and fell back and split his head open on the kerb.'

'Is he dead?'

'I don't know. Maybe. I just ran away from there as fast as I could. I'm sure they would have beaten me to death if I'd stayed.'

'*Dios mio*, Ramon. They will be out looking for you. Do you think anyone can identify you?'

'Maybe. Maybe not.'

'For God's sake, are they going to be looking for you or not? Do they know I'm your brother? Are they going to come here?'

'Well, I was with some comrades. They know my name and they know I'm from Jerez.'

'So the Guardia Civil could well be looking for you here. Why the hell did you come back to Jerez then?'

'I wanted to see you. You're my brother.'

'But you do realise what you've done; you've put us all in danger now. They will track me down and then they will find you.'

'Now why would they do that? You're a working man. You don't even belong to a political party, more's the pity.'

'How did you get here?' asks Ana, no longer smiling at her brother-in-law.

'A friend got me on a lorry that was going to Jerez.' He picked up the *bota* and poured some more sherry into his mouth. 'That's where this came from. Good isn't it.'

Pedro stands up. He would like to grab the wineskin and throw it at his brother, but he thinks better of it and instead takes it from him and drinks some more. 'You can't stay here. It's too dangerous. I don't want anything to happen to my family, or to me for that matter. If I get arrested how will they live? Tell me that. They will starve.'

'Don't be so dramatic, brother. Why would they arrest you?'

'Where can he go?' asks Ana. 'If he can't stay here, where can he go?'

'Let me think. In the meantime prepare us some food.' Pedro is still holding the wineskin and decides to drink some more.

'It's your own fault, Pedro. I know you voted for the centre-right,' says Ramon, staring at him. 'You should join the Spanish Socialist Workers' Party; that's the party of the people. We have to stick together; it's the only way the working man can win.'

'What do you know about the working man? Have you any idea what my life is really like? I am a *bracero*. How do you suppose we can live on what I earn, five pesetas a day? Five pesetas when a loaf of bread costs three. When I have work for just half the year and then only if I don't upset the foreman. What do you think I am supposed to do in the winter when they don't need me at the vineyard? It's easy for you to talk about demonstrations and strikes and demands for better pay; all I want is to know that I will have work each and every day.' He can hear his own words and he knows he should feel angry at his situation but all he feels is helpless. Helplessness and hopelessness, he does not have the energy for anything else. What can he do to change his life. What can anyone do. He is stuck in this quagmire of poverty and there is no escape.

'I'm telling you, that's why you should support the Spanish Socialist Workers' Party. They tried to change things in 1931 but all those changes are being undermined. They want to help the working man, but you have to support them,' his brother continues. He is blind to the reality of Pedro's situation.

'That's easy for you to say, Ramon. You are single. You have no-one that depends on you. You have no wife and no children. Of course I would like to vote for the Spanish Socialist Workers' Party, or any party that will make my life better, but I can't. We *braceros* are forced to vote the way Don Luis wants us to, the *cacique* way. It's that or no more work. I would like nothing better than to tell that bastard of a foreman what he can do with his *cacique* system but I can't. They have us over a barrel; if I refuse to vote the way they want I will get no more work. And all the workers feel the same as I do. We hate giving in to them but we just can't risk voting against them.'

'Here, eat it while it's hot,' says Ana coming out with a cauldron of something that smells delicious.

Pedro hears a rumble from his empty stomach and smiles at his wife. He is proud of her; she is determined to make their meal as pleasant as possible despite the fact that all she has to offer them is a broth made with a few vegetables and thickened with stale bread.

'So this is your youngest?' asks Ramon, picking up a toddler who has crawled out from the hut.

'Yes, that's Amalia. She's not been baptised yet but we called her after her grandmother,' says Ana, taking the child from him and placing her at her breast.

'Not baptised? That's not like you, Ana. I remember this young lad's christening as being a very happy occasion,' he says, looking at their son, a skinny child with a soot smeared face and a runny nose.

'That was five years ago and I've had no new clothes since. How could I go to church looking like this,' Ana says, pointing to her bare legs and torn skirt. 'The priest wouldn't allow it. He would not let me past the door.' She sounds angry, but with whom, the Church or her husband?

'Pepe is almost six now. He's a good boy,' says Pedro, rumpling his son's hair. He is ashamed that he does not earn enough money for his wife to have a decent dress and stockings to go to church, even though she never complains; this is the first time he has heard her speak about it and it feels like another blow to his heart. When his mother died he had rescued a few of her clothes but they are no better than rags either. 'Wipe your nose, lad and come and have something to eat.'

The boy sits on the ground between his father and his uncle. He does not speak but takes the bowl of broth from his father and begins to eat it hungrily.

'I will leave as soon as I have eaten,' says Ramon.

'But where will you go?' asks Ana. Pedro knows she is anxious for his brother's safety, as is he.

Ramon shrugs. 'Don't worry about me. I never should have come here; I just didn't think. I'm really sorry, the last thing I want is to bring you any trouble.'

'No, at least stay the night. Give me time to think about where you could hide.' Pedro glances across at his son who is staring at Ramon and listening to every word. 'We will discuss it later, when the children are asleep.'

'Why not speak to Adolfo,' whispers Ana, leaning closer to her husband so that Pepe does not hear her.

He nods. 'Any more of that sherry left?' he asks his brother who shakes the wineskin and nods.

Later, when all is quiet and his family are asleep, Pedro walks across the compound to where his old friend, Adolfo, is sitting by a small fire. 'It's turned cold tonight,' he says by way of a greeting.

'Aye, it has.'

'I've brought you something,' he says and hands the half-empty wineskin to the old man.

'What's this? Have the Three Kings arrived and I missed them?' He smiles a toothless smile as he takes it from him.

'My brother brought it. He came to see Mother.'

'Bit late then, isn't he.' He pulls out the stopper and takes a swig from the *bota*. 'That's good stuff. *Dios mío,* I don't know how long ago it is since I've tasted anything as sweet as that. 1915 maybe.' A faraway look comes into his eyes.

Pedro squats on the ground beside him. He realises his friend is about to start reminiscing and he does not want that. 'I need your advice, Adolfo.' He knows from the tales he tells to anyone who will listen, that the old man had spent a large part of his younger life living with a gang of bandits in the hills.

Adolfo sticks the stopper back into the wineskin and looks at him, warily. 'What sort of advice?'

'If someone wanted to hide from the Guardia Civil where is the best place for them to go?'

'Are you in trouble, my friend?'

'Me? No. It's possible that my brother is, though.'

'Very well. Don't tell me any more; I don't want any details. But why have you come to me?'

'Well, I know you lived with the *bandidos* once and that you were never caught. Surely you can tell me how you managed it.'

'I was careful who I talked to for one thing. If your brother has done something to upset the Guardia Civil, or even if they think he has—which is almost the same—you must not mention it to anyone. They will come looking for you and even though you deny having seen him, they will take you away. Even if you are telling the truth they won't listen to you. It probably won't matter to them which brother they have, so as far as they are concerned you will do just as well.'

Pedro feels sick when hears this; although he has eaten his stomach is still not full and he can taste the broth lingering in his throat. 'You are the only person I have told that he is here. He is leaving tonight, but I don't want to just turn him away with nothing. He is my brother and I ought to help him if I can.'

The old man grunts and takes another draught of the sherry. 'When I was young, we hid in the Sierra Morena.' He rubs his hands together and stretches them towards the fire. '*Dios mío* it was bloody cold at night up there.' He turns to Pedro. 'That would be no good for your brother. It's too far away; they would catch him before he could get there.'

'So where then?' Pedro is feeling desperate. He cannot bear to think of his brother being locked up by the Guardia Civil, or worse, being shot. He may not take part in the demonstrations but he knows what happens when the police arrest the demonstrators; there will be no trial. His brother is running for his life but he does not seem to realise it, or if he does, he does not care.

The old man is staring at the flickering flames of his dying fire. 'I know. Of course. He should hide in plain sight.'

Pedro stares at him. 'What do you mean? Where?'

'*Dios mío,* lad. I can't tell you any more. What good would it do you to know where he is.'

Pedro shakes his head. Does he mean the wilderness on the other side of the river? That doesn't sound like a good idea. It is too close. What if they find him and connect him to Pedro and his family? No, he has made a mistake asking Adolfo for help;

he has involved him for nothing and worse still, he has told him that his brother is here.

'It just doesn't sound like a very good place to hide,' Pedro says, rather weakly.

'Ah, but you're wrong. It is an excellent place to hide. There are hectares of woodland and marshes and deserted beaches over there. One of my fellow *bandidos* has lived there for twenty years, undetected. Sometimes the best hiding places are out in the open. Look at me. I am a wanted man in Seville, Huelva and even Córdoba, a *bandido* with a list of crimes as long as your arm,' he says proudly. 'Yet here I am and nobody comes to bother me. Trust me, your brother will be safe there. I would offer to go with him, but my legs are not up to walking all that way anymore. Send him to me and I will explain what he has to do.'

'But...'

'Do you want to save him? Or do you just want rid of him? If so, then turn him in to the Guardia Civil and your problem will be solved.'

That thought has already passed through Pedro's mind, but he knows he could never betray his brother, not even for the sake of his wife and children. 'Very well I will send him to you.'

'Believe me, my friend, he will be safe. You will see. Tell him to come here two hours before daybreak, and I will instruct him where to go. It's best if you and your wife do not know any of the details. Ignorance may keep you safe. Now I want to have a few hours' sleep. Thank you for the sherry.' The old man kicks at the fire, scattering the half burned sticks so he can relight it later and retreats into his hut.

Pedro gets up and walks slowly back to his family. The night is still and the sky is clear. He can hear an owl calling for its mate and from somewhere in the distance, the cry of the lynx. He has never had a reason to cross the river, but he has heard people talk of the rich hunting grounds that lie beyond it, the wild boar and deer that roam the woods and the stories of the ancient people that once inhabited the land. He hears that some men will pay four *duros* for a lynx, and three *duros* for a fox; it sounds easy money but he knows he does not have it in him to kill an animal that he is not going to eat, a wild boar yes, but they are fierce creatures and not easy to kill. They hunt them on horseback, armed with long, sharp lances; he has neither a horse nor a lance. Pedro has heard the old men retelling the local myths of strange animals that roam the dunes, of gold and silver hidden in underground tunnels and of the bandits and cutthroats that live there. Does Adolfo really intend to send his brother to that ungodly place across the river? He looks up at the moon and sighs; as his friend says, it is best that he does not know.

CHAPTER 4

Her mother has gone to check up on Juliana, leaving her to deal with this enormous pile of pine cones. Clementina has been tapping them against the rock one by one for ages and has gathered a lot of nuts in this manner, but there are still many more cones to do. She picks up one of the tiny nuts and peels it with her teeth then pops it into her mouth. They are sweet and delicious but very small. The little pile of nuts lying on her neckerchief will not last long with all their hungry family; she will have to gather some more. She pushes the empty pine cones onto the ground; they will be used later to start the evening fire.

Mama thinks it is her duty, as the sister-in-law of the patriarch, to look after all the women in the clan, not just the unmarried ones. Juliana's mother died last year and now that Juliana is pregnant again, Mama is taking her under her wing, even though there is no need; the girl has aunts and sisters, plenty of womenfolk to help her. She has just had her eighteenth birthday and this is her third pregnancy. Clementina shudders; that is not for her. She is never getting married and never having children; she does not care what her parents say. Why would she willingly want to undergo all that pain and suffering to have a child for whom she is then going to have to be responsible for years. She remembers Juliana's wedding quite clearly; she looked like a fairy princess she was so lovely. Everyone was happy for her; everyone congratulated her and Juliana looked radiant, but that has all changed now. She often sees Juliana going down to the stream to wash her clothes, with the baby strapped to her back, a little girl toddling behind her and the basket of dirty clothes balanced on her swollen belly. She looks tired and older than her eighteen years. There is no radiance now. She looks like all the other *gitano* women in their clan, tired and irritable. Well that is not going to be her life. Clementina would rather leave the clan and all her family than end up like that. But despite her brave words, she realises it has already started, the preparation for marriage and motherhood. It started when she was twelve. That was when her mother said she must stop helping her father with the wild horses, like her brothers did. It was unbecoming for a girl to canter around the marshes with the men. No-one would want to marry a girl who behaved like that. She remembers how she had cried and pleaded with Papa to let her continue working with the horses, but he had stood firm and supported her mother, although she knew he was sorry to lose her help. He could see she had the gift, a gift that none of her brothers had inherited. She only had to stroke one of the horses on its nose, or whisper in its ear and it would follow her as meekly as a lamb.

'Where's Mama?' asks one of her sisters. It is Maya, and she has her two children with her. 'I want to leave the twins with her. I have to go into Almonte; it's market day.' She has a large basket of dried lavender over her arm.

'She's not here. She's gone to see if Juliana is all right.'

'She's always fussing about other people. Doesn't she realise that she has her own grandchildren to worry about.' She smiles at Clementina in the way that she has when she wants her to do something for her.

'No, I can't look after them. Mama has me doing a million things,' she says before Maya can speak. Her nieces are actually very sweet children, but she does not want to be lumbered with them all day. 'What about Kati? She loves looking after children.'

'Our sister says she is too busy.' Maya leans across and helps herself to a handful of pine nuts.

'Hey, stop that. Now I'll have to gather even more,' Clementina says.

'Say you'll look after the girls and I'll put them back.'

'No. You keep them. Just leave the girls and go. I expect someone will look after them.'

Maya does not need to be told twice. Clementina watches her sister run down the path and join her husband who is waiting in the wagon. The wagon rolls down the path pulled by two of the Marsh horses that Papa keeps for trips into the town. Clementina has never been into Almonte; her father will not allow it. The two little girls sit down beside her and begin to play with the pine cones.

'Why don't we go and gather some more cones,' she says and instantly the girls are up and running towards the woods. Clementina picks up the empty sack and follows them.

'You don't have any babies, Auntie. Why not?' asks one of them. She can never tell who is who because they are so alike. Maya says she ties a different colour ribbon in their hair so that she can distinguish them. Clementina is not even going to try. She knows one of them is Mari and the other is Ana, so she calls them both Mariana.

'Because I don't like babies,' she says. 'Except to eat.' She runs towards them with her arms outstretched and they run away shrieking with delight.

'I found some pine cones,' shouts one of the girls. 'Here, Auntie. Over here.'

Clementina sits down on a fallen log and watches as the girls rush around gathering pine cones. Her thoughts keep returning

to Hugo. It had been such a surprise to see him but she had recognised him immediately. They were great friends when they
were young; her brothers had been either too old to play with
the young son of Don Luis or too embarrassed, so she and Maya
had played with him. Now he is a man, and such a handsome
man. She had been hiding behind the stable and heard him tell
her father to send for her, but she knew her father would never
do that; he guards her as though she is a rare jewel. Sometimes
she finds his attitude pleasing and is flattered that of all his children he treats her so well, but other times it irritates her. She
was tempted to casually walk over to them and greet Hugo, but
who knows how her father would have reacted. He might have
lost his temper and offended Hugo and his friend and that could
have led to trouble. Despite what her mother thinks, Clementina
is learning the ways of the world, and knows that no matter
what her father may think of Don Luis and his family, he needs
their patronage.

'Is that enough, Auntie?' asks one of the nieces, sitting down
beside the pile of pine cones.

'Yes, but let's check them first. I don't want to carry them all
the way home just to end up throwing them on the fire. Let's
see. No. This one is no good. Look, it's already been eaten by a
squirrel. This is a good one. That's what you must look for, light
brown with a tinge of green.'

'So this one is no good either?' asks the other niece, holding
up a blackened pine cone.

'No, Mariana. That one is for the fire. Check through them
carefully and then we'll go and look for some berries before we
take them home. You like blackberries?'

'You know we do, Auntie.'

Clementina sees her mother sitting by the entrance to their home. She is sewing a brightly coloured apron and looks up when she hears the children laughing.

'Where is Maya?' she asks.

'She's gone to Almonte. She wanted you to look after the kids, but I told her you were busy.'

'So you're keeping an eye on them. That's nice of you.'

'Not really. They have been helping me with the pine nuts.' She glances down at the two little girls, their hands and faces are stained blue with the blackberry juice.

'Blackberries?' says her mother. 'Did you bring any back with you?'

Clementina shakes her head. 'They ate them all.' She turns and addresses the twins, saying, 'Right, now we have to finish removing the pine nuts from the cones. You are doing such a good job, you might as well carry on.' She picks up one of the pine cones and hits the rock with it. The girls squeal in delight when they see the pine nuts fall out onto the ground. 'Not too hard now. You don't want to smash them up.' She watches them for a moment to make sure they are doing it correctly and then goes and sits by her mother.

'You're a natural mother, Clementina. I've always said so. Well soon you'll have children of your own.' She is beaming at her daughter.

'Don't be ridiculous, Mama. I don't like children and I'm not getting married anyway. Ever.'

'You have no choice, my dear child. You can't live at home forever; you're fifteen already. We can't afford to keep you, so you will have to find a husband to do that. That's the way of the world, whether you like it or not.'

'Are you happy, Mama?' she asks, looking at her mother as though for the first time. She tries to see her as a woman instead of just her mother. Her hair still has a shine to it, and beneath the tired skin she can see that once she was beautiful. The lines on her face tell of a hard life but her eyes gleam with an inner fire.

'What sort of question is that, child. Don't let your father hear you talking like that or you will be in trouble.'

'Well are you? Did you love Papa when you married him?'

Her mother is looking confused. 'My parents found me a good husband. What more could I ask for? Now enough of this silly nonsense. We already have a very nice young man picked out for you. That's what is important, a good match.'

'So you didn't love Papa? Did you love someone else?'

'Stupid girl. Watch what you are saying or you will regret it.' Her mother's face is scarlet.

Clementina can see she has hit a raw nerve. So her mother was in love when she was young, but with whom? Was it the man she was forced to marry or someone else? She feels sad for her mother. 'I'm sorry, Mama. I don't know what I was thinking. I didn't mean to upset you.' She puts her arms around her mother and lays her head on her shoulder.

'You didn't upset me, child. It just grieves me to hear you talking such nonsense. There are more important things in life than being in love. You will find that out, soon enough. Now, go and sort out those girls or we will never get the pine nuts ready for tonight's meal.' She pats her daughter gently on the back. 'And when you've finished go across to the charcoal burners and buy me a sack of charcoal.'

'But, Mama, the charcoal will stain my dress. Can't you send one of the boys?' Her mother does not answer; the look on her face says it all. 'Oh, all right.'

CHAPTER 5

Ramon is not sure that he is doing the right thing. He should never have come to see his brother. He should have stayed in Seville. Now he is following the directions of some befuddled old man, a thief and a liar who believes he is still top of the Guardia's wanted list. He does not realise that the world has moved on; the police are more interested in apprehending dissidents than bandits these days. Still Ramon has no choice. If he stays he will be putting Pedro in danger and he does not want his brother to pay for his mistakes. Not that he regrets taking part in the demonstration, no, what he regrets is not keeping control of his temper. His mother always said his fiery temper would get him into trouble one day; now he is glad that she is not here to see it.

It pains him to think about Mama; he should have been there for her, to help her, to hold her hand when she passed away. He chokes back a sob. Whatever Pedro might think, that was what he was trying to do, help her and all the other women like her who struggle all their lives to bring up children in a world which does not want them. He remembers how she would tell them stories when they were little; how she scraped and saved to pay the teacher who came to their village and taught him and Pedro to read and write. He can still hear her strong determined voice saying to his father that she did not want a child of hers to have the humiliation of having to sign his name with a cross. She had never been to school herself but that did not mean that she could not see the importance of education for her sons. If she thought that by educating them she might help them escape from the poverty in which they lived, she never said so. And when his father asked her why she thought it was important for them to read and write all she said was that it would help them to understand the world they lived in. In that she was right. By the time he turned sixteen Ramon had come to realise that the system was broken, so he had left home and looked for people who thought like him, and he had found them in Seville, groups of anarchists, socialists and communists. He met teachers and intellectuals, artisans, labourers like his father, peasants and sharecroppers. Political tensions in the city were high and each group had its own demands but they shared one thing in common; they wanted a better life for themselves and their families. Ramon was poorly educated but he was stimulated by their discussions and soon began to form his own ideas. He did not agree with all of them—that was an impossibility as many of their views were extreme and even he could see that they would not work without tearing the country apart—and gradually he allied himself to the socialists.

He stops and listens. There is no sound of anyone or anything moving, just the distant screech of an owl. He guesses that he has been walking for almost an hour so he must be close to the river by now. Surely that is running water he can hear; he continues walking straight ahead and the sound of the river grows steadily louder. It is almost dawn and the birds are waking up; he can hear the screech of seagulls in the distance and smell the salt of the sea in the air. He must be close to the estuary now. The old man has warned him that the Guadalquivir estuary is wide and deep, so once he reaches the banks of the river he must follow it downstream until he comes to the small port of Bonanza. Here, according to Adolfo, there is a ferry which will take him across the river to the dense woods of the Coto Doñana and safety. He walks cautiously, still not sure that following Adolfo's advice is the best decision he has made in his life.

By the time Ramon reaches the ferry, a pale gleam of light is just appearing over the horizon. He looks around him; there is no-one about and the ferry seems to be closed, but then he notices a small rowing boat moored a little upstream. He must have passed it just now without seeing it, so intent was he on looking for the ferryman. He clambers down the bank and heads towards it. As he starts to climb into the boat he hears an angry shout.

'What the hell? Where do you think you're going?' A man is crouched in the undergrowth, a fishing net spread on the ground next to him. He picks up an oar and gets up slowly, his eyes never leaving Ramon as comes towards him. He carries the oar as though it is a weapon.

'Are you the ferryman?' Ramon asks.

'Why do you want to know?'

'I need to get across the river.'

'You can swim, can't you?' the man says with a smirk.

Ramon shakes his head. This is going to be difficult. He has hardly any money to pay for the crossing—he had given most of his money to his sister-in-law before he left— and although he calculates that he can overpower the man quite easily and take the boat, he does not want to do that. He has had enough of violence for now. 'I just need to get across. Can you help me?'

The man continues to stare at him. 'Where are you from?' he asks. 'Are you one of those Bolsheviks?'

'No. Of course not. I've been to visit my mother in Jerez. My brother sent me a message to say she was ill but by the time I arrived she had died. Now I must get back to work or I will get the sack. I just can't lose my job. I have five children to feed. My boss is such a bastard; he pays me a pittance as it is. I know he will get rid of me if I so much as put a foot wrong.' He says the first things that come into his head and prays that the ferryman will not ask him where he works.

'Ten centimos and I'll take you across,' the man says at last. He bends down and rolls up the net, but not before extracting two small fish that he has managed to catch and putting them in a bucket.

Ramon heaves a sigh of relief. 'Not much luck then?' he says, nodding towards the fish.

'Just get in if you want to cross.'

Ramon hands the man a ten centimo coin and climbs into the boat. He is reluctant to start a conversation with him and the ferryman seems disinclined to chat anyway, and sits staring at the receding bank in silence. Ramon remembers Adolfo's advice, the least anyone knows about him the better.

The river is turning from black to silver as the sun rises. It flows gently but unwaveringly towards the sea. Is this his life now, he wonders. Is he too on an unstoppable path towards his destiny? But what is his destiny? At the moment it looks as though he has a choice between death, prison or at best, exile. He feels the rage grow inside him again. What the hell is he doing here? And for how long must he remain in hiding? These are the questions that race around in his head. He should never have left Seville; it was a coward's way out.

The rowing boat pulls up alongside the bank. 'Out you get,' the ferryman says, steadying the boat with one hand and swatting at a mosquito that has settled on his neck with the other. 'Damned *bichos*.'

As Ramon stands up he can feel something under his foot. He bends down to look; it is a dead Mallard, freshly killed. So it is not just fish that the ferryman wants to catch in his net, it is wildfowl too. He smiles to himself. Poacher cum ferryman, well why not. His stomach is so empty he is tempted to slip the duck into his bag while the ferryman is busy steadying the boat, but decides against it. Why make an enemy of him; he may need his services again. He realises that the ferryman has no intention of taking him any closer to the bank and hesitates, looking down into the murky river.

'Come on. What are you, a damned Marquess? Out you get.'

Ramon reluctantly steps into the cold water and climbs up the bank. The forest looms darkly in front of him, unknown and forbidding. He is tempted to ask the ferryman if he knows where the charcoal burners live, but decides that is too risky. Normally a chatty, talkative man by nature, he must learn to curb his tongue; he cannot trust anyone now.

He steps gingerly onto the path leading into the forest and peers into the undergrowth. The old man has warned him about the wild boar that roam the woods and Ramon does not fancy encountering one of them in the dark as he has brought nothing with which to defend himself, so he decides to wait until the light is stronger before looking for the *carboneros*. He turns and watches as the ferryman rows back across the river and disappears into the early morning mist that is now drifting across the surface of the water, then he takes cover in the undergrowth and curls up to wait for dawn.

Ramon seems to have been going round and round in circles and is getting no nearer to finding the charcoal burners. Adolfo had led him to believe it would be easy, that he would smell the slow burning wood as soon as he grew near the charcoal *bolich-*

es. The woods are full of smells; he recognises the stink of foxes' piss, and maybe where a lynx has marked its territory, but the overwhelming scent which fills his nostrils is that of the pine trees, a sweet, sharp smell which for some reason seems to invigorate him. He has no idea how far into the woods he has wandered and is thinking of retracing his steps towards the river—if he is able to—when he notices it, that bitter, acrid smell of smouldering wood. He looks up at the sky and through the tree tops he sees a narrow column of smoke drifting upwards. He has found them. *Gracias a Dios.* At last. Carefully Ramon heads towards the clearing where he finds six *boliches*, conical mounds of logs, covered with a layer of sand and reeds; smoke is drifting lazily out of them. A man is stretched out on the ground beside the *boliches* but he ignores Ramon as he walks towards the nearest one and inspects it. He has never seen a charcoal oven before although he has often used its product; the design is impressive but how does it work? He peers at it closely; there is a small hole in the top of the mound which acts like a chimney and it is from here that the smoke drifts slowly into the air. He is about to ask the man to explain the process to him when a large dog bounds up to him and starts barking. Ramon does not move; he is unused to dogs and not sure of what to do next. The dog does not appear to be very friendly and begins to growl and show its teeth. Ramon looks across at the man on the ground who is ignoring the presence of both him and the dog. Ramon is tempted to pick up the charred log on the ground near his feet but if he does that the dog might take it as a threat and attack him. Instead he decides to talk to it, 'All right, old boy. You have nothing to worry about from me. All right now. Good dog. Good dog.'

The man is watching him now and smiling, but does not move.

'Niño,' a girl's voice calls. 'Here. Come here.'

The dog turns and runs off in the direction of the newcomer. Ramon still does not move, but this time it is not from fear but from surprise. Coming towards him is the most lovely young girl he has ever seen. She is wearing a white dress and there is a scarlet and black shawl around her tiny waist, a flowery scarf holds her dark hair back from her face. She is like an angel and he wants to pinch himself in case he is dreaming.

'He's perfectly harmless,' the girl says. 'He just likes to make a lot of noise, like most males,' she adds with a laugh which reveals the daintiest, whitest teeth he has ever seen.

He cannot speak; just looking at her fills his whole being with pleasure.

'Are you all right?' she asks. 'I assure you, he is quite harmless.'

At last he manages to pull himself together and says, 'I'm fine. Thank you.'

'Are you lost?' she asks.

'I don't think so,' he answers rather vaguely. He can see she is beginning to think there may be something wrong with him, so he adds, 'I am looking for Jorge, the *carbonero*.'

'Jorge? Jorge Bandido? He's dead. He died three years ago.'

His mouth drops open. What on earth is he going to do now? 'How did he die?' he asks, not from interest but just so he can keep this lovely creature standing there a little longer.

'He was gored by a wild boar. He was too old to be out hunting on his own; he should have waited for his son, everyone said so.'

'He has a son?'

'Yes, his name is Jaime.' She points to a path leading through the trees and adds, 'If you go along there you will come to the *chozas* where he lives. I can show you if you like. I'm going there to collect some charcoal for my mother.'

'That would be very kind.' He has forgotten why he is here; all he can think of is how to remain in her company a little while longer. She leads the way, walking along a narrow path, closely followed by the dog and with Ramon bringing up the rear. He is desperate to talk to her but he finds himself tongue-tied; he who can be so eloquent when declaring the rights of the worker cannot even introduce himself to a young woman. What is happening to him? His heart is pounding, his mouth is dry and all he can think about is the vision walking in front of him.

After a short while they come to a clearing encircled by a thick briar hedge, and inside the clearing are a number of small *chozas* and people sitting on the ground, eating. The smell of fresh meat drifts across to him and once again his stomach reminds him of how hungry he is; he has eaten nothing since the watery broth at his brother's home the night before.

The girl stops and turns to him. 'That's Jaime's *choza*, over there,' she says, opening the gate into the clearing. 'I must go now. I have to collect the charcoal and get back or my mother will be angry. She is always saying that I spend too much time day-dreaming and not enough working.' She laughs as though it does not really matter to her what her mother says, and once again he gets a glimpse of those perfect white teeth and his heart skips a beat.

'Thank you,' is all he manages to say. He wants to ask if he will see her again, but knows he cannot do that; it would be much too forward of him, and anyway why would she be interested in a man who was hiding from the Guardia Civil. He waits for a moment longer, watching her walk across the clearing and speaking to one of the *carboneros*.

'Are you looking for someone?' A woman asks. She is wearing a loose smock over her dress and her face and hands are stained with smears of charcoal. A dirty scarf is tied around her hair.

'Jaime Bandido. Does he live here?'

'Who are you and what do you want with him?' she asks, looking at him suspiciously.

'Well, actually I came to see his father, Jorge, but that young lady told me he is dead.' Ramon points in the direction of the girl in the white dress, who is now leaving with a large bag of charcoal on her back.

'Clementina? Did she now. She's very free with her information, like all of her family, I might add. Well wait there and I'll go and get him.' She ducks down and enters the conical structure that is Jaime's home.

A few minutes later a young man emerges. His face, hands and beard are stained black from the charcoal and his clothes are filthy, but he smiles pleasantly at Ramon and says, 'You wanted to see my father? Well as you have heard he is no longer with us. What business did you have with him?'

Ramon hesitates. Can he really trust these people? Adolfo seems to think so. He looks around him. Apart from Jaime and the woman, nobody is paying any attention to him. 'An old friend of your father's sent me. Adolfo. He said that Jorge would help me.'

'You're hiding from the Guardia Civil?'

Ramon is surprised at his abruptness. 'Yes.'

Jaime looks at him and begins to stroke his beard, and by doing so covers it with even more charcoal. 'Are you hungry?'

Ramon nods his head.

The woman ducks back into the *choza* and comes out with a hunk of bread and a piece of sausage.

Ramon almost snatches it from her hand; he has not had sausage for a very long time. The smell is wonderful. 'Thank you,' he mumbles with his mouth full.

'I don't want to know what you've done or why you are here,' says Jaime. 'The less you talk about yourself, the better. If you stay here you will have to work. You will get paid. Not much, but enough for you to eat. In your spare time you can build yourself somewhere to live. There is wood aplenty in the forest. You might even get someone to give you a hand.'

'I don't know anything about making charcoal,' Ramon says.

'You'll soon learn. Kiko, come here, son.'

A young boy runs over to them; he is even dirtier than his father, the black charcoal dust is engrained in his youthful skin. 'My son will help you settle in and show you what to do,' he says. 'There is one thing though; we never go into the town or leave the forest except to deliver the charcoal. We keep to ourselves and you will have to do the same if you want to live with us. If the Guardia find you, they will punish all of us, not just you. So bear that in mind before you decide if you want to live here with us.'

Is this to be his life now? Making charcoal and living in the forest? Yes, he will be safe but it will no longer be *his* life, the life he has dreamed of. 'I understand,' he says, trying to sound positive.

'Very well. You can leave your things in our *choza* for the moment then go with Kiko and he will show you what to do.'

Ramon steps inside the *choza* and looks for a space to leave his bag. The building is twice the size of Pedro's mud hut and is built with saplings of pine, cut and trimmed into poles which form the sloping walls and roof of the hut. Much like the *boliches*, the *choza* has a fire burning in the centre of the room with an opening in the roof for the smoke to escape, but it is a sturdy building and even has two large beds at one end. How his sister-in-law Ana would love a home like this. Even the floor, although mud, is beaten hard and coated with something to reduce the dust.

'Everything all right?' Jaime asks.

'Yes. I was just admiring your house.'

'Time enough for that later. You've got wood to chop.'

The boy is hunkered down on the floor outside the *choza*, waiting for him. He smiles at the lad and follows him to the edge of the clearing and through the gate. He is about eight or nine-years-old and, like most of the children Ramon sees, he is very thin but he looks strong and wiry for his age. 'Do you go to school?' he asks him.

'What? No, of course I don't. I have work to do here. There's no money for stupid things like school books. What good would it do me anyway? You don't need books to be a *carbonero*,' he says, obviously quoting his father. He picks up an axe which is nearly as big as he is and hands it to Ramon. 'We have to build a new *boliche*, so we need to chop down some trees. To do that we need to go deeper into the forest.' He bends down and picks up a branch. 'This should do if we meet any wolves,' he says.

'Wolves? Are there wolves in the forest?' Ramon does not like the sound of that.

The boy bursts out laughing. 'Don't look so worried; they never attack during the day. They will be sleeping somewhere until it gets dark.'

'But there are wolves in Doñana?'

'Not many. Papa told me that there used to be lots of them when he was a boy, before the hunters shot most of them. He said that my grandfather had seen them.' He looks proud of this information. Ramon presumes that he is referring to Jorge Bandido. 'He was a brave man, my grandfather,' the boy adds. 'And he taught me lots of things.'

By now they have lost sight of the *chozas* and as they move deeper into the woods, the pine trees are taller and more densely packed, but the boy does not slow down; he seems to know his way through this gloomy forest and soon they step out into a sunlit clearing where two men are already chopping at the trunk of one of the trees.

'Watch out, lads. This one is about to fall.'

Ramon stands back and watches as a giant pine tree, as straight as a flag pole, crashes to the ground, causing a flock of grey-legged geese to fly up from a nearby pond honking in protest.

'It's all yours, lads,' says one of the men as they move on further into the forest.

'What does he mean?' asks Ramon. 'What have we got to do with this?' He points to the fallen tree.

'Turn it into charcoal, of course.' The boy looks at him as if he is stupid.

Well maybe he is. 'And how do we do that?' he asks.

'First we have to cut this tree into logs of an equal size.' He takes out a piece of charcoal and makes a mark on the side of the trunk. 'They all have to be this size.'

'But why? You're going to burn it, aren't you? Not make a piece of furniture.'

'I can see you have a lot to learn,' the boys says, as though he is speaking to a small child. 'You will see later when we empty one of last week's *boliches*. For now, just do as I say.'

They divide the work between them, Ramon chopping the logs according to Kiko's instructions and Kiko filling the hessian sacks. It is hot work and Ramon's hands are soon sore from wielding the axe.

'That's enough for now,' the boy tells him. 'We'll take this back and I'll teach you how to build a *boliche*.'

When they get back to the group of *boliches*, Ramon notices that two men are busy dismantling one of them and raking out the charcoal; he recognises the man who was lying on the ground earlier.

'Is it finished?' he asks Kiko.

'Yes. Come and have a look.'

'*Buenos días*, kid. What are you up to? Going to give us a hand?' One of the men asks. He ignores Ramon.

'I'm teaching this guy how to be a *carbonero*,' he says. 'He's a friend of Papa.'

'Oh, another of them, is he,' says the second man, turning away. He makes it sound as though Jaime Bandido helps a lot of fugitives. 'Well, you'd better come closer if you're going to learn anything.'

'This is the last stage,' says Kiko.

Ramon watches attentively as the men rake the glowing charcoal from the embers of the fire.

'This took ten days,' the boy says proudly. 'I told you it has to burn slowly. And it has to be watched night and day so that it doesn't suddenly flare up and burn too quickly. That's the skill, keeping it burning steadily. Slow and steady does it.'

'Not burning, lad. Smouldering. We don't want any flames. That's no good at all,' says one of the men.

The boy looks chastened and says,' Yes, that's what I meant to say. It takes a lot of skill to keep it just right.' He points to an old hut nearby. 'That's where they sleep, close to the charcoal ovens, so they can monitor them all the time.'

'Is that all they do?' asks Ramon, hoping he will not be asked to monitor the *boliches*.

'Yes, but usually it's only the more experienced *carboneros* who do that. The rest, like me,' he says puffing out his chest, 'prepare the *boliches*.'

'How about you stop talking about it and get on and do it,' says the other man.

Kiko signals for Ramon to follow him and they take the sacks of wood to an open space. 'This will do fine,' he says. 'We need to stack the wood into a big pile, but carefully, not just any old way. Watch me.' He picks up some logs and begins stacking them vertically to form a cone shaped mound of wood. 'The heat must be even. Not too hot in one part and cool in another.'

'What about the hole for the smoke?' asks Ramon.

The boy scowls at him. 'I'm coming to that. Now you can see how to do it, you can help me stack the logs. But be careful.'

Ramon sets to, handing the logs to the boy who continues stacking them. He wonders how old Kiko was when he started building these charcoal ovens; he seems to be very competent.

They work at building the pyre for a couple of hours until it is finished. They have set a small fire of brushwood and wood chips in the centre of the *boliche* and have covered the outside layer with a thick coating of reeds, moss and earth.

The boy stands back and admires his handiwork. 'That's it ready,' he tells Ramon. 'Hey Javi, it's finished,' he shouts. 'Are you going to light it?'

The two men have finished dismantling the other oven and are shovelling the charcoal into the hessian bags that the logs were in. 'Just a minute,' Javi shouts.

'It's very impressive,' says Ramon. 'You certainly know how to build a good *boliche*. How long have you been doing this?'

'Since I was six.' He is beaming with pride. 'You'll soon be able to do. It's not that difficult, it just takes practice.' He bends down and smooths the mud coating. 'You see you have to control the flow of air otherwise it burns too quickly and then there will be no charcoal.'

Ramon smiles sadly and nods. So this is Kiko's life now, to become a *carbonero* like his father. No schooling, no chance to learn that there are more opportunities for him than making charcoal and no chance to explore a world beyond these woods.

Javi comes across and inspects their work. 'A fine job, lad,' he says. 'Right, let's get this lit.' He has a burning taper in his hand and leans over and inserts it through the hole they have left open. Soon a wisp of smoke is rising from the *boliche* and the man checks that no smoke is escaping elsewhere. 'That looks fine. We'll keep an eye on it now. You can carry those bags of charcoal over to the shed.'

'So what will they look for?' Ramon asks the boy. 'How will they know it is working properly and making charcoal?'

'The most important thing is to keep it burning very, very slowly,' Kiko emphasises this with a sweep of his hand. 'Any sign of flames is bad. But the fire mustn't go out either. That's just as bad.'

'So how do they know what's happening without opening it?'

'That's the trick. The *carbonero* watches the smoke. If it's thick and grey then the wood is still raw. Look, like that one over there. That was only lit five days ago. But if it's blue smoke then it means it's making good charcoal.' He points to another *boliche*.

'How long does it take for an oven of that size to make the charcoal?' asks Ramon, picking up one of the sacks and putting it across his shoulders; it is much lighter than it looks.

The boy shrugs his shoulders. 'Each one is different. Anything from one week to two. This carbon took eight days. But it was not easy because last week we had a lot of wind and one of the *carboneros* had to watch it all the time. He has to control the draught so that it doesn't flare up.' He takes another of the sacks and sets off for the woods. 'Follow me.'

'Is that why he is making those holes in the side of the oven?' asks Ramon. He has spotted one of the men making small punctures in the mud coating and then resealing others.

'Yes. I'm not allowed to do that yet,' says the boy. 'It's skilled work.' He looks across admiringly at the *carbonero*.

Ramon is growing to like the lad; he is a serious child and very bright. Again he thinks about what Kiko's future could be if only he has an education.

They deposit the charcoal in the shed, alongside a dozen other similar bags and then head back for the rest. Suddenly the boy stops.

'What is it?' Ramon asks.

'It's my mother. What does she want? She hardly ever comes into the woods.'

When Ramon looks round he sees the woman who had given him the bread and sausage standing on the path; she has been running and now her chest is heaving with the exertion.

'Are you all right, Mama?' the boy asks.

'The Guardia Civil are in the woods. You can't go home just yet. Kiko, take our friend into the dunes and stay there until dark. I must go back before I am missed. Here take this.' She thrusts a piece of bread and a lump of cheese into her son's hand and immediately starts running back the way she has come.

'Come on. We can't stay here. The Guardia love to nose around our sheds and often help themselves to a few sacks of charcoal. They say they are looking for contraband but we don't believe them.' Kiko does not look at all upset at the news.

'So this often happens?'

'Not really, but sometimes. We don't trust anyone from outside, and especially not the police.' He sounds like an old man, and in a way he is because he has had to grow up quickly in this hard world. He thinks about his own niece and nephew; their future is even bleaker than Kiko's, at least he has work and food. It may not be much but it is honest work and the *carboneros* have their independence.

'Come on. We need to hurry. Bring some of the charcoal with you.'

Ramon picks up a couple of bags of charcoal and follows the boy. Why are they helping him? He realises how dangerous it is for them, so why are they doing it?

CHAPTER 6

Hugo has to admit that it was a shock to see the change in Clementina. More than that, it was a revelation; she was such a tom-boy when she was young, always preferring to play with him and her brothers—when they would let her. But it is more than that. He cannot quite put his finger on what it is about her that has disturbed him; maybe she reminds him of someone. He shakes his head. He is being ridiculous; she was a child when he last saw her and now she is almost a grown woman. He thinks back to when they were children; she had always been a far better rider than he was, despite being younger and smaller. She was quite fearless when she was on the back of a horse. He wonders if she still rides. He imagines her sitting on their lovely Retuerta, her skirts caught up around her waist exposing her long brown legs, her hair loose and blowing in the breeze. He sighs.

'You're very thoughtful,' says Cristóbal. 'Or are you dreaming of that lovely gypsy girl?'

'I'm just hungry, you idiot. Come on. Papa gets irritable if anyone is late for dinner.'

They make their way into the elegant dining room and Hugo pours out two large glasses of Amontillado sherry and hands one to his friend.

'Ah, Cristóbal, you're still here,' says Don Luis coming in and sitting at the head of the table. 'Pour me one, if you would, Hugo.' His wife follows him; she is dressed in a gown of dark blue silk that ripples and reflects the light as she walks, and her long greying hair is piled on top of her head.

'Yes, I thought I'd stay a while longer, if you don't object. That chap in Doñana says he needs a couple more days to train the stallion before I can take him.'

'Well if he says that, then it must be true. He knows what he's doing. You are more than welcome to stay here as long as you like.' He looks at his wife, who smiles and nods her approval. 'We will be in Seville tomorrow, as you already know.' His wife is smiling contentedly at the thought of her day in the city.

'In that case, how about we go hunting again tomorrow?' suggests Hugo. 'You've never hunted in the Coto de Doñana, have you? It will be a treat for you. We'll go first thing tomorrow morning.'

Cristóbal bursts out laughing.

'What is it? What's so funny?' asks Don Luis, looking at him in surprise.

Hugo scowls at his friend but Cristóbal will not be contained. 'Hugo has fallen in love with a beautiful gypsy girl. That's why he wants us to go back to Doñana. He is hoping for a rendezvous with her.' He looks around the table and his face drops; he has made a dreadful error of judgement.

Don Luis immediately stands up, knocking over his glass. 'I do hope you are joking, young man. I can assure you that my son would never, I repeat, never entertain any sort of relationship with a woman of that class.'

A silence falls over the table, even Doña Isabel looks uncomfortable. Hugo can see that his friend is dying of embarrassment and is unable to find a way to retrieve the situation. He is about to assure his father that it is just a joke and they are referring to Clementina, the little girl he used to play with, when his brother joins them at the table.

'You're late,' snaps Don Luis. There is no smile of welcome for Felipe.

Hugo's brother looks around the table. 'What's happened? Someone died?' He pours some sherry into a glass and picks up an olive and pops it into his mouth. 'Well? What's happened?' Felipe repeats.

'Your brother is planning to bring disgrace on this family,' Don Luis says. 'But I won't have it. I will disinherit him rather than have our family name ridiculed.'

Hugo is unable to speak. He cannot understand why his father is reacting so dramatically; it is not as though Cristóbal has said that he is about to elope with her. Why so much fuss over a silly joke? Was his father never young himself? He sometimes doubts it. He swallows the last of his glass of sherry and pours himself another.

'Is anyone going to tell me what's going on? Cristóbal, you're a sensible lad, what is happening here?' asks Felipe.

This appears to be too much for Cristóbal, who stands up and leaves the room without a word.

'*Madre mía*. Have I walked into a mad house?'

Suddenly Hugo can stand it no longer. 'I'm not hungry. Sorry, Mama,' he says and walks out. He can hear his brother shouting; Papa has told him about Tina.

Cristóbal is sitting outside in the garden, smoking a cigarette. 'I'm so sorry, Hugo. I really didn't mean to cause all this fuss. I thought your father would join in the joke.'

'It was a bit crass of you, but there was really no need for father to be so upset. I just can't understand his reaction. And did you see Mama's face? She looked as though she was going to be sick. Something's not right.' He accepts a cigarette from his friend and lights it.

'So what will you do? It is a joke, isn't it? You're not in love with this girl, are you? You're not planning on doing anything stupid, I hope?' Cristóbal asks, searching Hugo's face for an answer.

'Of course not, you idiot. But she is a lovely girl; what man wouldn't want to kiss her. Still I don't see why you should be deprived of a day's hunting in Doñana, just because my father can't handle a bit of banter. We'll go early, before breakfast. He'll change his tune when we bring him back a few wildfowl, or maybe even a deer.' Hugo throws the cigarette on the ground and says, 'Come on. We'll get something to eat from the kitchen. I'm starving.'

At first they limit their hunting to the marshes and very quickly manage to bag three ducks, a goose and a few pigeons. 'That should appease the old man,' says Hugo, tying the birds to his saddle. 'How about we try to shoot a deer later?'

'Does that mean going near the gypsy encampment?' asks Cristóbal.

'Not necessarily, but we do need to go deeper into the woods. Even if we are nearer to the gypsies, we are unlikely to see Tina.' He feels excited at the thought that they might in fact see her again. 'But we need to wait until it's evening; that's when we will have a better chance to bag one.'

'Well, it's your funeral. Your father did not look very pleased yesterday when I mentioned her. But don't worry; I won't say anything this time.'

They sit down by a stream and unpack the lunch that the cook has prepared for them: smoked ham, bread, cheese and a couple of bottles of wine. The sound of a woman singing drifts across the water towards them.

'Who is that, do you think?' asks Cristóbal.

'Probably one of the gypsy women washing her clothes in the stream.'

'Are there other people living in Doñana? Other than the gypsy horse traders?'

'There are a few *carboneros* and their families, some fishermen down by the beach and the Marquess's people who work on the estate and at the palace. He employs quite a number of gamekeepers to look out for poachers.'

'Oh, isn't that what we're doing? Poaching?' Cristóbal looks worried.

'No, of course not. My father has permission from the Marquess; we can hunt here whenever we want.' He lies back and watches the flamingos who have gathered on the far side of the lake. The singing grows louder; it sounds as though the woman is coming their way. He props himself up on one elbow and looks towards the edge of the forest and then he sees her. It is Tina; she is carrying a basket full of wet clothes and she is heading towards them.

He looks over at Cristóbal but he has his eyes closed and appears to be asleep, so taking care not to disturb him, Hugo gets up quietly and walks towards her.

'Tina. How lovely to see you after all this time. I thought it was you when we came to look at the horse.' He hesitates.

'Hugo. I knew it was you. You haven't changed.' She smiles at him and her whole face lights up with pleasure. 'I mean, well you have of course, but I could recognise you straight away. How is your family?'

He shrugs. 'They're fine. Was that you singing?'

'You could hear me? Yes. Don't you recognise it? I used to sing that song all the time when I was younger. I suppose it was seeing you yesterday that reminded me of it.'

He nods. He does remember her singing it; all the girls used to sing that song and some of the older boys too, strumming their guitars in accompaniment.

'So what are you doing here?' she asks, looking at the remains of their picnic spread out on the riverbank.

'We came to do some hunting. My friend has never hunted here before.' He lowers his voice; the last thing he wants is for Cristóbal to wake up.

'I don't remember him,' she says, looking at the figure stretched out on the rug. 'From the old days.'

'No, you wouldn't. He's from Seville. His father is our family lawyer.' He wants to say something more to her, but he can't. All he can do is look at her. Even with her hair awry and her dress wet from the river; she is so lovely.

'Well I must go. Mama is waiting for the clothes,' she says.

She is still smiling at him and Hugo begins to feel that there is no one else in the world but them. 'Here, let me carry it for you,' he says at last and takes the basket of wet clothes from her.

She doesn't protest but asks, 'What about your friend?'

'My friend?' He looks across at the supine Cristóbal, who has now begun to snore. 'He will be all right. I'll be back before he knows I've gone.'

Together they walk along the path through the woods and before they know it they are laughing and joking about the times they shared as children, and now Hugo feels he is in love.

'I'll take it now,' she says, stretching up and relieving him of the basket. 'Papa will be cross if he sees me talking to you.'

'Can we meet again?' asks Hugo.

She smiles. 'I don't think it is a good idea, do you Hugi? We are no longer children. Your father would not approve and neither will mine. In fact they will both be very angry. I don't want to upset my father.'

Hugi. She says his name just like she used to. It sounds like music on her lips. 'Tomorrow?' he whispers.

Clementina smiles again and walks away towards the gypsy encampment leaving him standing there in the woods, grinning like a fool.

'I love you, Clementina,' he calls after her. 'I always have.'

'Where have you been?' asks Cristóbal. 'I was beginning to think you had got lost, or eloped with that beautiful young lady.'

'What young lady?' Hugo asks, feeling the blood rush to his face in embarrassment.

'You know. The one you just walked off with. You don't think I was really asleep, do you?' He sits up and grins at him. 'I must say your courtship technique is not very slick. I was beginning to think that the cat had got your tongue and I should run across and give you some tips.' They both laugh at this because normally it is Cristóbal who becomes embarrassed and tongue-tied when they meet any young women.

'That'll be the day when I need lessons from you,' says Hugo.

'So? Are you seeing her again?'

'I'd like to, but I don't know. I don't want to cause any trouble, but to be truthful, I don't think I can keep away. I think I'm falling in love with her.'

'Oh, Hugo, Hugo. It's just a fancy. I know you. We've been here before. You meet a lovely woman and then you immediately think you are in love with her and want to spend the rest of your life with her. Until the next one comes along, that is. Forget it; it's just infatuation.'

'No, Cristóbal, this is different. I really do feel something for her. It's not a fancy. There's something that is drawing me to her. I have never felt like this before. Never.'

'You're too right, it is different. There's something about that girl that your father cannot bear; I could see it in his face. And remember her father when we were here last time, he wouldn't let you see her either. You are likely to be disinherited if you continue this time; that's if her father doesn't kill you first. You mustn't get involved with her; it will only lead to trouble.'

'I'm not going to inherit the business anyway. That's going to Felipe when Papa dies. All my inheritance will consist of is the chance to keep on working at the bodega. He might leave me a little money, but I doubt it. So I don't really care if he does cut me out of his will.' Hugo pauses. Maybe Benito knows what is in his father's will. 'Your father drew up the will for Papa, didn't he?'

'Yes, I think so. It would have been some years ago, though.'

'Why does Papa want to see your father, I wonder?'

'No idea. I can ask him if you like, but I know he won't tell me. He is very strict about client confidentiality.'

'No, don't bother. I'm sure Felipe will get it out of Papa and then we will all know, especially if it's something he doesn't agree with.' Hugo picks up a bottle of wine. 'There's a little left if you want some,' he says.

'No, you have it. I'm going to have a siesta.'

'Good idea, and then we will go and find ourselves a nice fat buck.'

CHAPTER 7

Don Luis is still feeling angry about his outburst at dinner; it was stupid to reveal his feelings like that, and undignified. And for what? Hugo is always falling in love with some unsuitable female; this one will be no different. By the time he has been to England for a couple of weeks he will have forgotten all about Clementina. He knows she is the one Cristóbal was talking about. It has to be; he remembers her as a very beautiful child. Nevertheless it is time Hugo got married and settled down; then it will be up to him if he wants to dabble in a little extra-marital sex, as long as it is not with her. He will talk to his wife about bringing forward Hugo's marriage to Mari Carmen de Almudanza. Yes, it is about time they invited her and her parents to dinner again; they will do that before Hugo goes to England. He smiles to himself; it will be a wonderful match, something he has always longed for, a union between his company Butler & Rodriguez and Almudanza & Watson, the two biggest and best bodegas in the region. Better still, Mari Carmen is an only child —her mother died in childbirth and Juan has never remarried— so she will inherit the company and, in time, his grandchildren will become the owners.

'*Señor* there are some people to see Doña Isabel,' says his major-domo. 'Father Sanchez and two other gentlemen.'

'Well, show them into the drawing room and let her know. Why are you bothering me?' He continues to look out of the window. Hugo has never shown much interest in the business;

he does what he is asked to do, but without enthusiasm. Maybe when he is married he will view things differently.

He hears the sound of male voices. Strange, Isabel does not often have visitors, and never men unless they are from the Church. Maybe he should go and see who Father Sanchez has brought along with him this time. He will be after money again no doubt. Isabel is an easy touch for the priest; she believes that the more of his money she gives to the Church, the more likely they will both go to heaven when they die. He has tried to explain to her that that is not necessarily what happens but her faith is strong. Strong enough for both of them luckily or he would be destined to go to a hotter destination when he dies.

The major-domo opens the door to the drawing room for him. Don Luis sees the bulky figure of Father Sanchez perched on the edge of an armchair like a huge black crow. Two men in the blue uniforms of the Falange are sitting side by side on the sofa and his lovely wife is sitting opposite them listening attentively. What the hell is going on?

'*Buenos días,*' he says, striding into the room. The men all leap to their feet.

'Don Luis, how nice to see you,' says Father Sanchez, looking slightly embarrassed. 'We did not know you were at home or we would have come directly to you.'

'Well now you know.' He turns and looks at the two Falangists, who promptly salute him. 'And you are?' he asks.

'*Buenos días, Señor.* Capitán Moreno, *Señor.*'

He seems very young to be a captain, but then the Falange is a new organisation, formed only two years earlier. Before he can ask them their business, the priest begins to explain.

'Don Luis, these gentlemen are here to ask your lady wife if she would be so gracious as to help with the *Sección Femenina.*'

So not money this time. What then? He perches on the arm of his wife's chair and asks her, 'What is this all about, *Cariño*?'

'They are just about to explain, my dear. The *Sección Femenina* is an organisation to help families and ensure that women lead good, clean lives,' she replies.

'A charity? Run by a political party?' He cannot keep the sarcasm from his voice. He has heard a little about this new party; they are great supporters of the Catholic Church and consider themselves to be the party of law and order, in other words not great advocates of democracy. Maybe that's not such a bad thing; the country needs someone to keep these damned Communists in their place.

'More than that, *Señora*,' the captain interrupts. 'It is to educate women on how to be good wives and mothers. Our founder, Primo de Rivera, understands that women do not have the same intelligence nor creativity as men and therefore need help to lead useful lives in society. With the help of the Church, we have drawn up a number of rules for women to follow in order to fulfil their roles as good wives.' He pulls out a printed sheet of paper. 'I will leave this with you.'

'Are you suggesting that my wife is not fulfilling her duties correctly?' asks Don Luis, frowning at them.

The captain looks horrified. 'No, *Señor*, of course not. These courses are open to all women but particularly the young, unmarried women, so that when they enter into the holy state of matrimony they are well prepared to submit to their husband's needs. No, we are here today to ask Doña Isabel if she will help us to set up a branch of the *Sección Femenina* here in Jerez. We feel she would be a shining example of the perfect wife and mother.'

'Indeed.' Don Luis looks at Isabel. Her face is impassive. 'Well, I am sure my wife will give you her decision in good time.' He stands up, a signal for them all to leave. His mind is analysing what the young captain has just said; maybe he can see an opportunity here.

Once they have left, he asks his wife, 'Did you know that they were coming to see you today?'

'No, of course not. I would never have agreed. Now they have left me with very little time to get ready for our trip to Seville. What on earth shall I wear for Mario's? You know how elegant all the women are in Seville.' A tiny frown creases her forehead. 'What time is your appointment with Benito?'

'Midday. Go and get dressed. We can talk about this on the way.' How subtly his wife has changed his meeting with their lawyer into a social outing.

He picks up the sheet of paper that the Falangist has left on the table and starts to read it. It is headed Advice On Preparation for Marriage. He skims down the list and concludes there is nothing radical about this advice; it is something he would tell his own daughter, although when he thinks about Adriana he is not sure that she would take much notice of him. Still it is excellent advice for women of the lower and middle classes; he considers himself and his wife to be part of the upper echelons in society even though they are not part of the aristocracy.

While he waits for her to get ready he walks around the garden. It was not his idea to plant so many shrubs and bushes; it had been Isabel's design. She said it would be somewhere nice to sit and watch the sunset and he has to admit that she is right; it is a pleasant enough area and so it should be, given the amount of money she has spent on it. He pulls out a cheroot and lights it, sucking in the smoke greedily as he considers this new Falangist enterprise.

Father Sanchez has been very astute in suggesting Isabel to the Falangists; she will be an excellent person to run the local branch of the *Sección Femenina.* The more he thinks about it, the more he likes the idea. During the first few years of the Second Spanish Republic women had been allowed to do much as they liked. It had led to chaos and discord, what with giving them votes and allowing them to divorce their husbands the women had lost respect for the Church and the family. Luckily that has stopped now since Azaña came to power and the more conservative right-wing politicians have taken over control, but it could happen again. Politicians come and go, but women need to learn their place in society from a young age and this seems to be an excellent way to ensure they do so. He reads through the aims of the *Sección Femenina* again, this time paying more attention. Yes, he likes the part about women being subordinate to their husbands and honouring their marriages. However he feels that some of the items are a bit too detailed, such as removing her husband's shoes and making sure that he is asleep before she puts her hair in rollers. Was it Father Sanchez who came up with these ideas? Most likely. Well maybe it is necessary to point out these things to women of the lower classes, but he cannot imagine Isabel removing his shoes for him or getting into bed as quickly as possible so as not to keep him waiting. If anything, she is always the last to come to bed and then she likes to talk rather than go to sleep.

Still it looks like a good idea and what is more if his wife becomes the president of the Jerez branch it can only be good for his reputation. He stubs out the remains of his cheroot on the wall and heads for the garage. He is looking forward to the meeting with Benito; they have a lot to discuss.

As they enter Seville, the car suddenly jerks to a stop.

'What is it?' asks Don Luis.

'It looks like a demonstration, *Señor*. We will have to make a diversion, but it shouldn't be a problem,' the chauffeur informs him.

Don Luis does not even bother to ask the reason for the demonstration; there seem to be people constantly parading through the streets waving their banners and shouting their demands to anyone who is stupid enough to listen to them. It will be the same old rubbish. Communists most likely. If the Falangists get into power they will soon get these demonstrators under control; they are exactly what the country needs, strong ideas and firm leadership.

'Where are the police?' asks Isabel. 'Surely they should be controlling the mob.'

'Well don't wait to find out, Diego. Just drive through the back streets. I don't want to be late for my appointment.'

'*Si Señor*.'

Don Luis notices some women in the demonstration waving banners demanding Votes for Women. 'Do you see that, Isabel? Votes for women, indeed. Look what happened before when they had them; they didn't know what to do with them then and they won't know what to do with them now. You can't give the vote to women; they are just not ready for it.'

'Is that what you think, Luis?'

'Well, maybe one or two exceptional women would be capable of making a decision, but not the majority. Even so, a woman must vote the way her husband does, don't you agree?' He does not want his wife to think his remarks are directed at her; she can be very sensitive to criticism.

'So not much point in them having the vote,' his wife says.

He is not sure whether she is agreeing with him or being sarcastic. 'Exactly. By the way Isabel, have you decided to accept the position of President of the Jerez branch of the *Sección Fe-*

menina? I think you should. You will make an excellent president.'

'I'm not sure. I don't like political parties and I thought those young men were rather impolite the way they spoke about women.'

'But it's not just the Falangists, my dear, the Church is backing this too. I believe Father Sanchez says that it is the Church who drew up those rules for newly married women. If he sanctions it then it must be all right.' He knows how his wife slavishly believes every word the priest says.

'Yes, that's what's confusing me. I don't want to go against Father Sanchez; he is a very good man. I'm sure he wouldn't be supporting this if he didn't believe in it.'

'Exactly what I think,' says Don Luis. 'And I believe the *Sección Femenina* is run by Pilar Primo de Rivera, the sister of the man who founded the Falange party. They say she is a very devout Catholic.' He has been making enquiries about the Falange Party and he is sure this information will be enough to convince his wife.

'Yes, Father Sanchez mentioned her.'

'So you will accept?'

She sighs. 'If you want me to, *Cariño*.'

He sits back and looks out of the window; it is all starting to look possible. He is sure that his wife's connection with the Falangists will help him with his plan.

They drive for a little while longer then the chauffeur says, 'We are here, *Señor*. What time do you want me to come and collect you?'

Don Luis looks at his wife. 'What do you think?'

'At four o'clock. That will give us plenty of time to have lunch.'

'Very well, *Señora*.'

'What about the demonstration?' she asks.

'You don't need to worry about that, *Señora*, that is on the other side of the city, near the university. You will be all right here,' assures the chauffeur.

'I will meet you in Mario's then at two o'clock. Please don't spend all my money,' Don Luis tells her.

She laughs and climbs out of the car. 'See you later, *Cariño*.

He watches his wife walk away. He is a fortunate man; his wife is still as beautiful as the day he married her.

Benito Herrera de Vega is sitting in his office waiting for him. He leaps to his feet when Luis is shown in. 'How good to see you, Don Luis, my dear friend. It has been too long. It sounds as though you have a problem that requires my skills.'

'*Buenos días* Benito. You are right; it has been a while, but we have had the pleasure of your delightful son staying with us lately.'

'Yes, Cristóbal. I hope he is not making a nuisance of himself.'

'On the contrary, I think he is a good influence on Hugo. Has he told you that he has bought himself a horse, a real beauty by the sound of it.'

'I think you mean, I have bought him a horse. He tells me you have been kind enough to let him stable it at the bodega.'

'Yes. It's no problem for us—we have a number of empty stables— and it means we will see more of him, I expect.'

'Can I offer you something? A glass of sherry?'

'Yes, why not. It was a long, boring drive, not made any better by having to take a diversion to avoid that awful demonstration.'

'Ah, yes. That is unfortunate. I would have suggested you come another day, but I know you are a very busy man.' He opens an ornate mahogany cupboard and takes out a bottle of dry sherry and two glasses. 'It's not yours,' he says, looking at the bottle. 'Although I do have some Butler & Rodriguez if you would prefer.'

'No, that is fine.' Don Luis recognises the label; it's from the bodega Almudanza & Watson. 'I'm familiar with that brand.'

'Of course, isn't that the bodega belonging to Hugo's future father-in-law?'

'It is. I am hoping Mari Carmen will soon be his wife, but it is still to be arranged.'

'That will be a great match. Together you will have the largest control of the sherry trade in Jerez. Is that what you wanted to talk to me about?'

'No, it is something quite different. In fact, it's your advice and hopefully your support I'm after.'

'Very well, tell me what is bothering you, my friend.'

'Many things are bothering me at the moment, Benito. Like all businessmen I am concerned by the current political situation; I am not sure the government is keeping strong enough control over these rabble rousers. If we are not careful there will be another general strike like there was last year.'

'I don't think so, my friend. General Franco and his African troops soon put an end to that one. Surely you aren't suggesting that they didn't come down heavily enough on the strikers then, what with three thousand deaths, twice that number wounded and almost thirty thousand in prison. I would call that a crushing defeat, wouldn't you. I don't think there will be any more strikes for a while.'

'Well I'm not so sure. They are still out there demonstrating. Just look at today. The police don't seem able to keep the rabble under control. My driver was unable to get through; we have had to drive through the most unsavoury part of the city to get here, and my wife was in the car. It isn't good enough. I don't know what we pay our taxes for if they can't keep our streets safe.'

Benito nods and says, 'But you have something specific you want to discuss with me? Yes?'

'I was coming to that,' Don Luis says, a little curtly because he has the feeling that Benito is pressing him to come to the point. 'You are not in a hurry, are you?'

'Of course not. I am just curious about what is so urgent that you have come all this way today, when there is a big demonstration in the city.'

'Well I'll tell you. I've spoken to no-one else about this because I wanted your advice first.' He pauses and smiles at Benito. 'I'm thinking of going into politics.' This news seems to take the lawyer completely by surprise; for once he is lost for words. 'Well? Nothing to say?'

'But, what about your business? The bodega, the vineyard?'

'Oh, Felipe will handle all that. He does most of the work as it is. Of course I won't be stepping down entirely, just stepping back a bit.'

'I see. So how can I be of help to you?'

'Let me tell you what I am thinking,' he says, leaning forward and putting his elbows on Benito's desk. 'I thought I would run for mayor. Don Ignacio Rubio is planning to retire. He is getting on now and I believe his health is not too good. I see that as the perfect opening for me to enter into politics.'

'Indeed.'

'I have one problem.' The lawyer is waiting for him to finish but he wants to keep him in suspense. 'I can't decide whether to stand as a right-wing conservative or a member of this new Falange party.'

'The Falangists? They are rather extreme, Don Luis. Why would you consider representing them?'

'Because they are the party of the future and I intend to be such a mayor. I want our future to be one of stability and tradition. That's what I will represent. No more strikes and demonstrations. What the country needs is law and order. In fact two of their men were at my house this morning, which is why I had the idea of joining them. They want my wife to be the president of the Jerez branch of the *Sección Femenina*. It is quite an honour,' he continues eyeing the lawyer carefully. Benito is not looking convinced. Does this mean he is a liberal at heart? Or a socialist? No that is impossible. Still he has always been very cagey about his politics and if it turns out he has left-wing leanings then he could lose most of his clients. 'So, what do you say, my friend? Is it a good idea? Will I get the support I need to win? Would you support me?'

'You have asked for my opinion, Don Luis, so I will give it to you. I don't think it will be easy for you. If you were standing as a conservative, you might have a chance, but as you say, this is a very new party— if I remember correctly only formed in 1933 by Primo de Rivera— and they do have some very extreme views, especially regarding women. Very extreme. I would almost say they are fascists, and most certainly racist. I cannot see them as the party of the future; as far as I can see all they want to do is to return Spanish society to where it was before the Republic, with everyone knowing their place.'

'Is that so bad? Surely you are not a supporter of votes for everyone, including women? Why give votes to illiterate workers and empty-headed women? No, it's the educated classes that must run the country. I have faith in this party; it is strongly supported by the Church, you know. What more can we ask?'

'Maybe you're right,' says the lawyer, but he does not look convinced. 'What does Doña Isabel think about it all?'

'She doesn't know about this mayor business; it will be a surprise for her.'

'And she has agreed to be president of the *Sección Femenina?*'

'Mmmn. Well, not yet but she will. Isabel always does what I tell her. She is an excellent wife.'

'Well, as you say they do have the full support of the Church, so maybe it is a good idea.'

Don Luis beams at him. He is not convinced that Benito is being completely honest but that is what he wants to hear. 'Excellent. In that case I'd like you to be my agent; contact the Falange Party on my behalf and offer my candidature as mayor of Jerez. Then we'll see some changes in the town; there will be no more demonstrations for one thing.' He leans back in the chair feeling very pleased with himself. 'What about something for us to drink to my new venture?' he says.

'A spot of brandy? I have an extremely good one for you to try.'

'Excellent idea.'

CHAPTER 8

You only have to look into his steely grey eyes to see the hardness of his heart, a heart without pity, without compassion, without understanding. All Felipe understands is money. Don Luis's elder son measures everything in pesetas and weighs its worth in gold. His employees hate and fear him, not surprisingly as he has the power of life and death over them; one word from him and they and their families would starve and he would think no more of his actions than if he had stepped on a cockroach. Their lives mean nothing to him; there are always others queuing for work, eager and willing to take their place. The men arrive each and every morning begging for a few hours labour. If they are lucky they get to work from dawn until sunset. If not they trudge home to explain to their waif-like wives and hungry children that there is no work today and therefore no food.

These are the thoughts that run through Pedro's mind as he stands shivering in the cold light of a pale dawn. He has been waiting along with the rest of the men who hope to be employed today on the Butler & Rodriguez estate; they are all *braceros*, the landless labourers who are the most wretched of all Spain. For half the year they are employed and can feed their families; for the rest of the year they have to make do on what they can scavenge, and Felipe does not care. He does not care if their children starve, nor if they are sick and have no money for a doctor. He does not care if they have to eat scraps that they have found in the bins of others, or grub in the ground for roots as though they were animals. He does not care if the water they drink is foul and contaminated, nor if the women have to walk two kilometres to collect it from a well that is also used to water the vines. This is the most economical way for the owners of the vineyard to employ the men so why should they pay them for being idle half the year, he argues. It does not make sense, he says. The families have roofs over their heads. What more do they want? he asks.

As he contemplates his life, Pedro feels more and more depressed. There is no escape. It does not matter what Ramon says. All that fighting-talk will come to nothing, just more hardship and more violence; the children will still be hungry and his beautiful wife will still looks ten years older than she is.

At last the foreman drives up in the lorry. Immediately the air is charged with expectation and hope; the men shuffle forward hoping that today they will be lucky.

'I only need twenty of you for the pruning,' Enrique says, jumping down from the lorry and opening the tailgate. 'You, you and you.' One by one he points to those he wants and they climb up onto the back of the lorry.

Pedro holds his breath. 'Me, choose me,' are the words repeating themselves in his head. 'Please choose me.'

Enrique stares at him for a moment as though weighing him up and then waves him aboard.

Pedro sighs with relief. He has had work every day this week, which is quite unusual. The harvest is over, the grapes have been picked, de-stemmed and crushed. The work on building up the *asperpia* to catch the winter rains has finished and all that is left for men like him is pruning the older vines. He does not often get picked for that work, so it is a surprise when Enrique drops him off at the most northerly part of the vineyard and says, 'Make sure you don't prune any of those young vines, only those that are more than four years old. If you've got eyes in your head you can see which they are. And remember, stick and thumb only.'

'Yes, *Señor*.' By this last remark the foreman means that he must prune one trunk of the vine short and leave the other long. He does not know why he is telling him this; Pedro has been working in the vineyards since he was ten-years-old. Does he do it to make him feel a lesser man, ignoring the facts that Pedro knows how to do every job there is in the vineyard, from levelling the *asperpias* again in the Spring and planting new vines, to the harvesting in the Autumn and the planting of new root stock in the winter. He actually enjoys the work, or he would do if the owners treated him better. There used to be nothing he liked more than working outside in this beautiful countryside, but nowadays the poverty is killing his soul. Nowadays he cannot see the beauty that he knows lies around him because he is always tired and constantly hungry; he is a failure. He knows it. He lets the foreman humiliate him just so that he will be given a few hours work. He is constantly in debt and has to beg the local shopkeeper for food with promises of payment when he can make it, just so he can feed his family.

Pedro is not the same man he was when he met Ana; then he was a man in love with life. Now he is a bitter man, a loser who is angry with the world and everything in it. He picks up the shears that the foreman has left for them and begins pruning the vines; it is back-breaking work but he is used to that. That is not what bothers him; he has always been a hard worker.

'What on earth do they want?' says the man working in the row opposite him. He spits on the ground as if to say what he thinks of them. Pedro turns to see who he is talking about. His companion is looking at a green and white car with the Guardia

Civil insignia on the side. 'The blue light's not flashing, so what are they doing here?' he continues, beginning to look worried.

That is how it always is; even if you have done nothing wrong you still feel guilty when you see the green uniforms and tricorn hats. 'Looking for someone,' suggests Pedro. He feels his stomach tighten, a sign of his recurring anxiety. He has seen the man working next to him before, but doesn't know his name. He knows very few of the *braceros* by name; there is no time for idle chatter and to be honest, little inclination.

'They must be looking for someone. Poor bastard, whoever it is. Look they're talking to Enrique, now.' The Guardia Civil officers have got out of the car and are chatting to the foreman; their tricorn hats are clearly visible from where Pedro is standing. 'Hang on. What on earth is Enrique up to? He's pointing up here. Stupid bastard, why is he sending them up to us?' Pedro's companion pulls his hat down to shade his face and returns to the pruning.

Pedro stands and watches the two officers clambering up the slope towards him. His stomach has turned to water now and he is frightened he will crap himself. It's about Ramon; he knows it is. The old man's words echo in his ears: *It will not matter which brother they have; you will do just as well.*

'Hey, you. Put down those shears.' The officer has a Mauser pistol in his hand and it is pointing at Pedro. 'Are you Pedro Molina Moreno?'

He nods, nervously. The shears lie on the ground at his feet where he has dropped them. He steps away from them as if they might bite him.

'What? Speak up,' snaps the second officer.

'Yes.'

'Yes, *Señor*,' barks the first policeman.

'Yes, *Señor*.' Pedro can feel the sweat running down his neck. What the hell do they want? This could cost him his job; the owners don't like the Guardia Civil coming to the vineyard.

'Is Ramon Molina Moreno your brother?'

'Yes, he's the youngest.'

'When did you see him last?'

Pedro hesitates. Adolfo is right; it does not matter what he says they will find a way of punishing him anyway, so he replies, 'Not for a long time. I can't remember exactly; it must be almost two years.'

'But you know where he lives,' the older of the two officers says, stepping closer to Pedro.

He wants to step back out of range of the man's fists, but he cannot move. 'Not really. The last I heard he was working in Osuna.'

'Is that so? And how did you hear that?' The younger policeman asks, thrusting himself in front of Pedro so that his hat is almost touching his face.

'Well, that's where he said he was going when he left. I assumed he had found work there because we heard no more from him.'

'Assumed, eh? Assumed, indeed. Well I assume that you're lying. I think you do know where your murdering brother is, and before the day is out you are going to tell us where to find him.'

'What's he done? Why do you want him?' Pedro at last picks up enough courage to ask.

'He killed a member of the Guardia Civil,' the policeman says. 'So now you know why we want to find the bastard. I think you had better come along with us to the station.'

'But I'm working,' Pedro protests. The words come out as a squeak; he is so frightened.

The young policeman hits him across the head with the butt of the Mauser, causing Pedro to stumble and fall to the ground. Blood drips down his face; it tastes bitter in his mouth.

'Get up. Hands behind your back,' says the other officer, taking out a pair of handcuffs and fastening them to Pedro's wrists. 'I can see you're going to be trouble. It obviously runs in the family,' he adds.

Pedro staggers to his feet. 'Hey there, will you let my wife know what's happened,' he shouts to his fellow worker who has not once even looked their way. 'Please let her know where I am.' The man does not reply, but Pedro knows he will tell her; someone will let her know. They will all be talking about this for days to come.

'Get a move on,' says the policeman, shoving him in the back. 'You don't need to worry about your wife, by the time you get back to her she will have forgotten all about you.'

Enrique is standing by the police car, watching as they descend the hill. He is smiling. 'So your brother is a communist, is he? Well, if they ever let you out of gaol don't bother coming back here. The boss doesn't want any bloody communists working for him.' He spits on the ground in front of Pedro. He is enjoying this; it is written all over his pock-marked face. 'Oh and don't worry about your pretty little wife; I'll tell her what has happened to you.'

Pedro is not normally a violent man but he would give anything to have his hands free at that moment so he could smash them into the foreman's smirking face. And if he finds out he has been anywhere near Ana, then one day he will hunt him down and do just that. But there is no time for idle dreams, the Guardia Civil officer pulls him roughly by the arm and shoves him into the back of the car.

'Where are you taking me?' Pedro asks, trying hard to keep his voice steady. 'I haven't done anything wrong.' He is going to say more, but his protest ends in a grunt as the officer's answer is to whack him around the head with the butt of his rifle again. Pedro feels he may lose consciousness and struggles against the dizziness and pain that flood over him. He leans back and closes his eyes. He can feel the blood running down his cheek but he is unable to wipe it away. So this is it then. It is exactly as Adolfo forewarned. It does not matter which brother they arrest; one is as good as the other. Fear begins to creep over him like a cold mist that he cannot escape. Is this the end? He has heard the rumours of what happens in the police cells, the torture, the starvation, the beatings, the mock trials, the summary executions. He will not survive any of it. He is not a brave man. Thank goodness Adolfo did not tell him where Ramon is hiding; he cannot betray him if he doesn't know where he is.

The drive to the Guardia Civil headquarters in Seville seems to take forever; the man sitting beside him never speaks a word but the two policemen in the front of the car chat away happily to each other throughout the journey. They appear to be two normal men chatting about their families and their favourite football teams, like anyone else you would meet in a bar or at the bullfight, but he is not comforted by this. Their reputation is such that the very mention of the Guardia Civil strikes fear into most people's hearts and he is no different. The sight of those tricorn hats is enough to turn his stomach to water. They may sound like normal men but it is an illusion.

The car stops and the senior officer turns to the man in the back and says, 'Take him in and charge him. We'll see what he has to say for himself later.'

Pedro does not resist when he is pulled out of the car and taken up the steps into the police station. There is a group of women standing outside the main entrance, and the policeman pushes his way through them, dragging Pedro behind him. Some of the women are crying, others look angry. They are all dressed in black and one of them is on her knees praying. '*Señor*, help us. Where are our sons? What have you done with them?' they cry as the two men struggle to pass them. 'We just need to know. Please, *Señor*, tell us where they are.'

'Get out of the way, you stupid bitches, or you'll be joining them,' the policeman says, ignoring their pleas and pulling his baton from his belt.

At the sight of the wooden baton, the women shuffle away, leaving them a clear passage into the police station. Pedro is frightened to look at them; he cannot bear to see the suffering in their eyes in case he weakens. He tries not to think about what is ahead of him. Instead he focuses on what his brother had said to him; they are fighting for their children's future. They are fighting for change. If he survives this nightmare he will look for his brother and he will tell him that now he understands.

Ana cannot stop crying. The news that Pedro has been arrested has already reached her but nothing more, no information as to his whereabouts, no reason for his arrest, nothing about when or if he will return to her. She pulls out the clay pot tucked behind the stove and tips the contents onto the floor. She has already counted it, the money that Ramon gave her before he left. She has been keeping it for an emergency, but she never thought that it would be this, that Pedro would be arrested. She tries to remain positive for the sake of the children, but she is not a stupid woman, she has heard of too many people going missing, sons, brothers, husbands. All it takes is for someone to suggest that their neighbour has been talking to a Red or a communist and the police sweep in and take them away for questioning and they are never seen again. She removes a couple of coins and puts them in her pocket then replaces the rest of the money. If she was not so desperate she would throw it away; this was all Ramon's fault. Why did he have to visit his brother? He knew that the Guardia were after him so why didn't he go as far away from here as possible? She is furious with him for implicating her family in his actions, but at the same time she understands how he feels. She knows nothing about politics but she too wants things to change. Nobody listens to the wives and mothers who have to watch helplessly as their families go hungry, who when their children get sick have no money for medicine, whose husbands are beaten down by poverty and take it out on those closest to them. For not the first time in her life she wishes she had been born a man. She places the pot back in its hiding place and steps out of the hut.

'Ana,' one of the wives of the *braceros* calls across to her. They greet each other with hugs and kisses, and more tears. 'I'm so sorry to hear about Pedro. It's awful news.'

'Have you heard anything? All I know is that he was arrested this morning while he was working. I don't know what it's all about.'

The woman follows Ana into the hut and lowers her voice. 'He has done nothing wrong. It's his brother they are after. They say he is a communist.'

'His brother? We haven't seen him in years. He didn't even come here when his mother was dying. You remember? I told you how upset Pedro was.'

'Yes, I remember. That was very sad.'

'Do you know where have they taken my husband?' Ana asks, biting her lip until it bleeds.

'To Seville. They just want to question him about his brother, if he knows where he is, or what he had done?'

Ana begins to cry again. This is worse than she thought. 'But he doesn't know anything about his brother, I told you. He hasn't seen him for years,' she repeats. She prays that none of her neighbours noticed Ramon at their home that night.

'I'm so sorry, Ana. How will you manage? If there is anything I can do for you I will try to help but you know how it is.' The woman looks genuinely upset. Everyone knows how ruthless the Guardia Civil can be.

Ana nods and tries to smile. What can any of them do. They are all in the same boat, families to feed and very little money to buy food. 'I will be all right for a little while; Pedro was a very careful man with his money,' she lies. 'Thank you, anyway.'

'I have to go. Please don't tell anyone I told you where Pedro is. I can't afford to get involved. You understand?'

'I understand.' She kisses her goodbye and once she has left Ana can hold the tears back no longer and begins to sob as though her heart will break. Without Pedro she will never be able to manage. Ramon's money will only last a few weeks and then what will she do? She knows she is never going to see her husband again. They will question him and whether they get an answer from him or not he will still rot in prison. She needs to do something to help him. What about Adolfo; he helped Ramon, surely he can help Pedro as well. She wipes her face on the hem of her dress and heads for Adolfo's hut.

The old man is sitting outside his humble dwelling, hunched over a tiny fire which gives off more smoke than heat.

'Adolfo,' she whispers. 'Have you heard?'

The old man nods his head. 'I'm sorry this has happened,' he says.

'I need to find Ramon,' she says, sitting down beside him. 'He has to give himself up. I know he will do it as soon as he realises they have arrested his brother. He is an honourable man; he won't let Pedro be punished for his crimes. I know he won't. I must find him and tell him. I have to get my husband home. Adolfo, you have to help me. You know where he is. Please tell me.'

The old man does not reply and continues to stare at the flickering flames.

'Adolfo, do you hear me? You are the only one who can help Pedro. You must tell me where his brother is hiding.'

'It will do no good, my dear child. It will just mean that they will have both brothers in custody and both will suffer. Your husband is unlikely to return to you now. Sad though it is, you have to face the truth. His brother killed a Guardia Civil officer and for that someone must be punished.'

'I realise that, Adolfo, but if Ramon gives himself up then they will let Pedro go,' she insists.

'And if they don't? Then two men will have been sacrificed for what was after all, only an accident.' He stands up and kicks at the fire, scattering the ashes. 'I'm going to bed now, child. You should do the same. There is nothing we can do to save your husband. I'm sorry.'

Ana cannot speak; her heart is too full. She stands looking at the dying embers of the old man's fire and curses her brother-in-law.

CHAPTER 9

His father has not spoken to him since the outburst over dinner. In fact Hugo has tried to avoid both him and his mother; he feels sure that his love for Clementina is written all over his face and they will see it.

'Hugo, I think I should leave on Monday; I don't want to outstay my welcome,' says Cristóbal as they sit outside on the terrace watching the moon rising over the vineyard. He relights his cheroot, which he has let go out.

'You don't need to worry about that,' says Hugo. 'You are always welcome here. Mama is very fond of you, as is Papa.'

'I'm not so sure now after my indiscretion the other night. Anyway I have received a message to say that I can collect my horse tomorrow.' He beams at Hugo. 'I am so excited about riding him.'

'Well then, you should stay at least a couple of days more so he can get to know you before you return to Seville.'

'No, I think I ought to leave as soon as possible.'

'Is this because of Papa? I know he flew off the handle last night, but that was very unusual for him. You are very welcome here; you always have been. My father likes you. It was me he was angry with, and to be honest, I'm not sure why. Stay for a few more days.'

'No, I really should get back to my studies. Papa will be angry if he thinks I'm wasting his money. You know I can't afford to fail my exams.'

'Just a couple of days won't matter. We'll think up some excuse for your father.' He sees his friend hesitate.

'Well, if you are sure that your father won't object I must admit that I am tempted to stay a little longer. But I don't want to upset him or make things worse for you.'

'You won't. I told you; it's me he is angry with, not you.'

'All right. You're a very persuasive chap, Hugo. Although I'm not sure it is entirely all for my benefit.' He grins at his friend.

Hugo feels himself blushing. He is not very good at lying to Cristóbal, who is quick to realise that his friend is looking for a credible excuse to go back to Doñana. 'I don't know what you mean. Anyway I think I can hear dinner being served. We'd better go in. I don't want Papa to have something else to moan about.'

Don Luis glances up at them as they enter the dining room, and nods in greeting. He does not speak; he is busily engaged in conversation with his elder son. Hugo sighs with relief; the less attention his father pays to him, the better.

'So what did they want?' Don Luis asks. 'Two Guardia Civil officers on my land? Did you speak to them?'

'No, Papa. Enrique handled it; he's the foreman. That's his job.'

'So did Enrique tell you why they were there?'

'They were looking for a communist who took part in the riots in Seville. He murdered a policeman.'

'What? And he was working for us? That's not going to help my candidacy for mayor; who is going to vote for me if they think I'm employing communists. Bloody Reds; they should all be shot. What were you thinking of, Felipe?' He nods at the servant to pour him some wine.

'I'm trying to explain, Papa. He isn't a communist. He is the brother of a communist. Anyway he's one of the *braceros.* He doesn't count as an employee.' He picks up a piece of bread and breaks it in two.

'Same thing. I expect the whole family are Reds. So where is this communist now?'

'He said he didn't know, so the police have taken him away to question him...' Felipe stops abruptly and stares at his father. 'What's that, Papa? What did you say? You are going to stand for mayor?' he asks, his jaw tightening. Hugo can see that his brother's temper is rising; the nerve in his temple is pulsating as he struggles to contain himself.

'I am. So I want you to bear that in mind when you go chasing these young fillies.' Don Luis looks around the table. 'I want you all to bear it in mind; how you behave reflects on me and my chances of becoming the mayor of Jerez, for better or for worse. Make sure it's for the better.' He smiles, but there is no warmth in his smile.

'But what about the business, Papa?' asks Felipe, as calmly as he can muster. 'Why didn't you discuss this with me before putting your name forward? How on earth will you be able to manage the duties of being mayor and running the bodega? It will be impossible.'

For a moment there is a deathly silence then Don Luis says, 'The last time I looked, I was the owner of Butler & Rodriquez. Why should I ask you for permission to stand as mayor? Anyway I don't see a problem; I have two strapping sons. It's time they both took on their full share of the work, instead of spending their time hunting and fishing. You can't expect to live off me forever.' He looks from Felipe to Hugo and back again.

Hugo thinks Felipe will explode; his face turns puce as he struggles to control his temper. Always volatile, now he is incandescent. 'That's hardly fair, Papa. I have been managing the bodega for six years now. The only time I have off is on the Sabbath, and when I do go hunting, it is usually then after Mass. How can you even think that I am living off you, never mind say it in front of a guest?' He glares at Cristóbal. 'This place would fall apart if it were not for me,' he continues. His anger is now barely under control.

Hugo silently agrees with him. Papa may be the owner but it is Felipe who manages everything. Why does his father always have to be so hard on him? Not for the first time he wonders why his father treats Felipe as if he is an employee rather than his son and heir. His brother always does whatever Papa asks him to. If he is honest with himself, Felipe has been a far better son to him than Hugo.

'You may consider yourself indispensable Felipe, but I can assure you, you are not.' Don Luis glares at his elder son.

Normally that would have been enough to silence his brother, but by now he is in full swing. 'I just don't know how can you say that. I work hard for my money. Bloody hard.'

Felipe's wife, Beatrice, is playing nervously with her rosary. She stretches out her hand and places it on top of her husband's then whispers something to him but he snatches his hand away and scowls at her.

'Really. And who pays you your exorbitant salary? Who lets you and your family live here in luxury, for nothing I might add? You just take my generosity for granted,' Don Luis continues.

'It was you who suggested we live here so that I could be on hand twenty-four hours a day. What more do you want from me, Father? Blood?' Felipe is almost shouting now.

'Well now you are both going to have to step up to the mark, because I will not have as much time for the business when I am the mayor,' his father continues. 'Let me make that clear right now.' He nods for the servants to bring in the first course, a dish of seafood soup. Hugo knows his father, as far as he is concerned the conversation has now ended.

But Felipe is not finished. 'And what about him?' he asks, pointing to Hugo. 'How dare you compare my contribution to this business with his. He is an idle, useless wastrel, and if anyone is taking advantage of your generosity, it is him.'

Hugo decides he will say nothing. He believes his father is being unfair to Felipe, but he is not going to cross him. They have had these arguments before. His father and his brother are so alike it is inevitable that they will clash, but he knows one thing; his father will always win. Perhaps that's it; maybe Papa can see the worst of himself in Felipe and does not like what he sees.

'I'm not hungry,' Felipe says, waving away the bowl of seafood soup that is being placed in front of him. He starts to get up.

'Sit down. You will not behave like that in front of the servants. The food has been prepared and you will eat it. If you wish to discuss my plans for the future in more detail, we will talk tomorrow morning. Now sit down and don't make a spectacle of yourself,' Don Luis says nodding at the servant to replace the bowl of soup. He turns to Cristóbal. 'Please forgive my son; he forgets that we have a guest. So tell me, when do you get the Retuerta stallion?'

Felipe gives a snort and sits down again, then begins to eat his soup, deliberately slurping noisily to annoy his father.

'Well, actually I am going to collect it tomorrow. I feel quite excited about it, just like I used to feel when I was a child on the eve of the Three Kings.' Cristóbal grins.

'How lovely for you,' says Doña Isabel. She has said nothing so far, but the look on her face shows Hugo that she is glad the conversation has taken a more civilised turn.

'I hear that Father Sanchez visited you, mother,' says Hugo. 'Have you been skipping Mass?' He likes to tease his mother. She is very religious and would no sooner miss attending Mass than walk through the streets naked.

'No silly boy, he came to ask me if I could help him with something.'

'Don't be coy, Isabel. Tell them what they want you to do,' says Don Luis. When he sees her hesitate he continues for her, 'Your mother has been asked to be the President of the *Sección Femenina*. It is a great honour.'

'What exactly is that?' asks Hugo. 'Another of Father Sanchez's schemes for getting money out of you?'

'Don't be like that, Hugo. Father Sanchez is a good man,' his mother says, smiling indulgently at him.

'It's the Falangists,' says Don Luis. 'Something they've come up with to make sure newly married women toe the line.'

'I think it's meant for all married women,' Isabel says quietly.

'Is that a good thing, Mama?' Hugo asks. 'You don't look very enthusiastic about it.'

'Of course it's a good thing,' says Don Luis. 'Women need to know their place. After all, who wants anarchy in the home; it's bad enough when we have to tolerate it in the street.'

Hugo looks at his mother. She smiles and gives just the slightest shrug of her shoulders. So she is not convinced but, just like the rest of them, she will never contradict Don Luis.

Hugo can barely contain the excitement that is building up inside him at the thought of getting even a glimpse of Clementina again. He knows he will be heading for trouble if he approaches her, but he cannot help how he feels.

It is early afternoon when they arrive at Doñana. Hugo is driving the horse box and Cristóbal is fidgeting beside him, like an excited schoolboy.

'I can smell something cooking,' his friend says, leaning his head out of the window. 'I say, I think there's a party going on.'

Hugo can hear the clicking of castanets in the distance and the strumming of a guitar. The sound of a man singing *Canto Jondo* echoes through the woods, and for a moment the singer holds the note in a howl which is more of pain than pleasure. Hugo tries to remember if today is a religious holiday, if so they won't be pleased to see them. He parks the horse box in the usual place and climbs down; the stables are quiet and there is no sign of Vano. Maybe that was him singing.

'I think they're over there,' he says, heading to where a thin column of smoke is floating up through the canopy of trees. 'Come on; let's see what they are up to.'

'Maybe we should come back tomorrow. We don't want to intrude.'

'Don't be ridiculous. If he sent you a message to say that your horse is ready then he will expect you to collect it. I just can't understand why he isn't here.' He studies Cristóbal's face. 'What is it?'

'It's just that, well, he didn't actually send me a message. I just thought that the horse must be ready by now.'

'But he said three days. Well, I suppose that explains it. I didn't think that Vano would just leave us hanging about like a couple of idiots. He knows only too well which side his bread is buttered. Well, we're here now, we'll go and tell him we want your horse today. If you're sure that's what you want. It might not be fully trained. Are you happy with that?'

'Yes, now that we're here, I'd like to see it. Is that all right? You're not just doing this because you want to see that girl again?'

'Come on. You worry too much.'

They do not have to go far before they come to a clearing in the woods where a large fire has been lit and Vano and his family are sitting around it. It is not Vano who is singing, but a younger man who looks very like him and is probably one of his sons. Vano is clapping in time to the music and all eyes are on the singer, a tall, dark-skinned youth with hair that reaches to his shoulders. He is accompanied by an older man on the guitar. A woman wearing a bright pink flamenco dress sits beside him clicking her castanets and joining in the singing from time to time. The delicious smell which is making Hugo feel hungry is coming from the carcass of a young deer that is being roasted over an open fire. The young boy attending to it turns the spit slowly, stopping occasionally to baste it with some juices. He looks up and sees them before anyone else notices. The woman in the pink dress has just begun to dance and all eyes are now on her.

'Papa,' the boy calls. 'Visitors.'

Everyone stops and looks to where the boy is pointing then the music resumes and they turn away again. The woman in the pink dress lifts her skirts so that they can see her black high-heeled shoes beating out the rhythm of the music on the wooden board where she dances. Her head is held high and her back is straight; she glances his way and gives him a haughty look and a toss of her hair. Hugo catches a glimpse of her slim brown thighs before she turns away, dipping and swaying to the music, turning faster and faster until she throws her arms into the air and stops. Cheers of 'Olé,' ring out from her audience and everyone claps. Hugo and Cristóbal join in the clapping.

'Señor Hugo, Señor Herrera de Vega,' Vano says coming over to them. 'Is everything all right? I wasn't expecting to see you today.'

'My friend has had a problem and needs to return to Seville as soon as possible,' says Hugo. 'He would like to take his horse now as he is not sure when he will be back.'

'Well I did tell him that the animal is not one hundred percent tamed, but then when is a stallion ever completely domesticated. I'm sure you want him to retain some of his original spark,' he says, turning to Cristóbal.

'Yes, a little wildness is an attractive thing,' says Hugo, thinking more of Clementina than the stallion.

'I'm sure the horse will be fine,' says Cristóbal. 'I just want him to get used to me before I have to leave.' He looks past Vano at the family gathering. 'Are you having a party?'

'Yes, you could say that. It was my grandson's christening today. Now we are celebrating with all the family.'

'Was that your son singing? He has a lovely voice,' says Cristóbal.

'Yes, that's Álvaro; don't you recognise him?' he asks, looking at Hugo.

'Of course, yes.' Now he remembers that Álvaro was the one who played the guitar and was always singing. The other brother preferred to play soldiers and they and Clementina would trek through the woods looking for the enemy. Sometimes Vano had let them ride his ponies. Yes, he remembers them all.

'Well, you'd better follow me and I'll get you the stallion.' Vano heads back towards the stables, leaving Hugo and Cristóbal with no option but to follow him.

'The meat smells good. Do you normally celebrate with roast venison?' asks Hugo. He knows and Vano knows that the gypsies have poached the deer from the Marquess's estate, but he is reluctant to accuse him. Nevertheless he wants him to realise that it has not gone unnoticed. If he tells the Marquess then Vano and his family would probably be thrown off Doñana, and there are a number of reasons why he does not want that to happen.

'This is my first grandson, so it is something special,' Vano says.

He is walking more quickly now; any minute Hugo thinks he will break into a run. Although Vano would never dare to be openly rude to them, it is becoming clear that they are not wanted here; there has been no suggestion that they should join in the festivities.

'So all your family are here today?' Hugo asks, wondering why he hasn't seen Clementina.

Vano grunts an assent, and keeps on walking.

'I was hoping to see Tina,' he says at last. 'I didn't get the chance to speak to her last time.'

'I don't know where she is,' Vano says, through tight lips. He is looking angry now.

Cristóbal taps him on the back. 'Leave it, Hugo,' he whispers. 'It will only cause trouble.'

'Papa,' a girl's voice calls. 'Papa, wait for me.'

Hugo spins round. It is her. Clementina is running down the path towards them, her shiny black hair streaming out behind her and her face flushed from the exertion. He stops and stares at her. 'Tina, what a lovely surprise,' he says, trying hard not to grin too broadly.

'What is it child? Can't you see I'm busy. Whatever it is will have to wait,' snaps her father, continuing to stride towards the stables.

'Don't be grumpy, Papa. I'll walk with you and then when you've finished your business I can tell you the news.'

'So, Tina, you are an auntie now,' says Hugo walking beside her. He would love to take her hand in his, but that would certainly cause problems with her father. He knows that Vano has a reputation for being violent so he does not want to aggravate him, certainly not here with his family close by.

'Yes, he's the most lovely little boy and so good...' She begins to tell him about the new baby and how the christening has gone, but Hugo hears not a word; he is too absorbed in the closeness of her body as she skips along beside him, of the fresh woodland smell of her hair and the gleam of her bare arms. 'You should stay and join us for lunch,' she says. 'Papa, you must invite Hugo and his friend to stay and eat with us. There is plenty of meat.'

'Don't be so stupid, child. These gentlemen have better things to do than eat in the woods with the likes of us,' says Vano, without slowing down.

'We have already eaten,' says Cristóbal before Hugo has a chance to accept. 'And we are expected at the *cortijo* for dinner; we cannot be late for that. Another time, maybe.'

'Ah, I see you've brought a horse box,' says Vano. 'Good. I'll get the stallion for you, if you'd like to wait here for a minute.'

'May I come with you? I'm so looking forward to seeing him again,' says Cristóbal.

'Of course.' Vano is not particularly happy at this suggestion and gives his daughter a hard stare, which she appears to ignore. 'Follow me.'

Once Cristóbal and the gypsy have disappeared into the stables, Hugo turns to Clementina and says, 'I was hoping to see you today.' He tries to take her hand but she pulls away.

'Don't be foolish Hugo. We will always be friends, I hope, just like when we were children, but we can never be anything more. My father would sooner I was dead than married to a *payo*. And your father would probably have our whole clan kicked out of Doñana if he thought you were in love with me, which I am sure you are not. You can understand that, can't you?'

'I have never seen anyone as lovely as you, Tina,' he says. Hugo knows she is right, but he refuses to accept it.

'That's silly. You must meet plenty of beautiful women and one day you will marry one of them. We have nothing in common, you and I, but what is the same for both of us is the fact that you will marry whomever your father chooses for you and so will I. My parents have already picked my husband. I have to trust them to pick someone who will treat me well and who is not too ugly.' She laughs at this last comment.

'How can you find it funny? I'm in love with you, Tina, don't you understand? I won't marry whoever my father chooses. I intend to marry for love. I want to marry you.'

'Hugo, you are such a child still. You already know who you are going to marry. I heard your friend talking about it the other day. Some rich heiress from Jerez. So why are you playing games with me?'

He looks down at her, this slight, fragile beautiful girl whom he wants to crush in his arms, understands the world better than he does. Her rejection only makes him want her more than ever. 'Just give me a chance,' he whispers as he spots Vano leading the stallion across to the horse box.

'Here's Papa. I have to go, now.'

'Hugo, come and see this lovely creature,' shouts Cristóbal. 'He must be the most magnificent horse in the whole of Spain.'

For a moment Hugo watches Clementina walk back towards the party then he goes to join his friend. Give him time and he will show her that he is not playing games with her.

CHAPTER 10

Her mother has sent her down to the dunes to see if the tide is out and look for cockles. Clementina wanders along the foreshore, enjoying the feel of the wet sand between her toes until she comes to an outcrop of rocks covered in seaweed. She gathers some and places it in her bucket then sits on a rock staring out at the sea. There's little chance of finding any cockles this morning as the tide has barely turned, but she is in no hurry to go home.

Her thoughts drift back to Hugo and how pleasant it was to see him again. They had a lot of fun together when they were children; he was always doing something he shouldn't and there were lots of times when they had to run and hide from her father. But that was then; things are different now. He has changed. Before he was a cheeky young boy who didn't have a care in the world; it didn't bother him that he often went home with a ripped shirt from scrambling in the blackberry bushes or wet, mud-stained trousers from trying to catch a duck or a fish from the lagoon. Her mother would invite him to eat with them and they would sit by the fire sharing a plate of *migas,* or cracking and eating pine nuts. Now she sees him as a handsome, immaculately dressed, but rather haughty young man, someone who is sure of his place in the world and his superiority to others. She wonders how many years it is since he last tasted a dish of fried breadcrumbs flavoured with olives and garlic.

She admits that it would be nice to see him again, but she knows it won't be the same as when they were children. She is still fond of him, likes his company even, but not enough to risk upsetting her father by meeting him again in the woods. Hugo has told her he loves her but how many other young girls has he said that to, she wonders. She is certain that as far as he is concerned, this is just another flirtation. Common sense tells her that his father would never allow him to go out with a gypsy girl, not in a million years.

Clementina is aware that boys find her attractive. The boys her age don't actually say anything to her, but they smile at her in a special way and sometimes one of them will give her a flower he has picked in the woods. Her sister, Maya has even told her that her brother-in-law has confided to her that he would like to marry Clementina, but she has met him and knows that is unlikely to happen; he is a lot older than his brother, ugly and leers at her every time she sees him. If he were the last man on earth she would not marry him.

A wave comes in closer than expected and splashes against her legs, wetting the hem of her dress. The sea is vast, she stares at it and wonders what lies beyond it; some days when the light is right she catches a glimpse of mountains on the far shore. Her father says it is Africa, a country where they don't speak Spanish and the people look very different to them. Clementina has never left Doñana and although she has no great desire to visit places like Africa, she often feels she is missing something. She can see a blue and white fishing boat in the distance; it is heading for a harbour further along the coast. That's somewhere else she has never been.

It is not that she is unhappy with her life, but she can't help wondering what sort of life would she have if she left here. If she marries the man her parents want her to marry, the one they have picked for her, her life will remain the same, no better and maybe, if she is unlucky, worse because he is from Huelva and she will have to go and live there with him. If that happens then she will hardly ever see her family or visit Doñana. Her mother promises her that he is a good man, young and handsome, but how does Mama know; she has not seen him since he was a boy and the betrothal was arranged. Clementina thinks of her sister, Maya. Her husband is a nice man and Maya never complains about him, but Clementina knows that her sister does not love him even though they have two lovely daughters. Her mother always says that love is not that important, but a good match is. She is not sure that she believes her.

Of course life with Hugo would be much more interesting than life in Huelva. They could travel; he would take her to England with him. But the reality is that his friends would never accept her and they both know that; she is well aware of how the *payos* treat *gitanos*. No matter what Hugo thinks he feels now, he would come to despise her humble roots and be ashamed to be seen with her. No wonder her father is angry. He does not want her to go anywhere where she would run the risk of being humiliated; he may not be a rich man but she knows he is a proud one. If only there were not so many narrow-minded ideas about what women can and cannot do. She feels frustrated. Her father knows she has a much better connection with the wild horses than either of her brothers but now that she is no longer a child he won't let her work with them, and she never gets to ride any more. When she challenges him, his only excuse is that it is not suitable work for a woman. What would people say if they saw one of Vano's daughters training the horses? He would lose everyone's respect and all his customers. She tells him she does not care what they say; she is good at it and he knows that. Surely that is all that matters. Unfortunately her mother agrees with Papa; they both think that nobody will want her as a wife if she is seen mucking out the stables and riding around the paddock on a wild horse.

What can she do? If she wants to be happy she has to convince her father that she does not need to marry anyone, at least not until she is older; this way she can try to delay the inevitable. In the meantime she must be careful about speaking to Hugo, although it is all quite innocent, because if her father finds out she is defying him it might push him into bringing her marriage forward. She definitely does not want that to happen.

CHAPTER 11

The boy begins to run towards the sea, with Ramon close behind him. Is this his life from now on, constantly living in fear of the Guardia Civil? He might just as well be living in Seville as here in the middle of nowhere.

'Hurry up,' calls the boy. He scampers over the dunes like a young deer and is soon out of sight.

'Kiko,' he shouts. 'Are you all right? Where are you?' The boy has disappeared from view. Ahead of him stretches a desert of fine sand and the only thing moving is the wind as it whips the sand into the air and batters against the marram grass.

The boy's head pops up from behind a clump of grass and grins at him then disappears again. Ramon clambers up the side of the dune, struggling against the wind which is blowing the stinging sand straight into his face. Once at the top he stops to catch his breath and looks about him. Ahead is the Atlantic, grey and unwelcoming, its white-topped waves lashing against the shore and relentlessly moving the sand towards them. To his right and to his left the beach extends into the distance, kilometres of white sand which over the years has gradually encroached on the pine forests that border the dunes, burying the trees bit by bit, centimetre by centimetre until only the topmost branches are showing, and the trees are gradually drained of life. The wind does not ease, not for one moment; it batters against him incessantly. He pulls his hat down further over his eyes, trying to protect them.

'Don't just stand there gawping. We're supposed to be hiding. You stick out like a sore thumb up there. Come down here, where you can't be seen.' The boy has wrapped a scarf around his head and face, covering his mouth and nose. He looks like a pocket-sized Moroccan with only his eyes showing.

Ramon slithers down the other side of the sand dune and drops the bags of charcoal beside the boy. He is about to ask him what they plan to do next but suddenly he cannot speak. He points along the beach and at last manages to stutter, 'What the hell is that?'

Kiko swings round to see what he is pointing at, then bursts out laughing. 'Haven't you seen a camel before?'

'A what?'

'A camel. It's like a mule but with a hump on its back. Papa says they used to use them all the time in the old days to carry heavy loads, but now there are only a few wild ones left.'

'What happened to them?' Ramon asks, still staring at this mythical creature.

'The hunters used to shoot them. Papa says the meat is very good, but a bit on the tough side. I expect that's why they are hiding in the dunes too, so they don't get shot.'

'So what do we do now?' asks Ramon.

'Nothing. We just sit here and wait until someone tells us we can go home.'

'Won't the police be able to follow our tracks in the sand?' asks Ramon, edging up the slope so he can look back towards the woods.

'Only if they are very quick. The wind will soon cover them with fresh sand; there will be nothing for them to follow. We just have to be patient and wait.'

'You've done this before, haven't you?'

'Yes, it's nothing to worry about. They will soon get fed up and move on.'

Ramon sits down beside Kiko and the charcoal, with his back to the sea and asks him, 'So why does your father do it? Why does he risk his life helping people like me?'

'He likes helping people I suppose.'

'But he doesn't even want to know why the Guardia Civil are after me. I don't understand how he can take such risks with people he doesn't know.'

Kiko shrugs his shoulders. 'He never talks about it. Sometimes people come and stay for a short while then they disappear. Sometimes they stay longer and become *carboneros*. I don't ask questions. Nobody does.'

Either Kiko has been taught not to discuss the people that his father helps, or he does not know anything about them other than that they are hiding from the Guardia Civil. Either way, Ramon, who has had little to do with children, is amazed at the confidence and resourcefulness of the child.

He does not know how long he has been asleep but when he wakes the sun has moved across the sky and it is now way past noon.

Kiko's mother stands over them. She has removed the charcoal stained smock and has draped a shawl around her shoulders instead. She carries a basket over one arm and beams at them, revealing a big gap where her two front teeth should be. '*Buenas*,' she says. 'They have gone.' For a moment Ramon does not know what she is talking about. He blinks at her in confusion. 'The Guardia. They've gone. And taken two sacks of charcoal with them, the bastards,' she continues.

'Do you have anything to eat, Mama?' asks Kiko, sitting up and rubbing his eyes. 'I'm starving.'

'You're always starving,' she replies fondly and hands him a hunk of honeycomb.

At the sight of it Ramon can feel his mouth begin to water. The smell of the honey is wonderful; he cannot remember when he last saw a honeycomb, never mind tasted one.

'Would you like some?' she asks him. 'I'm sorry it's only honeycomb, no bread. I collected it this morning. Luckily I managed to hide it before the Guardia arrived or they would have taken that as well.'

'Thank you. That's very kind of you.' The honeycomb melts in his mouth and its sweetness trickles down his throat reminding him of the long past days of his childhood. He is sure that life was not so hard when he was a boy; they were not rich but his father was usually able to work and most days there was food on the table. Life seemed so simple then.

'Well I'm off. You need to get to work too,' she says and slithers down the side of the dune and heads back into the forest.

Kiko licks his fingers clean and says, 'Come on, you heard what Mama said, we need to get back to work now. I hope someone has been keeping an eye on our *boliche*.' He picks up two sacks of charcoal and motions for Ramon to do the same.

It is two weeks since he last saw Clementina, but he has not stopped thinking about her; there is something about the young woman that fascinates him and it is not just her beauty. At times he thinks he has imagined her, that she is a spirit that drifted out of the woods to bewitch him and steal his soul. So when he sees her struggling across the clearing with two pails of water that she has collected from the well, he is relieved to see that she is after all just flesh and blood. '*Buenos días,*' he calls. 'Here, let me help you with those.'

/

121

'*Buenos días*, Ramon. I hear that the Guardia Civil were looking for you.' She gives him that smile of hers which seems to say he must do more than that to win her heart.

His mouth drops open and once more he is tongue-tied. He takes the buckets from her and grins like the idiot he undoubtedly is; why would such a lovely creature want to talk to him.

'Well, where have you been? Are you still running from the Guardia?' He doesn't know if she is joking or whether someone has told her what he has done. 'Don't look so worried; they weren't looking for anyone in particular,' she continues.

'How do you know?' he manages to say at last.

'Because they just like to keep us on our toes. They visit all the *pueblos* in turn and occasionally come into Doñana. They are looking for troublemakers, they say, but everyone knows they are opportunists who like to help themselves to a chicken or two, or frighten people into giving them information about their neighbours. We make sure to keep out of their way.'

'This time they took some charcoal,' he tells her. 'I went into the dunes to hide with Jaime's son.'

'I thought so. You've got sand in your hair. Come on, we'll go this way,' she says, and skips down a narrow path through the trees. 'So tell me something about yourself. Why are you here?'

He hesitates and shakes the sand from his hair. She is very young; he needs to be careful that she doesn't find out why he is running from the Guardia and tell anybody. He does not believe that all the people who live in the woods are generous like Jaime; he has discovered that life is not like that. There will always be someone who will sell information, true or false in order to get something for themselves, be it money, food or the confidence of the police. 'I was looking for work and someone told me that I could find some with the charcoal burners if I didn't mind living in the woods,' he says. It is only a half-lie, after all.

She stops and looks at him. 'You can tell me, you know. I won't tell anyone.'

He does not reply.

'And be careful with the buckets, you're slopping the water all over the place. I will have to go back and refill them,' she scolds.

He looks down at the buckets; she is right they are only half full now. 'I will get some more,' he says and tips the water from one into the other. 'Wait here.' He takes the empty bucket and runs back to the well. An old gypsy woman dressed in black is slowly winding the pulley to bring up her bucket. 'Would you like me to help?' he asks.

She stares at him and at first does not reply. 'That girl is betrothed,' she says, scowling at him. 'Her father is the patriarch's brother. He will not be happy if he knows you are talking to her. I am warning you because you look like a good man, but let me tell you that news travels fast in this place and especially news like that. Unless you want to end up in a ditch with your throat cut, keep well away from her.' She unhooks her bucket and staggers off in the opposite direction.

For a moment Ramon is tempted to abandon Clementina's bucket and head for the charcoal burner's house, but then he thinks about her smile and her dainty feet as she skipped along the path, like a carefree child. What harm can it do to talk to her. He doesn't have to tell her everything.

Clementina is waiting for him near the gypsy encampment. 'You took a long time,' she says taking the bucket from him.'

He explains about the old woman, but does not tell her about the warning.

'Oh, that will be Lucia,' she says. 'She's a great gossip. I bet she had something to warn you about. What was it this time? Wolves eating the goats? Or a lynx that stole a baby?'

'No, nothing like that,' he says. 'Do you want me to carry the buckets?'

'No need. I am home now. Someone will come out and help me.'

He moves close to her and hands her the bucket. She smells of fresh lavender. 'Don't spill it,' he says.

'What a cheek. It was you who spilt the water, not me. I never spill a drop.'

He knows she is saying something but the words just pass over his head; his eyes are too busy tracing the slender lines of her neck and shoulders. He is mesmerised by her. Never has he seen a girl so beautiful.

'Are you listening to me?' she asks, a little petulantly.

'Of course. I heard every word; it was my fault the water was spilt.'

'Humph. All men are the same; they never listen to us women.' But she does not look angry, only bemused. He has the feeling that she is joking with him again.

He walks slowly back to the charcoal burners. It will be dark soon and the smell of roasting meat is in the air; women in brightly coloured aprons are preparing the evening meal for their families. One by one they have lit an open fire and are propping skewers of meat on the glowing coals. Those who have not been lucky enough to trap a rabbit or a wood pigeon to roast, hang their cast iron pots of vegetables from a tripod made of seasoned wood. Once again he is struck by the way these people, their skin stained black from the charcoal and cut off from the rest of the world, live far better than his brother does.

Thinking about Pedro and his family makes him restless. This is not what he intended to do, hide in the woods like a common murderer. The Guardia's death was an accident, committed in self defence. Is he going to let that change the course of his life? He still has to continue the fight for equality and a better standard of living. The conversation he had with Pedro comes back to him. He can hear his brother's voice: '...*after you disappeared, I couldn't find work for months and we had hardly anything to eat. We didn't realise it but Mama was giving her share of the food to the children; she grew so weak that she became ill and died.*' His mother had given her life for her grandchildren. The least he can do is continue to fight for a better future for them, and he knows he cannot do that from the sanctuary of Doñana.

"Ah, there you are, Ramon. Come and join us,' calls Kiko's mother.

The family are all sitting around the fire eating a stew of root vegetables and something, which from the smell, must be rabbit. He squats down beside Kiko and accepts a plate of food.

'So the Guardia Civil often come here?' he says, hoping to hear some scrap of news from the outside world. 'What did they want today?'

'They don't say and we don't ask,' says Jaime. He pulls a leg of rabbit out of the pot and begins to chew it. The juice runs down into his beard. He wipes it away with his sleeve.

'They just like to nose about,' says his wife. She hands Ramon a hunk of bread that she has dipped into the pot. 'Here, eat this. It will fill you up.'

'So he wasn't looking for anybody in particular?'

'No. Mind you, if they see a new face then they start to ask questions. That was why it was best for you to keep out of sight,' says Jaime.

'Do they know you help people like me?'

'I certainly hope not. Remember, they shoot first and ask questions afterwards. We have never given them any trouble, so they leave us alone.'

'Well, apart from helping themselves to free charcoal,' adds his wife.

'A small price to pay,' Jaime replies.

'So you don't know anything about what is happening in Seville?' he asks as casually as he can. He is desperate to know.

'No, and I don't want to. We keep out of politics; that's the only way to stay safe these days. We keep our heads down and we keep away from those revolutionaries.'

'But you help people like me,' Ramon says, a little puzzled by his attitude.

'Helping people in need is another matter, but here there is no judge and no jury. We don't need to know what you have done in order to help you. If a friend tells me that someone needs help, I will do what I can, but I want no details.' He glares at him as if to say that he wants to hear no more about it.

Ramon dips his bread in the stew again and chews it slowly. So this is the choice he is offered. He remains here and thinks no more about politics or he leaves and risks imprisonment or execution. He looks around at the *carboneros* enjoying their evening meal; the light from the cooking fires flickers on their blackened faces making them appear like dark shadows of themselves. Maybe that is what they have become, shadows of men. Yet they seem happy, chatting and laughing with their families while their children chase each other around the fires playing tag, and the active *boliches* glow in the darkness. There are worse places to live. Here they have work. They have food and a roof over their heads. It is a simple life but it is an honest one. Surely he could accept such a life for himself; he could find a wife, maybe even Clementina. They could have children and grow old here. Even as these thoughts run through his head he knows he is lying to himself. He would last a month, maybe two or even three but then he would become restless and have to leave. It was foolish of him to have come here in the first place. Ramon knows he has to be careful and he does not want to put the charcoal burners at risk, but he cannot stay here. He will wait a few weeks until things have quietened down and the Guardia have moved their search away from him and on to some other poor wretch, then he will leave.

One of the older children comes up to Jaime and whispers in his ear. From the expression on his face, Ramon can see that it is not good news.

'What is it husband?' asks his wife.

Everyone looks at Jaime expectantly, but instead of answering, he stands up and motions for Ramon to follow him. Once they are out of earshot he turns to him and says, 'I'm sorry to tell you this but your brother has been arrested.'

'Pedro? *Dios mio*, what have I done.' This is all his fault. He was such an idiot to visit his brother; he should have known that they would find out eventually. 'What happened?'

'I'm sorry I have no more information than that. It's best not to speak of it to anyone else. But I do have one question for you. Did your brother know where you were going?'

Ramon shook his head. 'No, nobody knew except that old man.'

'Adolfo? Are you sure?'

'I'm positive.'

'Well, you can stay here for now but if the Guardia come looking for you, you will have to leave. I can't put the rest of the *carboneros* and their families at risk. You understand?'

'Yes, I understand.' So the decision whether to stay or leave has been made for him. As soon as he can, he will leave Doñana. He probably cannot help Pedro but he can help his wife and children. It will be dangerous but it is the least he can do for his brother's family.

CHAPTER 12

Cristóbal has left for Seville and Hugo is sorry to see him go, partly because he is good company and partly because now he no longer has an excuse to visit Doñana again. He is sure that his father has told Felipe to keep him as busy as possible because between running around doing errands for his brother and trying to plan for his trip to England, he has not had a minute to himself. Now his mother has sent for him. He is beginning to feel like a child again as he climbs the marble staircase to his mother's room.

'Mama, you wanted to see me?' he asks, trying to keep the irritation out of his voice.

'Yes, Hugo. I just wanted to be sure you had no plans for this evening.'

'No, Mama. I don't have any plans. I am too busy to have even the shadow of a social life.' He throws himself down on the chaise longue under the window. His legs are too long for it, and his feet hang over the end.

'Good. That's all right then.'

'What? What's all right? What have you got planned?' His mother is a great schemer and planner.

'Just a small dinner party. Your father has invited Don Manuel de Almudanza and his daughter, Mari Carmen, to dine with us tonight.'

'I know who Mari Carmen is, Mama. And I know why Papa has invited them to dinner. You are wasting your time.'

'Now, don't be like that, Hugo. You have known about the arrangement between your father and Don Manuel for a long time. She is a lovely girl and has such a sweet smile. You and Mari Carmen were very close at one time.'

'When we were ten years old, yes. That doesn't mean I want to marry her.'

'I'm not asking you to marry her tomorrow,' his mother replies. 'I just want you to be nice to her over dinner. They are old friends of ours and I don't want you insulting them. Is that understood?'

'Of course, Mama. When have I ever insulted any of your friends?'

'This is very important for your father, not only would a marriage between our two families be very advantageous to all of us, but Don Manuel's support in the election could be very useful.'

Hugo bites his tongue. It is not his mother's fault. His father has put her up to this. 'So my father wants me to marry someone I do not love just so that he can become mayor of Jerez. So much for family solidarity.'

'Just be pleasant this evening and don't upset your father. It's not as though you have to propose to her tonight, although that would please your father immensely. Just be nice to her.'

'Of course I will, Mama. I actually quite like Mari Carmen. I wonder if anyone has bothered to ask her if she wants to marry me.' He swings his legs round and sits up. 'Tell me, Mama, what's going on? Why is father so angry with me? Is it to do with that rubbish that Cristóbal came out with about Tina?' A flush of pink colours his mother's cheeks, a sign that she is embarrassed at this turn in the conversation. 'Well? I'm right, aren't I? Why is he so scared that I will talk to Tina?'

'You know very well that we have a position to keep up in society. Just leave it alone and do as your father tells you.'

'Like you do, Mama? For years I've wondered when you were going to stand up to him. All this nonsense about the *Sección Feminina*, that's not you. You know it isn't. I've met him, you know.'

'Who do you mean?'

'José Antonio Primo de Rivera; he started the Falangist party and it's his sister who has come up with this feminine nonsense, strongly backed by the Church of course.'

'Don't be like that, Hugo. They just want to help women live good clean lives. That's not a bad thing, is it?'

'I suppose not, but it sounds more like they want to control them, to me.'

'What is he like, Primo de Rivera?'

Hugo wrinkles his nose and says, 'You wouldn't approve, Mama; he's rather a playboy. Nothing like his sister who comes across as a bit of a dragon.'

'Listen Hugo, if it will help your father, I'm happy to do it,' she replies but he can see she does not really mean it. 'Don't let's quarrel, my dear boy. Sometimes we cannot have everything we want in life.'

His mother looks sad. There is something she is not telling him, but he won't press her. Another time, maybe, 'Very well, Mama. I promise not to upset Papa or Felipe or our guests and I will be pleasant to Mari Carmen.' To be honest, he can not guarantee the first two but it will be nice to see Mari Carmen again. He is actually quite fond of her and she is very attractive, with her pale skin and blonde hair, all part of the English blood passed down through the family from Richard Watson. He knows she will make someone a wonderful wife, just not him.

'Excellent. I knew you would understand and when you get back from England we will discuss plans for your wedding.'

He groans. Is nobody listening to him?

It has been a cloudless day and now that night has fallen the sky is filled with stars. It is unusually cold tonight and when the guests arrive, they are well wrapped up against the winter chill in heavy coats and warm scarves. The maid relieves them of their outer garments and shows them into the lounge where Don Luis is sitting by the fire with his feet on the fender.

'Welcome, dear friends. Come in out of the cold.' He gets to his feet to greet them, beckoning them towards the fire which is radiating a warm glow around the room. Then he snaps his fingers and a servant appears carrying a tray of crystal glasses and a full sherry decanter. 'Something to warm you up,' he says. 'This is the latest vintage.' He pours the golden brown liquid into one of the glasses and hands it to Don Manuel. 'What do you think of that? Good, yes? Not too sweet?'

Don Manuel sniffs at the sherry, then swirls it around his glass and holds it up to the light. He nods. 'An excellent Olorosa, my friend. A very good year. And of course I see you already have the DOP on the label.' He turns to his wife. 'Here, try this, Victoria. I'm sure you will like it.'

'Yes, being able to put Denomination of Origin on the label is something I've wanted to do for a long time.' Don Luis beams with pleasure. 'I don't know why it took them so long to approve it. Now it will stop towns like Montilla calling their wines sherry when they are nothing like ours.' He savours his wine; it is one of the best they have produced.

Why does Hugo not understand what a great opportunity he has before him; a marriage into the Almudanza family will consolidate   their corner of the sherry market and make them all rich. 'Ah, there you are, my dear,' he says as his wife enters the lounge. He watches her as she greets their guests, kissing them on both cheeks and asking after their health. He was right to marry her; she has been an excellent wife, loyal and supportive in everything he has wanted to do. A tiny black cloud floats into his head; except once. Just once she stood her ground and defied him and although he had been angry, he had given in to her demands. Now he knows he was wrong to have done so.

'Have you recovered from your trip to Seville?' Don Manuel asks Doña Isabel. 'I hear you were caught up in those riots. How awful for you.'

'There were riots, but we kept well away from them,' she replies. 'Still it wasn't very pleasant. We were quite worried, even though we had Diego with us.'

'He wouldn't have been much use if the mob had attacked us,' adds Don Luis.

'Still we were glad he was there,' says his wife.

'I don't know what the police were doing. They should have stepped in as soon as the riots started. The country is falling apart.'

'You are quite right, political unrest is growing daily. It will end badly, mark my words,' says Don Manuel.

'I believe a number of people were hurt, including some of the Guardia Civil,' says Victoria. 'But I expect they will soon have it under control, like they did with the general strike.'

Hugo turns to her and says, 'By killing three thousand workers and injuring thousands more, you mean? Well I suppose that's one way to put down a strike.'

'Watch your tone, young man,' Don Luis snaps. Hugo seems determined to annoy him lately.

Victoria has turned pale. 'That must be an exaggeration,' she says timidly. 'I'm sure they would not do that.'

Hugo is about to respond but his mother is too quick for him; she turns to Mari Carmen who is standing by the door, nervously playing with her shawl, a pale green silk square with gold flowers embroidered on it. 'And how are you, my dear? You are looking very well.'

'She always looks well, Mama. It's all the fresh air and exercise she takes,' says Hugo, smiling at her. 'Isn't that right, Mari Carmen?'

'If you say so, Hugo. I do like to take the dogs out every morning and just lately I have taken to playing tennis with Henrietta MacVie a couple of afternoons in the week,' she replies.

'I believe that exercise is very good for your health,' says Isabel. 'It's one of the things that the *Sección Feminina* recommends.'

'It is indeed, and cleanliness too,' Victoria replies. 'If only our workers would understand that. Honestly, I really don't know why they are always so dirty. And their clothes are just filthy. I sometimes think they are lower than the animals.'

Hugo opens his mouth to respond, but his mother's stare stops him.

Don Luis is becoming confused. Hugo and Mari Carmen are getting on so well; they act like old friends, which is what they are, he reminds himself. But what was that she just said about playing tennis with the McVie girl? The McVies are new to the area and to the sherry business. He views them with suspicion. Just recently they bought a declining and bankrupt vineyard which he has had his eye on for a while but was waiting until the price dropped before he made an offer. Then the McVies suddenly stepped in before he could do anything about it, paid the asking price and imported some new healthy vines from America to improve the stock. Now it looks as though Harold McVie might be interested in an alliance with Almudanza &

Watson. This is not good news. 'How is their son,' he asks. 'Has he got married yet?'

'No, and I don't think he is planning to either,' adds Victoria. 'These young people are not so eager to get wed as we were in our day. I can't understand it, personally. Maybe we pamper them too much and that's why they don't want to leave home. My nephew is just the same; quite happy to live with his parents forever it seems.' She laughs and looks at her husband for confirmation.

'Well, he will have to make up his mind soon or all the lovely girls will be married off,' Don Manuel says, but he does not seem overly concerned.

'You make it sound like a meat market,' retorts his wife.

'I suppose that's what it is,' says Hugo. 'Selling your children off to the highest bidder.' He laughs.

Don Luis tries to give his son a warning look but Hugo is talking to Mari Carmen now and avoids looking at his father. What the hell is his son trying to do to him? They haven't even sat down at the table yet and Hugo is attempting to upset him. Well he is not going to allow it. 'Why don't we go into dinner, now that we have all gathered,' Don Luis says, beaming at his guests. He is determined that Hugo will not rattle him.

'What about your older boy, Felipe? Isn't he joining us?' asks Victoria.

'Maybe later for a nightcap. He is very busy at the moment.' There was no way he wanted Hugo and Felipe to start their usual bickering in front of his guests; Felipe could eat elsewhere for once.

Isabel, as always has planned an excellent dinner, designed to show off their range of sherry wines. A large platter of seafood, fresh from the Atlantic is delicious with their dry, pale Fino, and then when the venison is served he offers them a glass of golden Amontillado. He looks around the dinner table and feels pleased with himself. Hugo and Mari Carmen appear to be getting on very well so maybe his son is actually beginning to understand how beneficial their marriage could be for everyone concerned.

'It's all delicious,' says Victoria. 'Absolutely delicious.'

Her husband nods in agreement and helps himself to another glass of the Amontillado. 'Yes Luis, an excellent meal and this sherry is the perfect accompaniment to the venison.'

'Well, I have a little surprise for you, Manuel; a Palo Cortado which will go beautifully with the dessert. It's a new sherry for us, but I think it will sell well. Hugo is going to England in a few days to find some buyers for it.' He nods to the servants and they bring in a selection of fruit and pastries and place them on the table.

Don Manuel sips the Palo Cortado and says, 'Yes it has a good fresh taste and is a beautiful colour, but I'm afraid I have a preference for a nice cream sherry with my dessert.' He takes a grape from the table and pops it into his mouth. 'But that's just a matter of taste; it's a perfectly rounded wine. I think it should sell well.'

'Are you two going to spend the whole evening talking about business?' asks Isabel. She turns to Victoria and says, 'How are the rest of your family getting on? I hear your brother came to visit you.'

'Yes, but he didn't stay long. He wanted to tell me that he is getting married to Rachel Watson; she's the great niece of our founder. She sounds a bit young for him but he seems to be happy about it.'

'So how will that affect Mari Carmen's inheritance?' asks Don Luis, as casually as he can. This does not sound like very good news to him.

'Oh, it won't affect it at all. Victoria's brother doesn't stand to inherit anything from the company,' says Don Manuel. 'It will all go to Mari Carmen, *si Dios quiere.* Our agreement still holds good.'

'Has my husband told you he is going into politics?' asks Isabel, giving her husband a look that tells him he is going too far.

Don Luis knows his wife does not like him speaking so openly about the inheritance, so now she is changing the subject.

'Yes, I heard someone talking about it last week at the club. A big step for you, Luis,' says Don Manuel. 'So you think you can manage to run the business and be mayor of Jerez at the same time? Sounds a lot of work to me.'

Don Luis finishes the Palo Cortado before he replies. He does not like anyone questioning his ability, but tries not to show it and says, 'Yes, indeed. Unlike you, I have two very able sons who will take over my share of the work.'

'Ah, but I have a very capable daughter; she's as good as a dozen sons,' retorts Don Manuel. He smiles at his daughter and raises his glass to her.

'You exaggerate, Papa,' says Mari Carmen, and laughs. 'Only six sons.'

'So, Luis, you will be stepping back from running the company?' continues Don Manuel.

'No, no, not at all. Just leaving more of the day-to-day stuff to the boys. That's if I get elected of course.' He wishes Isabel had not mentioned the election.

'I'm sure you will. All your workers will vote for you of course and then there are your business contacts. I think they will jump at the chance to have someone in the sherry trade as their new mayor. What business is the current incumbent in? I forget. Import, export?'

'Something like that. I know he owns a lot of land and has a few businesses in Cadiz.'

'Well it's time he was replaced; I hear he has held that job for more than ten years. Some fresh ideas would be good for the town.'

'So I can count on your support then?' asks Don Luis.

'Of course. We will soon be family, after all.' Don Manuel takes Mari Carmen's hand and squeezes it.

Once his guests have left, Don Luis pours himself a glass of brandy and sits down by the fire. He stares into the flickering flames as a plan begins to form itself in his mind. Once Hugo has gone to England then he must get rid of the gypsy girl before his son returns. With her out of the picture, he is sure that Hugo will happily marry Mari Carmen. They make a perfect couple; he could see that very clearly this evening and when Hugo realises that nothing can come of his infatuation for Clementina he will gladly accept Mari Carmen as his wife. But how to do it? How can he get rid of her? He could pay her father to send her away. After all Vano probably has a suitor in mind for her anyway; he could pay him to bring the wedding forward. How old is she now? Fourteen? Fifteen? Certainly she is of a marriageable age. But would that work? Vano is a proud man. Would he accept Don Luis's money? Maybe he should try to get rid of the whole gypsy family. Get them to disappear, move to another part of the country; gypsies are usually very good at that.

'Still up, Papa? asks Hugo, coming in from the garden and closing the doors behind him.

'Yes, just enjoying a nightcap. I thought the evening went very well, didn't you?'

'The food was excellent, as usual, and it was nice to see Mari Carmen again,' he says, sitting down opposite his father.

'You two seemed to be getting along very well, I thought. She will make you a lovely wife, Hugo.'

'Papa, don't start. You know I'm not ready to get married just yet. Maybe in the future.'

'All right, my boy. I mustn't rush you. These things have to be approached carefully. I just feel that maybe she might change her mind and marry someone else while you are dithering. Now that would be a shame.'

'She's a very independent young woman, Papa. She will decide whom she will marry just as I will. At the moment we are just good friends. Let's leave it at that and see what happens in the future.'

So Hugo is not dismissing the idea; that is good. Don Luis is now even more certain that if he can get rid of Clementina then Hugo will marry Mari Carmen. 'By the way, Hugo, I want you to go to Bristol tomorrow. There is no need to wait until next week. The sooner you find us a new distributor, the better. Ask your mother to get your luggage ready. You can leave after breakfast. The car will take you to the station.'

'But why the rush, Papa?'

'I would like it done before the election, then I will only have one thing to worry about, my campaign.'

'Very well, but I really don't think you need to worry about either of them.' Hugo stretches his arms and stands up. 'In that case, I suppose I had better go to bed. *Buenos noches* Papa.'

'*Buenos noches*, son.'

As soon as Hugo has left, Don Luis goes in search of his other son. He finds him in the kitchen chatting to one of the grooms. 'Felipe, we need to speak,' he says. 'Come with me.'

'What is it now, Papa? I was just about to go to bed. I have to be up early tomorrow.'

'We have a problem and I want you to sort it out.'

'What now? Why is it always me who has to sort out your problems, Papa? What's that lazy brother of mine doing?'

'He's going to Bristol tomorrow and I want everything sorted out before he gets back.'

'All right, so what is it all about?' He follows his father into the library and shuts the door. 'Why so secretive?'

'You were there when Cristóbal told us about Hugo and that girl, Clementina, yes?'

'You know I was. The gypsy girl he's infatuated with at the moment. What of it? It won't last. Hugo is always the same. He meets a girl and all at once she is the one he can't live without. Then he meets another girl and the previous one is forgotten. I really don't understand why you are so concerned about her. By the time Hugo comes back from England he will have forgotten her and be in love with someone else.'

'That is what I am hoping, but I want to be certain and the only way to do that is to ensure that the girl has disappeared. If she is not here, then he will soon forget her and move on to someone else.'

'And you are hoping it will be Mari Carmen?'

'Yes. The alliance with her family is very important for our business.'

'So what do you want me to do?'

'Just that, make her disappear, her and all her family if that is what it takes.'

Felipe stares at his father. 'How the hell do you expect me to do that?'

'You'll find a way. Remember my reputation is at stake here. So just make it happen. If we allow anyone to think that there is something between that gypsy girl and Hugo, it will destroy any chance I might have of becoming mayor. You must do something. And don't stare at me as if I'm mad; you know I'm right. Get rid of her. As long as he knows she is there in Doñana he is going to want to see her. We can't let that happen. I'm relying on you, son.'

'Very well, Papa. I just hope you know what you are asking me to do.'

Felipe lies in bed thinking about what his father has said. It is always the same; whenever there is something difficult or dangerous he turns to Felipe. He cannot decide whether his father does this because he respects his ability or because he does not want to get his own hands dirty. Of course, if anything goes wrong it will be Felipe who will pay, not his father.

'What's wrong?' his wife asks him. 'You've been tossing and turning ever since you got to bed.'

'It's my father. He wants me to do something for him.'

'Well stop thinking about it and go to sleep. You can tell me about it in the morning.'

Except he cannot tell anyone. Whether he is successful or not, he will have to carry the guilt of what he is going to do alone.

CHAPTER 13

Vano is tired. He could not sleep last night for worrying about Clementina. The girl is so headstrong; he never knows what she will do next. It is his own fault; Lavinia is always scolding him for spoiling his youngest daughter. He cannot help it. Before Clementina was born he had thought that his family was complete, that he would never have any more children and then, suddenly, there was this angel, the most beautiful child he had ever seen. God had given him one more blessing. He wanted to ask the priest to hold a special thanksgiving mass but Lavinia was not happy about it; she said it was not right to put one child above the others. He could not understand her, but then he never could understand the workings of women's minds. What he considered to be women's things were best left to the womenfolk; he kept well clear of them.

'Papa, someone is coming,' says Álvaro.

'Well go and see who they are and what they want.' He walks across to the well and pulls up the bucket. He splashes cold water on his face and instantly feels better. He hopes it is the agent come to collect his horses and maybe to pay him for his trouble.

'Papa, Papa. Come quickly.'

'What on earth is the matter with you, lad? Why all the fuss?'

His son is grinning from ear to ear. 'Look who's come to visit us.'

Vano wipes his face on his neckerchief and turns around to see for himself what it is that is making Álvaro so excited, and

142

begins to smile. 'Well I never. Geronimo, is that you? As I live and breathe I never thought I'd see you again in this lifetime.'

'Well, here I am, dear brother.' A tall, swarthy man steps forward and clasps Vano in his arms. His grey hair is long and oiled; he has tied it back with a red headscarf, revealing a gold earring in his left ear. A grey beard covers his face, but it is not thick enough to hide the ugly scar that runs down the left side of his face. 'It's been a long time.'

'Too long.' Vano points to his face. 'Who did that to you? It looks fairly fresh.'

The man touches the scar. 'That's the reason we are here.'

'We? Who else is with you?'

'My family. We had to leave Osuna. Things were getting nasty.'

'So you decided to come here?'

'Yes, brother. There is no other choice. Anyway, I have missed Doñana. I don't think I have eaten any fish or fresh meat since we moved away.' He laughs. 'And you? How are you and your family?'

'Come with me and you will see for yourself. Álvaro, go and bring your uncle's wagon round.' He leads his brother towards his home. 'We will need to find somewhere for you to camp,' he adds.

'I see you have moved into my house,' says Geronimo.

'Well, I am the chief of those you left behind.'

'I didn't leave you behind. You chose to stay. I had to think of the whole clan; we were dying here.'

'Well, I don't want to quarrel with you, brother, but you have to realise that I am in charge here. You may be the patriarch in Osuna, but not here.'

His brother does not reply. Vano knows he is not going to accept this from his younger brother. Why the hell has he come here? If he has brought all the family then it isn't a passing visit. It is ten years since he left, so what is he after now? He takes a deep breath. Patience, he tells himself. Patience. Do not lose your temper until you know why he is here and, more importantly, if he intends to stay. Remember he is your brother and the patriarch of your clan.

'Lavinia, come and see who has arrived,' he calls to his wife, trying to sound pleased with the news. 'I think they will need some food; they have walked a long way.'

Lavinia comes out, carrying her new grandson in her arms. 'What is it, husband?' She stops and stares at Geronimo. 'Patriarch, what are you doing here? Is everything all right? Are you alone?'

'Lavinia, as usual with lots of questions. You are looking as lovely as ever, I see. Is this another child?' he asks.

'My grandson.'

'I see. A grandmother already. No, to answer your question, I am not alone; my wife is with me. She will be preparing some food for the family. Maybe you would like to help her.'

'Lavinia, please show the patriarch's wife where to get water and some wood for a fire, then come back here,' says Vano and turning to his brother adds, 'My wife is a very busy woman. I'm sure your wife is capable of organising your family without her help.'

'Of course. No need to be so touchy, brother. It's just that we have travelled all night and need somewhere to sleep, once we have eaten of course.'

Vano looks back towards the clearing; he can see the rest of the patriarch's family spilling out of the wagon. There must be at least thirty of them. 'It's a bit cold to sleep outside,' he says. 'I imagine you can sleep in your wagon tonight?'

'For now, yes,' says Geronimo.

Vano is beginning to worry about this turn of events. He is happy to see his brother but he does not want his life to change and it looks as though it might be about to do just that. 'I will ask Álvaro to see to your horses.'

'One of my sons can do that. Just tell him where to stable them.' The patriarch sits down next to the fire and stretches out his legs. He looks very much at home.

'I'll be back in a minute,' says Vano. He finds Álvaro chatting to one of his cousins. He has already helped him to unhitch the horses and lead them into the corral with the others. 'Well done, Álvaro. Is everything all right here?'

'Yes, Papa. I told them to camp on the edge of the clearing, near the stream. The women are getting everything organised.'

Vano nods at him. 'So I see. Well don't forget the agent is due to come today to collect his horses. Let me know as soon as you see him arrive.' He drops his voice and adds, 'Don't let him speak to any of our guests.' He does not want his brother knowing too much about his business or trying to undercut him.

'I won't, Papa.'

'And tell me if you have any problems.' He looks across at the new encampment in the clearing. 'I think I'll just check on the horses.'

Vano enters the corral and walks up to the horses he has selected for the agent to collect. He strokes them each in turn, speaking to them softly and promising them everything will be fine in their new home. Even when he knows he has to sell them, he still finds it hard to part with any of these lovely Marsh mares. Well at least he can console himself with the knowledge that they have been well trained and should be going to good homes. Their new owners will have nothing to complain about.

By the time he gets back to Lavinia and Geronimo, his wife has already heated up some of the dinner left from the night before and his brother is wiping the last of it from his plate with a hunk of black bread.

'You certainly eat well here. I had forgotten how easy it is for you to catch a rabbit or a wild duck. I see there's no shortage of food here, not like in Osuna.'

'We catch what we can, but it's not always so plentiful and we have to keep an eye out for the wardens. But you're right, we are not starving; there's always something in the woods to forage for.'

'What about the rest of your family?' asks Lavinia. 'Surely they are hungry?'

'They will be all right,' he says, stretching out by the fire again. 'What about a drop of beer to wash down that lovely meal?'

'We don't have any. I rarely drink beer,' says Vano, sitting down beside his brother. 'So, are you going to explain why you are here, brother? Are you running from the police?'

'No, not exactly. Well, yes. The mayor of our village had the Guardia Civil run us out of town, even though we hadn't done anything wrong. He just doesn't like *gitanos*.'

'The mayor of Osuna?'

'No, we lived in a small village just outside Osuna.'

'So why didn't you just move into Osuna? That would have been closer for you.'

'I can see it's a long time since you travelled anywhere, brother. You are living in a paradise here. People are starving in the towns and villages and Osuna is no better than most. There is no food and people have no means to grow their own, like you do.' He points to the vegetable patch that Lavinia keeps full of potatoes and beetroot, and whatever else is in season. 'There are no smallholdings. All the land is owned by big estates who don't even sow crops every year; they harvest the wheat one year, then the next year they leave the stubble and the third year they leave the land fallow. They say the land is too poor to produce crops more than once every three years, but that's because they keep the best land for hunting. They don't produce enough food to feed the people but they can still make themselves rich. There is no common land anymore and if anyone tries to grow their own food they are arrested for trespassing and thrown into gaol. I can tell you, we were already thinking of moving away from there before the mayor decided to move us on.'

'But surely there are other ways for people to earn a living?'

'Yes of course, there's soap making, olive oil factories, potteries, but there's not enough work to go round. And it is the same in all the villages we passed on the way here, people are struggling. Or to be more precise they are starving. A few years ago people would come out of their houses and give us food if we were passing by, or they would want their fortunes told or their knives sharpened. The children would skip along behind us as we went through the village, but not now. Nowadays they have no money and no food, and we hardly see a child.'

'So, that's why you came back? But what work do you think you can find here? You left Doñana because you wanted a better life, and now you're back.'

At first his brother does not reply, just sits staring into the fire. 'Well you seem to be doing all right, brother. Are you still stealing the Marquess' horses?' Geronimo looks past him towards the corral. 'I see you've got a few at the moment.'

'The horses are wild. They don't belong to anyone. I just take care of them.'

'Indeed. I wonder if the Marquess sees it like that?'

'What do you want Geronimo? Are you planning to stay here or have you just come to annoy me?' Vano is struggling to control his temper. He knows that what he does is against the law, but the local landowners welcome his skill with the horses. They are happy to turn a blind eye if it means that they can buy excellent animals for a fraction of the usual price. They are all complicit in his business.

'I don't know, yet. Right now, I just want to sleep.' Geronimo stands up. 'Thank you for the food, Lavinia. It's good to see you haven't lost your touch. We'll talk tonight, Vano.' The patriarch turns and walks back towards his family.

'What are you going to do, husband?' Lavinia asks as soon as her brother-in-law is out of earshot.

'What can I do? He is the patriarch. I can't send him away no matter how much I would like to.' He sits staring at the fire for a while then asks, 'Where is Clementina?'

'She's helping Zita to collect honey.'

'Isn't it a bit late for that?'

'No, she spotted a hive yesterday and so they are checking it out.'

'As soon as she gets back, send her to me. I need to speak to her, urgently.'

CHAPTER 14

Clementina gently lowers the last of the honeycomb into the box and covers it with a muslin cloth. The bees are dozy from the smoke of the small fire she and Zita have made and buzz peacefully above her head.

'Is that enough?' asks Zita. 'Shouldn't we collect that last little bit?'

'No, we have to leave something for the colony or the bees won't come back here.' She puts the box carefully on the ground then licks her fingers. 'It's lovely,' she says. 'Sweet but not too sweet and tastes of ...' She pauses trying to identify the flavour. 'Rosemary, pine trees. Oh, I don't know. But it's good.'

'I will sell it in the market tomorrow,' says Zita. 'Do you want to come with me?'

'No, Papa won't let me. He's been very strange lately; I'm beginning to feel like a prisoner.'

'Oh, don't worry. He was like that with me until I got married and then he couldn't care less about where I went or what I did.' She looks up at the sky. '*Dios mio*, it's almost dark. I must get back to the baby. Can you bring the honey if I run on ahead?'

'Of course. It's not heavy. I'll bring it to your house; if I take it home, someone is sure to want to taste it.'

'Álvaro, you mean.'

'Yes, he really loves honey.' She laughs. 'Do you remember the time he tried to collect some honey from the hive and got chased by the bees? The poor boy even had bees in his hair. I don't think he's been near a hive since then.'

'What was he, about eight? He should have known better.' Zita stamps on the embers of the fire to extinguish them. 'So I'll see you later, Tina.'

'All right. I won't be long.' She watches as her sister runs off in the direction of home and then picks up the box containing the honeycomb and begins to follow her. The path winds its way through the woods, past pine trees and eucalyptus trees, bushes of rock roses and fragrant lavender. The woods smell of the honey in her box and are far from silent. There is bird song all around her; this is a time of the year when migrant birds stop to winter here, arriving from somewhere in the far north. Her mother has told her about them and how they always return in the spring, flying thousands and thousands of kilometres to their homelands. Other less hardy species leave Doñana and cross the sea to Africa; if she goes down to the dunes she can sometimes watch then circling overhead, waiting until they are all gathered together before flying to a warmer continent. Her mother is a clever woman; she has been to school and now she likes to pass on her knowledge to the children in the clan. Not everyone wants her to teach their children, especially their daughters, but Papa has never objected and Clementina loves the time she spends with her mother learning how to read and write her name.

She stops; the birds have become silent. Someone is here in the woods. A stranger. She looks around her but cannot see anyone. She feels frightened and yet she does not know why; it is as though a cold wind is passing through the trees. Then she sees him and relaxes. It is Hugo's brother. She smiles; years have passed since she last saw him but she would recognise those ears anywhere. They used to tease him mercilessly about them when he was younger. She lifts her hand and waves.

'Clementina, so you remember me?'

'Of course I do, Felipe. How are you?' He continues to walk towards her, but he is staring at her rather strangely. 'What is it? Is something wrong?' she asks as he grows closer. Maybe he has been drinking.

'Keep away from my brother, you little fortune hunter.'

'What are you talking about Felipe? I have hardly seen Hugo. Yes, he came to see my father and we spoke, but that was all. Why are you so angry?'

'There's no way he is going to marry you, you know. Father would never allow it. If you know what's good for you you will heed my words.'

'What are you talking about? I have no intention of marrying Hugo. Whatever gave you that idea?' She is still smiling at him but he does not respond, just keeps walking towards her. This is not good. Something is wrong with him; she can feel it in her bones. Suddenly she knows she must get away from him and quickly. She turns and starts to run back the way she has come. She has no idea where she is going, just as long as it is away from Felipe. The box with the honey is heavy; she stops and throws it down on the path behind her. Her heart is beating so loudly she is sure that he can hear it.

'Come here, you little bitch,' he shouts.

She knows he is getting closer but she cannot run any faster; her skirt catches on a bramble bush and she hears it rip. For a second she looks down to see the damage and trips over a tree root; before she can save herself she falls flat on her face. Instantly she tries to get up, but he is too quick and pushes her back onto the ground; she can feel the weight of his body pressing down on her.

'By the time I've finished with you, no-one will want to marry you,' he whispers in her ear. His breath stinks of alcohol and tobacco.

She wants to be sick. Why is he doing this to her? What has she ever done to him? ´Felipe. Stop. Let me up. You're hurting me. It's not funny.'

'Lie still. There's no point struggling; I have you now.'

His body lies heavily on top of her, but still she struggles to get out from under him. 'Let me go,' she screams. 'Let me go. Why are you doing this, Felipe? My father will kill you when I tell him what you've done.'

He sits up, pinning her to the ground with his arms. 'I don't think so, little princess. He will want nothing more to do with you. What use is a deflowered daughter to an honourable man like Vano? What can he do with her? No-one will want to marry you after I have finished with you.' He unbuckles his belt.

Now she realises what he is about to do to her. She screams as loudly as she can, but she knows no-one can hear her; she is a long way from the camp and sound does not travel well in the woods. She is on her own. She must resist him no matter what he tries to do to her.

'Time to have a look at what it is my brother finds so attractive about you,' he says, turning her over and pulling at her clothes. Her blouse rips and lays bare her breasts. 'My, my,' he mutters and lowers his head towards them but she is quick and sinks her teeth into his neck. Felipe lets out an almighty screech. 'You little bitch. You're going to be sorry you did that,' he snarls and slaps her face so hard that her head snaps back and hits the ground.

The next thing she knows she is face down again and she can feel his hand travelling up her skirt. 'Help, somebody help me,' she screams but he shoves her face into the undergrowth and now she can hardly breathe.

'There is no-one to help you, little princess. You can scream all you want. Only the birds can hear you. I will...' He does not finish whatever he intended to say, instead she hears a muffled grunt and the full weight of his body topples forward onto her back. Something wet and sticky trickles onto her neck; it is warm. Clementina is too scared to move, even when the suffocating weight of his body has lifted; fear has taken all her strength from her. Whoever it is, she cannot fight them as well.

'Get up slowly, Clementina,' says a familiar voice. 'You will be all right, now. He can't hurt you anymore.'

'Ramon, is that you?' She sits up and looks around her. Felipe is lying on his back with a large gash in his head. 'Is he dead? Have you killed him?' she asks.

'No, more's the pity. But he'll be unconscious for a while. Here, put this on.' He hands her his jacket and she is suddenly aware how naked she is. She grabs it from him and covers herself up.

'What are we going to do?' she asks. She is not quite sure whether this nightmare is really over.

'Do you know him?' Ramon asks.

She nods.

'So who is he?'

'His name is Felipe Rodriguez; we used to play together when we were children. His father owns a vineyard; they are very influential people. I just don't understand why he would do this to me.' Tears are streaming down her cheeks.

'We can worry about that later, in the meantime you can't go home because as soon as he comes round he will go looking for you. You'd better come with me.'

'To the charcoal burners?' she asks.

'Yes, just until we can think of a better plan.'

'But my parents, they will be worried about me if I don't go home.'

'We will get a message to them, but for now we have to get away from here.' He helps her to her feet and takes her hand in his. 'Can you walk?'

She nods. She feels very cold and is beginning to tremble; at any moment she feels her legs will give way.

'It's the shock,' says Ramon, taking her shawl from where it has snagged on a bush and wrapping it around her shoulders. 'Don't worry, you will feel fine soon. Come with me, now. We must get away from here before he wakes up.' He looks at Felipe's bloody body and spits on it. 'I have a strong feeling that this is not over yet. He does not look like the sort of man who likes to lose; he will be looking to get his revenge on both of us.'

At first Felipe does not know where he is. It is night and he can see the moon shining through the trees. He touches his head; it hurts and he is bleeding. Gradually it comes back to him; he is in the woods in Doñana. Clementina. Did she do this to him? No, that is impossible. So who did? One of her brothers? Her father? No, Vano would not have left him alive; he is sure of that. He tries to sit up and a sharp pain runs through his head. Well, he cannot stay here waiting for the wild boar to find him. And if Clementina tells her family what has happened they will come looking for him, so he needs to get home and quickly.

CHAPTER 15

Ramon and Clementina walk back to the charcoal burners in silence. He is deep in thought about what he should do, while she is walking in a daze. The poor girl has had a traumatic experience and he is not sure what he can say to her to comfort her. It is probably best to wait until he has formed a clear plan in his head and then tell her about it.

He has already decided it is time to leave Doñana and today's events have strengthened his resolve but have also made it more complicated; he has Clementina to consider now. What if her family do not want her? He does not know much about the *gitanos*—they keep to themselves—but he knows how strict they are with their women. It will not matter that Clementina was not actually raped, the fact that she has been attacked puts her virtue in question. But what if it is not safe for her to stay in Doñana? Her attacker might return to get his revenge. Ramon's mind is in a whirl; he is responsible for Ana and the children now that his brother is in jail, but at the same time he feels responsible for Clementina. How on earth is he going to be able to care for two women and two children when he does not have a job, hardly any money and is on the run from the Guardia Civil?

Kiko is the first to see him when they arrive at the charcoal burners' *chozas* and runs straight across to them. 'What's happened to Clementina?' he asks staring at the girl. 'Is she all right?'

'Does she look all right?' Ramon replies, rather more abruptly than he intends. At the sight of the boy, Clementina begins to sob uncontrollably. 'Where is your father? We need to speak to him right away,' says Ramon. He attempts to put his arm around Clementina but she pulls away from him. 'It's all right. You're safe now. It's all right.' He is unable to find the right words to comfort her and feels helpless in the face of her distress.

'I'll get him.' Kiko turns and runs towards the farthest of the *boliches*. Ramon can hear him calling for his father.

There is no sign of Jaime but within minutes Kiko's mother is there, 'Ramon, what's happened to her?' she asks. 'Is she hurt? My poor child, what on earth is wrong?' Everyone has stopped what they are doing and now stand around watching them.

'I don't think she is injured, but she was assaulted.' He does not want to tell this woman what he saw; he will feel more comfortable speaking to her husband. 'Can you take her somewhere quiet? I need to talk to Jaime.'

'Of course. Come with me, child. Let's get you cleaned up and away from all these prying eyes.' She puts her arm around Clementina and leads her back to her *choza*.

Ramon sees Jaime and Kiko hurrying towards him and goes to meet them. 'Jaime, we need your help,' he says.

'Come with me. Kiko, I want you to go and help David; tell him I won't be long.'

'Yes, Papa.'

'So what is it?' he asks, walking away from the *boliches* and towards the dunes.

'Someone has just attacked Clementina. I was walking through the woods when I heard her screaming for help. By the time I got there, she was on the ground and he was on top of her. He had ripped off her clothing and was about to rape her. I only just got there in time.' He shivers when he considers what would have happened if he had been just a few minutes later.

'And? What did you do?'

'I had no choice but to stop him.' He pauses but he knows that Jaime wants more information. 'I hit him with the first thing that I could find. A dead branch. I didn't kill him but I did knock him out.'

'You are sure he is not dead?'

'Positive.'

'And do you know who this man is? Have you seen him before?' Jaime is looking very worried by now.

'I haven't seen him before, but Clementina knows who he is. Someone called Felipe Rodriguez. Have you heard of him?'

Jaime lets out a groan. 'Ramon, what have you done? *Dios mio*, he's the elder son of Don Luis, the owner of the bodega Butler & Rodriguez. There will be Guardia Civil all over the place before nightfall.'

'Well, I'm sorry about that but I couldn't just stand by and watch him violate her. Anyway he didn't see me. He doesn't know who hit him.'

'Do you think that matters to the Guardia? If they find you here there will be questions. Ramon, I can't believe you would do this to us. And then you bring Clementina here. Why on earth didn't you take her back to her parents? They are going to be worried sick about her.'

'I couldn't do that; it's the first place he will go to look for her. Don't worry, we won't be here for long, just until I can get a plan together.'

'A plan? You are going to need more than a bloody plan.' He strides off towards his home. 'Come on. Let's see what the girl has to say for herself.'

By the time they reach Jaime's *choza*, Ramon has already decided what he will do; he does not have much choice in the matter. His priority has to be Ana and the children; Clementina has her family and friends to help her, Ana has no-one. He will collect his sister-in-law and take her to Cádiz where her parents live. His brother should never have left there when he married her but the bodega offered Pedro work and somewhere to live so he had jumped at it. They were not to know then that their home would be so squalid and that there would only be work for Pedro for half the year. Once they were there, they were trapped; Ramon knows that Ana owes money to the local shop and although she tries to pay it back when she can she is caught in an ever increasing spiral of debt. Once he has Ana and the children safely in Cádiz he will come back for Clementina.

'Wait here,' Jaime says. 'And don't speak to anyone about this.' He ducks down and goes into the *choza*.

Ramon can hear them talking but he cannot make out what they are saying. He is desperate to know what Jaime will do; is he going to help them or just send him away. He does not have to wait long. The curtain is pulled back and Jaime's wife says, 'Come inside. See if you can talk any sense into her.'

'How are you feeling?' he asks Clementina. The girl has stopped crying and is quietly sitting in the corner of the room. Her torn clothing is in a pile in the corner and now she is wearing a faded blue dress belonging to Jaime's wife. She has draped her shawl across her shoulders and washed her face in an attempt to look normal.

'Better,' she whispers. 'Thank you.'

'It was very fortunate that you were in that part of the woods,' says Jaime. 'Although I have warned you, Ramon, about going near the gypsy encampment. You are supposed to be keeping your head down; that is what we agreed.' Ramon can see that he is angry with him and he understands why, but what choice did he have?

'Well, I'm glad that he was there,' says Jaime's wife. 'Otherwise who knows what would have happened to this poor girl.'

'I must let my father know that I am all right,' Clementina says.

'Don't worry about that. I will send the boy. I agree with Ramon; it will be better if you don't go home for a few days until we see what Rodriquez plans to do next.'

Jaime's wife leaves the *choza* and returns almost immediately with Kiko.

'Papa?'

'Kiko I want you to take a sack of charcoal to Vano. Do not give it to anyone else, do you understand? Only to Vano.'

'Yes, is that all? '

'No. Give him this message. Tell him Clementina is safe and to be careful. Felipe Rodriguez is angry.'

'What does that mean?'

'Never mind. He will understand. And do not speak to anyone else. Nobody at all. When you have given him the message and the charcoal, you must come straight back here. And be careful. Especially if you see any Guardia.'

'All right, Papa. I'm to tell Vano that Clementina is safe and Felipe Rodriguez is angry.'

'That's right. Good lad.'

'Is it safe to send Kiko?' asks Ramon. 'Why don't I go instead?'

'No, it would be too dangerous for you; you do not know the woods like Kiko does. He will be fine.' Jaime smiles at his son and ruffles his hair. 'Be extra careful, lad.'

'I will, Papa.' And before anyone can stop him, Kiko is gone.

'What about me?' asks Ramon.

'You must leave now. I'm sorry, Ramon, but your presence here puts everyone at risk. I realise that you have been feeling restless lately and I expect you are already thinking about moving on, so it's for the best if you go now.'

'I understand.' Jaime is right; it is best for everyone if he leaves now but it saddens him to go like this. These people have been kind to him; they have given him the opportunity to make a peaceful life with them and now he has to leave. It seems that no matter where he goes trouble follows him. He looks at Clementina; if only he could take her with him.

'You must take some food for the journey,' Jaime's wife says. She puts a flask of water and some bread in a cloth bag, then goes to the meat safe and takes out some dried sausage. 'It's not much but it should last until you find something else.'

'Thank you. I will go to...'

'No, no. Do not tell us where you are going. We do not want to know,' interrupts Jaime. 'Just take your things and leave now. The Guardia could be here at any moment.' The *carbonero* sounds brusque but Ramon knows it is because he is worried for the safety of them all.

'He will be spotted the moment he leaves,' says Jaime's wife. 'Then they will trace him back to us. He needs a disguise of some sort. Let him take the old mule and one of the carts; he can pretend to be delivering charcoal. No-one will bother him then.'

Jaime looks at his wife. 'We can't afford to give him a cart and one of our mules, even an old one. No, he's safer on foot; that way he can go through the forest and is less likely to meet anyone who might ask him awkward questions.'

'Take this bandana,' says Clementina. 'If anyone sees you wearing it they will think you are a gypsy.' She removes the red spotted bandana from her neck and stretches up and ties in round his neck. 'It's not much of a disguise but it might help.'

Ramon touches the bandana; it smells of Clementina, of her hair and the scent of the woods; now a sense of sadness threatens to overwhelm him. He does not want to leave these people, but he knows that Jaime is right, his continued presence will put them all in jeopardy. He gives Jaime's wife a hug. 'Thank you for everything,' he says and looking across at Clementina, adds 'Look after her.'

'We will. Don't worry. Now go.'

Ramon takes one last look at Clementina and leaves.

'Wait, you forgot the food,' calls Jaime's wife, running across the clearing towards him.

'Thank you. You have all been very kind to me,' he replies taking the bag of food from her.

The woman shrugs and smiles at him. 'My husband is a good man,' she says.

'He is, but why does he take these risks? He knew that taking me in was a risk to everyone here. Why does he put you all in danger?'

She smiles sadly. 'It's a tragic story,' she says. 'Some years ago, before we were married, the Guardia Civil came into these woods looking for someone, a Communist they said. They searched everywhere but couldn't find the man they were after. Jaime had a young brother in those days, only seven years old, who was obsessed with becoming a soldier. Whenever he could he went into the woods playing at soldiers with his little friend. They even had wooden guns that his father made for them. Well, this day he was playing in the woods as usual with his friend, when the Guardia arrived looking for the Communist. The boys didn't realise they were there and they came rushing out from where they were hiding, pretending to fire their guns. One of the officers was spooked and fired at them. Jaime's brother was killed instantly and his friend was injured.'

'*Dios mio*. That is tragic. What did the Guardia do?'

'They said the gun went off accidentally. That it wasn't intentional.'

'He fired at two children carrying wooden guns?'

'To be honest, the policeman who killed him was very upset; it was his first patrol and he wasn't much more than a kid himself but the others wanted to cover it up. And so that's what they did.'

'And Jaime?'

'He was devastated and when he heard that the Guardia were not going to take responsibility for killing his little brother, he decided he would get his own back on them in other ways. Helping fugitives to hide is one of those ways.' She shrugs as if to say, what can I do about it.

Ramon is stunned. It was a tragedy for Jaime and his family to lose the child in that way, but is this really the best way to get his revenge? Maybe it is the only way. It is not as though he can take them to court. Who would ever listen to a family of *carboneros*, even if they could afford a lawyer?

'I must go. You take care. And don't trust anyone,' she says and heads back to the *choza*.

So now he knows. Jaime is a brave man, but does he realise that he is playing with the lives of his family and the others who work there? If the Guardia Civil had come and found Ramon, they would all have been punished. Was his revenge really worth it? He heads for the woods; now he must face his own responsibilities, he must retrace his steps to find Ana and the children. He knows it is risky but he has no other option. He reminds himself that it is because of him that his brother is in prison.

Clementina watches as Ramon heads for the woods and disappears amongst the trees. He saved her life; she is sure of that and she will always be grateful for what he did. She shudders when she remembers the touch of Felipe's hands on her leg, the stench of his breath and how his beard had rasped against her cheek. Never in her life has she been so frightened. Until that moment her life has been happy and carefree; her family do not have much money but they never go hungry and she has always felt loved and protected by them. She is shocked at how quickly her world can be turned upside down. She cannot go home now; Felipe might come back to Doñana looking for her. He will be angry and vengeful right now; she remembers how he was as a boy, not at all like Hugo. If only Hugo were here so she could talk to him; maybe he would know why his family hates her so much.

She wants to scream with rage. What is she going to do now? Who can she trust? The *carboneros* are good people but she does not want to spend the rest of her life with them. Now even Ramon has had to leave here; she does not know why but it must be something serious for the *carboneros* to send him away.

A tear trickles down her cheek and she wipes it away angrily; there is no point feeling sorry for herself. She has had a shock but that is all; she is unhurt and her virginity remains intact. Clementina knows how important that is; if Felipe had managed to rape her she would be worthless. No man would ever want her as his wife; it is not just the *gitanos* who value virginity highly.

'Are you coming in, Clementina?' asks Kiko. 'Mama has baked some fresh bread.'

She manages to give the boy a smile and follows him into the *choza*.

CHAPTER 16

Vano stares at the ground in front of him, lost in thought. Things are not looking good; he needs to speak to the soothsayer. His brother has brought them bad luck, suddenly turning up like that. He has put him in an impossible position; it is many years since Geronimo left and Vano has become used to being treated as the leader of their clan, but now it looks as though he will have to stand aside and allow his brother to resume his rightful role as their patriarch. He is not happy about this but what can he do; it would be unheard of to go against the patriarch. And what is going on with Clementina? Why has she decided to take refuge with the charcoal burners? They are honourable people and they will look after his daughter but that does not explain why she is there. Is she hiding from someone? Or is she hurt? What did the boy say? *Felipe Rodriguez is angry.* What does that mean? He is a sly one, that Felipe. Vano does not trust him; some years ago Felipe Rodriguez wanted to buy a mare from him. Then he claimed that Vano had tried to fob him off with a lame horse which was therefore worthless; he kept the mare but refused to pay for it. It was all a pack of lies but there was nothing Vano could do about it, and Felipe knew it. He knows the man is a liar and a cheat, and now it seems that he is angry but with whom? With Vano? It does not make sense. He has not seen Felipe for many years, why would he be angry with him? No, the *carbonero* must mean Hugo, who else could it be?

There is a message hidden in those words, a warning from the *carbonero*, so he must tread carefully.

'Who was that boy?' Lavinia asks. 'What did he want? Does he know where Clementina is?'

'Nothing of interest to you,' he snaps. 'Go and tell my sons I must speak to them now.'

'Which ones?'

'All of them. Now.'

'Well, I don't know where they are. They will be working, I expect.'

'Talk to their wives and tell them I must speak to all my sons, as soon as possible. Get to it, woman. This is urgent.'

'I hope it's not something to do with your damned brother.'

Vano stands up and scowls at her. 'Now.'

'All right, husband. I don't know what's put you in such a bad mood. And where is Clementina, when you need her?' Lavinia puts down the bucket of water and runs to find her daughters-in-law.

As soon as she is gone Vano heads for the soothsayer's home on the edge of the clearing. The soothsayer is an old man, with long white hair; he has lived in this dilapidated wooden shack as long as Vano can remember. Nobody knows how old he is or where he came from; he has no family and no-one can remember who his parents were. 'Charo, it's me. I want to speak to you,' he calls, rapping on the open door.

A curtain is pulled back and the old man says, 'I have been waiting for you, Vano. Come in and sit down.'

He ducks his head and enters a tiny space, most of which is taken up by a low table and multiple cushions scattered across a grubby carpet. The tarot cards are already spread across the table. He sits on the carpet, directly opposite Charo. 'I need to talk to you,' he repeats. 'I need to know why this is happening to us?'

Charo adjusts the brightly coloured bandana that ties back his hair, picks up the cards and shuffles them. Then he spreads them out on the table again and selects three of them. The first one he turns over is Fortitude; Vano recognises the lion, it is a good card as it indicates strength and courage but it is pointing away from him. That is not good. 'Something bad is coming,' Charo says, 'but there is no point in fighting it. You must accept that it is what it is.' Vano takes a deep breath; does he really want to know his future? Was it a mistake to come here? The soothsayer is not looking at him; he is concentrating on the cards and slowly turns over the next one; it is the number ten, The Wheel of Fortune and this is pointing towards Vano. Change. His world is going to change. The old man looks at him sadly before saying, 'You must accept the transformation that is coming, my son. You cannot fight it. You must not fight it.' The old man stares at the cards; he seems to be lost in thought. Is he thinking about the remaining tarot card? Vano places his hand on his knee to stop it shaking. Why doesn't the old man get on with it and turn over the last card? What is he waiting for? 'Are you ready?' Charo asks. Vano nods. His mouth is dry. He cannot tear his eyes away from the cards. The lion of Fortitude is staring at him, the Wheel of Fortune does not move and the last one remains face down. Charo stretches out his hand and turns it over; it is number thirteen. A skeleton dressed in black armour and riding a white horse completes the set; Vano recognises it at once, Death and it is pointing directly at him.

'So I am going to die?' he asks, more calmly than he actually feels.

The old man looks at him. 'No, not necessarily. It's possible but remember this card also means chaos, that your world will be turned upside down. But you know all this already, so why did you come to me?'

Vano is surprised at his words. 'I just needed to be sure that I was doing the right thing. And now I know.' He tosses a coin on the table and gets up and leaves. The soothsayer was right; he already knew what the cards would tell him, but now his mind is calmer and the questions that have been spinning around in his head, although not answered, have slowed down.

As he walks back to his own home Vano continues to puzzle over the message he has received from the *carbonero*; he does not doubt its veracity but why say that Felipe Rodriguez is angry? That is the part he does not understand. It sounds like a warning. It must be because of something that his daughter has done and the reason she is now in hiding. He shakes his head in bewilderment. Clementina hardly knows Felipe; he is older than she is and, although he came over a few times when he was a child, Vano does not remember him having anything to do with his daughter. It was Hugo who liked to play with her. This must be to do with Hugo; after all Don Luis is no more likely to be pleased about Hugo hanging around Clementina than he is. Well, whatever the reason, if the message is a warning then he must be prepared; he can worry about why Felipe is angry at a later date. All that is important right now is that the charcoal burner wants him to know that he must be wary of one of the Rodriguez brothers.

'Papa, you want to see us?' It is Álvaro, closely followed by Mateo. 'What's wrong?'

'Where is Tomás?'

'He's just coming; he was training the colt.'

His eldest son jumps over the corral's fence and runs towards him. 'What's happened, Papa?'

'You are going to find this strange, but nothing, yet.' He sees their puzzled expressions. 'I want us all to be prepared and on the lookout for anything strange or unusual.' He explains about the message he has received.

'That could be a prank. I know that lad; he's quite the joker. I wouldn't worry about it, Papa,' says Mateo.

'Well, I am worried about it. That boy's father is an honourable man and he keeps himself to himself. Something must be about to happen if he has gone to the trouble of sending me a message, something bad.'

'So what should we do?'

'I want you to prepare for an attack. Release some of the horses into the woods and leave some of the wilder ones in the corral. Make sure everyone, including your wives, remains alert. Arm yourself with sticks and knives, but discretely. Fill some of the buckets with water from the stream—the women can do that —and take the children into the woods. If someone is going to attack us, I don't want any of the children getting hurt.'

'What about Uncle Geronimo? Do you think he's behind it?' asks Álvaro.

Vano shakes his head. 'No, but that does not mean he won't take advantage of the situation.'

'Should we tell him there might be an attack?'

Vano has been mulling this over ever since he received the message. Can he trust his brother to stand by his side? He has to decide, quickly.

'We would be stronger together,' says Tomás. 'I think we should tell him.'

'If it turns out to be nothing, we will never hear the end of it; we will be the butt of his jokes for ever and a day.'

'But if there is a real threat, it will be better to have him with us, especially as we don't know who is our enemy,' says Tomás.

'Very well. I'll go and see him now,' says Vano.

Geronimo is sitting on the step of his wagon, eating a hunk of bread. When he sees Vano he stands up and throws the remains of the bread to his dog, a moth-eaten cur with blue eyes. 'You've still got that gammy leg, I see,' he says, staring at Vano's left leg. 'Does it bother you?'

'Only when the weather's cold,' he says, leaning on his cane.

'And you still carry Father's cane. Mmn.'

'What does that mean? Mmn.'

'It means I remember it well; Father was quite liberal when dealing out the punishment with it. Or have you forgotten?'

He ignores this comment; he too has tasted his father's anger and prefers to forget it. 'I need to tell you something, Geronimo.'

'Well, spit it out. I expect you want me to move on, do you?'

'I have received a warning that we may be attacked. I wanted you to know. I have begun some preparations to protect my family, in case it is true. You are free to stay here or move on, as you wish.'

'That all sounds a bit vague. Can't you be more specific?'

Vano attempts to explain the little that he knows.

'So who sent you this message?'

'I can't tell you that, but I can say it's from someone I trust. And before you ask, I also don't know why he sent it to me.'

'It must have something to do with your daughter.'

'I think so, too. Otherwise it is quite a coincidence that I receive this warning the day after she has gone missing. Anyway, I thought you should know, in case anything does happen. You are my brother, after all.'

'And your patriarch.' Geronimo chuckles. 'Honestly, Vano, what a palaver. If you want rid of us so much you only have to say. It isn't necessary to invent such a complicated lie. I never planned on staying here anyway; we are on our way to Portugal. I fancy settling down by the coast.'

Vano stares at his brother. It is a waste of time talking to him. 'Think what you want. I have done my duty and told you. It's up to you what you do now.'

He turns and walks away as fast as his bad leg will allow him. Normally he never thinks about the accident. Accident. It was carelessness on his part; he had been an over-confident teenager and walked behind a particularly lively mare, with the result that the mare was spooked and lashed out at him. She broke his leg. The injury serves as a constant reminder to him that working with wild horses needs complete concentration.

'Well?' asks his oldest son. 'What did he say?'

'Nothing. He doesn't believe me.'

'But what about Clementina? Where is she?'

'She's safe for now. That's all you need to know. Now let's get the women and children into the woods.'

Vano walks back along the track that leads to the stables. Tomás has released the colt and it and its mother are grazing near the water meadow; it is a fine young horse and will soon be ready for sale. He opens the gates to the stables and lets the mares wander out. His thoughts keep returning to the message the boy had brought. It does not make sense. The charcoal burner must have mistaken Hugo for Felipe; that's what it is. Clementina must have rejected Hugo and that is why he is angry. He sighs. The sooner his daughter is married, the better. Thank goodness that his wife already has someone in mind. Once they have dealt with this threat, real or imagined, he will collect Clementina from the charcoal burners and get her married.

He hears the sound of his brother's wagons rumbling down the stoney path that leads out of the forest towards Almonte; so they really are leaving. Well, Geronimo has decided to believe him after all and is going before anything happens. It's just as well; life would be insufferable if he had chosen to stay.

'Papa, Uncle Geronimo is leaving,' says Álvaro.

'I can hear them, son. Don't worry, if anyone attacks us, we will be ready for them. We can protect ourselves.' He sounds far more confident than he feels. Don Luis is a powerful man and has the ear of the local Guardia Civil. One word from him and they will be swarming all over the woods.

'Is there anything else you want us to do, Papa?' asks Álvaro.

Vano shakes his head. What else can they do when they do not know where the attack could be coming from. 'We've done all we can for now, son. Let's get back to work. But don't drop your guard. We don't know when an attack might happen. We must all be vigilant.'

CHAPTER 17

Don Luis stands staring out of the open window at his wife's beautiful garden; even in winter it is full of colour. The bougainvillea, less lush than it is in the summer, trails purple flowers across an archway that leads to the sheltered lawn where she likes to sit most days, and bushes of scarlet and yellow hibiscus line the stone walls. He can smell the lavender and rosemary bushes through the open window. He pulls it shut. Unusually for him, he is feeling nervous; his hands are sweaty and he has not been sleeping well. He puts it down to the forthcoming elections which will be held very soon; he knows he has some fierce opposition, people who would jump at the chance to discredit him. The last thing he needs right now is bad publicity. If he does not do something about the girl, that is exactly what he is going to have; people love nothing better than a bit of scandal, especially when it concerns a local dignitary—he has started to think of himself as that.

'Everything all right, *cariño*?' His wife interrupts his revery. She seems to be in a good mood today; maybe she is coming round to the idea of him becoming mayor.

'Just thinking about the election,' he says, kissing her on the cheek. 'I don't think it's going to be as easy as I first thought.'

'Oh, I'm sure you will be all right,' she replies, sitting down in her usual chair and picking up her needlepoint. 'Felipe is looking for you, by the way. I don't know what he's been up to but he has got a dreadful bruise on his face.'

'Did he say how he got it?'

'No, and I didn't ask. He was in one of his moods. I don't know why he can't be more like his brother.'

'Mmn. I'm not sure we want two sons with their heads in the clouds. Felipe is a good worker, even if he does have a bit of a temper. I'd better go and see what he wants.'

'He was in the kitchen, the last time I saw him.'

His elder son is sitting on the kitchen table drinking a mug of hot coffee and talking to his foreman.

'You wanted to speak to me, Felipe?' He glances at Enrique, who mutters a brief greeting and leaves.

'Yes. We have a problem.'

I think you mean, you have a problem. What happened to your face?'

'One of those bloody gypsies attacked me.'

'Which one?'

'I don't know which one. They all look the same to me. The point is that I was attacked and I could have been killed.' He turns and shows his father the cut on the back of his head. 'We have to get rid of them.'

'That's what I said all along. You were supposed to get rid of them, and the girl. So what happened? Why did this gypsy attack you? There must have been a reason.' Don Luis is beginning to doubt his son's ability to complete the task he set him.

'I don't know but there's no point asking for an explanation. He attacked me and that should be enough of a reason to get rid of them.'

'So now I suppose I have to sort it out myself. *Dios mio*, why have I been blessed with two such useless sons?'

'Well, maybe you should have done it yourself in the first place,' snarls Felipe, 'instead of getting me to do your dirty work.'

Suddenly Don Luis can stand it no longer. He is furious with the whole situation, with Hugo for becoming infatuated with the gypsy girl and for Felipe for not clearing up his mess. 'Get out. Get out. You useless bag of wind. You can't even manage to do a simple task. I'll handle it from now on.' He has no option but to inform the Marquess about Vano's actions. The previous owner had not been interested in what the gypsies got up to; as long as they did not interfere with the hunting he was happy for them to live in Doñana. He probably guessed that Vano was stealing the wild horses but nothing had ever been done about it. Maybe the new owner would view it differently.

It has been a long time since he has visited the Palacio de Marismillas, the new property of the Marquess and his wife, and he is fortunate that now is the hunting season and that they are in residence. When the Duke owned Doñana it had always been the desire of the local gentry and certain businessmen to be invited to join the hunt. He wonders if the Marquess and his wife will be as generous. It would certainly do his campaign no harm if they invite him to join them one day.

'Don Luis. I will let the Marquess know that you are here,' says the butler, taking his coat and hat. He leaves him standing in the entrance hall, an area as big as his own lounge, while he goes to tell the Marquess. After a little a door opens and the Marquess steps into the hall. Don Luis gets a glimpse through the open door of a well furnished hunting lodge, with trophies of wild boar and a stag's antlers hanging on the wall before it closes again and he is left facing the Marquess.

'Don Luis. I do not believe we have met, although I am familiar with your excellent sherry,' says the Marquess, extending his hand to him. 'What can I do for you?' He does not invite Don Luis to go into the drawing room; instead he stands in the hall waiting for his reply.

'My Lord, I am reluctant to disturb you but I have some news that I feel would be of interest to you.' The Marquess says nothing but waits for him to continue. 'It's regarding the wild horses that live in the Coto Doñana.'

'Yes, what about them?'

'I have to report that someone is stealing the horses and selling them to whoever they can. It has only recently come to my attention that you were not aware that this was happening.'

'I was not. And who, pray, is the supposed thief?'

Don Luis swallows hard and continues, 'A gypsy named Vano. He pretends to be a horse trainer and has been telling everyone that he has the right to capture and tame the horses. Now I realise that this is a lie; they belong to you, Your Lordship.'

'Indeed. So what do you suggest I do about this thief, Don Luis?'

'It is not for me to say, Your Lordship, but personally, I would advise the Guardia Civil and let them take care of it.'

The Marquess nods his head. 'Indeed.'

Don Luis is starting to feel uncomfortable; surely the Marquess does not think he is involved in anything underhand or has anything to gain by telling him about Vano. After what seems to be an interminable silence the Marquess says, 'Very well, I will do as you suggest. Thank you for letting me know.' He turns and walks away, leaving Don Luis feeling rather slighted. He has never had much to do with the aristocracy; perhaps this is how they deal with everyone they consider to be inferior to themselves.

The butler suddenly reappears as if from nowhere, opens the outer door and ushers him outside. '*Buenas tardes*, Don Luis,' he says, handing him his coat and hat.

It is done. He has a sinking feeling in his stomach as he wonders if this is going to backfire on him. He tries to reassure himself. The Marquess is not going to get personally involved; he can see that he is not really bothered about the horses. Maybe if Don Luis had told him that Vano has been poaching he would have been more interested; someone stealing game from the reserve would have affected the hunt. It is too late now. There is little more he can do except wait.

As soon as he gets back to the bodega he sends for Felipe and tells him what has happened.

'Good. Once the Guardia arrive they will soon get rid of them.'

'Yes, but I don't want any violence. I want it all done quietly. I can't have news of this getting out and affecting my campaign.'

'You don't need to worry about that, Papa. Nobody will care if the Guardia chase off a few gypsies. They will probably give you a medal or it might even earn you a few more votes.'

He nods. 'Yes, you're probably right. I'm worrying about nothing.'

In fact two weeks pass before an officer in the Guardia Civil calls at his house. Don Luis invites him into his study.

'*Buenos días, Capitán*,' he greets him. 'Please be seated.'

The captain remains standing and says, 'The Marquess sent for me. He says you have made a complaint about some gypsies stealing horses and he wants us to deal with it.'

'Yes, that's right, *Capitán*. I must admit I am surprised it has taken you so long to see to the matter.'

'We need more information, *Señor*. We wouldn't want to arrest the wrong gypsies, now would we?'

Don Luis looks at him. Is he being sarcastic? 'There is only one group of gypsies living in Doñana; I don't see how you can arrest the wrong ones. They are all as bad as each other.'

'Very well, *Señor*. We will see to it right away.'

'Oh, one thing, *Capitán*, I do not want my name mentioned. To be honest it has nothing to do with me; the horses belong to the Marquess. I was just advising him of the situation.'

'Indeed, *Señor.*' He salutes Don Luis and leaves.

So it is done. Once the gypsies have left he will sleep more easily. Hugo will be surprised to see them gone, but he will deny knowing anything about it and his son will be none the wiser.

CHAPTER 18

Vano is beginning to believe that the warning he received was a hoax; so far there has been no sign of any threat to their safety. Everything is continuing as usual. 'I think we can relax,' he tells his wife. 'I'll get the boys to bring the horses back to the corral this evening. You let the women know that the danger has passed; they can return to their homes.'

'Are you sure?' Lavinia asks. She is looking anxious; a permanent line furrows her brow and there is no sign of her usual smile. Is it because of Clementina? Or is she just getting old and he has not noticed it before. He remembers when they were wed; she was a beautiful bride and she has always been a good wife and mother. And now she is a grandmother; no wonder she has a few lines on her face. He could have done much worse. 'Maybe we should wait a bit longer,' she suggests.

He looks away from her and replies, 'If we were going to be attacked it would have happened by now.'

'All right, if you are sure, I will go and tell them now. They will be pleased to hear it; it's been cold sleeping in the woods at night. They have all been moaning.'

Vano is not listening to her; he must concentrate on the matter in hand now. His main worry is how the horses have fared since he returned them to the wild. He had only just started training some of them; now he will have to begin again.

'Papa, there's someone to see you. It's urgent,' calls Álvaro, running across the clearing towards him. A man wearing a jacket with the Marquess' insignia on the sleeve follows him.

'Francisco, what is it?' Vano asks the man. He is one of the Marquess' wardens and also works on the estate as a gamekeeper; he and Vano have had a few run-ins in the past over his poaching of the Marquess' deer. He holds his hands up in mock surrender. 'It's not me this time, Fran. I haven't had a taste of venison since the last time you spoke to me.'

'I haven't come to accuse you of poaching, Vano. I've come to warn you. The Guardia Civil are on their way and they look as though they mean business; there's at least twenty of them and they are armed. You need to hide.'

Vano did not need to know anything more; he leapt into action. 'Álvaro, tell your mother. She's just gone to collect the women and children who are hiding in the woods. I'll tell the men. We need to arm ourselves.'

'Don't be ridiculous Vano. I've just told you they are armed and you know they won't hesitate to shoot if they think you are resisting them. Don't tempt fate; either hide and hope they lose interest or just let them move you on and then no-one will get hurt.'

He stares at the man. He is saying exactly what the Tarot cards told him; this is not a battle that he can fight and win. 'Why are you telling me this, Fran?'

'Because you are a good man, Vano and you don't deserve what is about to happen. Hurry. They will be here any minute.'

'What's this all about?' he asks the warden. 'Do you know?'

'All I know is what I heard a few days ago. Don Luis came to see the Marquess and told him that you were stealing his horses. It could be to do with that.'

'But why would he do that? He's bought many a horse from me over the years; he knew where they came from and he had nothing to complain about then. Unless...'

'Unless what?'

'Oh, it's nothing. His youngest son has been sniffing around my Clementina. Maybe this is his way of stopping him.'

'Oh, I don't know anything about that. But I do know you need to hurry.'

Vano holds out his hand. 'Thank you, Fran. I won't forget this.' He does not hesitate and runs straight to his house, grabs the bell he uses to call people to meetings and rings it as hard as he can.

They all know what they have to do and immediately people begin to collect their baskets of food, spare clothing and their animals, and hurry into the woods. 'Keep calm and make as little noise as possible,' he tells them, then he runs to the stables and lets the remaining horses loose, clapping his hands loudly to scare them into running away; luckily they are not so tame that they want to stay and they soon sense the panic in the air and gallop across to the water meadows. It is fortunate that the agent collected his horses the previous week and, miracle of miracles, actually paid him in cash and not with one of those useless bits of paper promising to pay him at some time in the future.

Vano just reaches the trees when he sees the dust from the first of the Guardia Civil's trucks. He ducks behind a bush and watches as the trucks rumble along the dirt track, one, two, three, four of them, all full of armed police. They pull to a stop one behind the other and the officers spill out from their vehicles and immediately start searching the site, pulling open doors, tearing down curtains, kicking over cooking pots left behind in the rush to leave. The anger swells up inside him but he knows there is nothing he can do; he must be satisfied with the knowledge that he has got his people out of there just in time. As quietly as he can he moves further and deeper into the woods. It will soon be dark and by then the clan will have dispersed according to his instructions. If they are lucky and do as he told them then no-one will get caught and they can reunite in a few days. He hears the crackling of a bonfire behind him and looks back in the direction of the clearing; a plume of acrid, black smoke rises into the air. The Guardia are burning their homes. Well, what did he expect? That they would come and arrest him for stealing horses or maybe let him off with a warning and a fine? That is not how they operate; if Don Luis was behind this he would expect them to burn their homes and drive them away. He would want to wipe them off the face of the earth; well that is not going to happen. As the volume of smoke increases and he sees the flames leap up and consume the thatched roofs of their houses the reality sinks in; they can never come back, never return to Doñana. There is a tightening in his chest when he realises that he must leave the place where he was born and where he has spent his entire life. He breathes deeply, wanting to fill his lungs with the smells and taste of his home and its destruction. He will not forget and he will never forgive.

'Papa, we must hurry,' whispers Álvaro.

Vano blinks the tears from his eyes and turns to his son. This is no time for sentiment; later they can ponder their loss and plan their revenge. For now he must put that out of his mind and concentrate on what lies ahead; the rest of the clan will be looking to him to lead them out of danger. He cannot let them down.

His wife and sons are waiting for him, as planned. They look at him expectantly, fear draining their faces of any colour. 'Yes, it's as we expected; the Guardia Civil are burning down our homes,' he says, struggling against the anger that continues to grow inside him.

His wife starts to cry. 'What will we do?' she sobs. 'And what about Clementina? How can we tell her where we are? We can't just leave without her.'

'We may have to; we cannot contact her without putting her in danger. Not yet, anyway. Later we will send for her. There is no point crying, *mujer*. What's done is done. We must all look to the future.' He does not tell them that he has some gold hidden in the woods; something he has been saving little by little in case it should ever be needed. His father had given him the idea, many years ago. He had said that a *gitano's* life is precarious, that he can never feel truly safe because there is always someone who finds the *gitanos* a threat and will want to get rid of them. They are a nomadic people and they should never forget that; their best hope of survival is not confronting their enemies but moving away from them. The young Vano thought that was a cowardly thing to do, but he did not dare say so to his father. Now, with the wisdom of age, he can see his father's reasoning is sound. What can a group of unarmed men, women and children do against unscrupulous armed officers of the Guardia Civil. Then later, when he was dying, his father had more to tell him; he warned Vano that he should be prepared for the day when his world would collapse, because that day would certainly come and he needed to be ready for it. In fact Vano has been lucky; he and his family have lived in relative peace in Doñana but despite that he has never been complacent and now the day has arrived and Vano is glad that he had taken his father's advice.

'Why has this happened to us now?' asks Álvaro. 'I don't understand. Who would do this to us?'

'It's possible that it was Don Luis. The warden told me that he visited the Marquess a few days ago.'

'That doesn't make sense,' says Lavinia. 'Why? After all these years. No, I don't believe he would do that to us.' She looks shaken at the mention of Don Luis.

'Do you think it's about Hugo?' asks Álvaro. 'He has been hanging around here a lot lately. Maybe his father did it to keep Clementina and Hugo apart.'

Vano looks at his son; he is an observant one. Nothing gets past Álvaro. 'What does it matter why he did it. We can't undo what has happened. The fact is that we can no longer stay here; if we try to rebuild our homes the Guardia Civil will arrest us.' He speaks calmly but his words are lies. It does matter. And he does need to know why Don Luis has done this to them. More importantly he needs to know that his daughter is safe, that Don Luis will not try to hurt her. Vano can understand that he does not want his son to marry her—he is in complete agreement with him about that—but why involve the Guardia Civil? Why did he not come and speak to Vano about it, man to man? They could have found a reasonable solution, but it's not reason that interests Don Luis, it's revenge.

'So what are we going to do?' asks Lavinia.

'We will hide here in the woods for a few days until we are sure that the Guardia have gone then we will head for Portugal.'

'Portugal,' she gasps. 'Please tell me you don't mean that. We can't go to Portugal.'

'Why not? We can be over the border in a couple of days and then the Guardia cannot touch us.'

'But Uncle Geronimo is going to Portugal,' says Álvaro. 'He told me.'

'I know, and I've changed my mind, I think it's time we joined forces with him; we are the same clan after all.' He sees them look at him in amazement. 'Once it is safe to leave the woods we will buy a couple of wagons from the *carboneros,* retrieve two of our horses and set off. The main thing is that the Guardia Civil do not catch anyone in the meantime; we must remain hidden.'

'And Clementina?'

'We will see, *mujer*. Don't fret. I am as concerned about her as you are.'

The Guardia Civil leave after two days, during which time the gypsy encampment is completely razed to the ground; it is as though no-one has ever lived there. Vano wanders through the ashes of their burned out homes in a daze, letting his anger grow stronger and stronger. He will get his revenge on whoever is behind this, he swears to God he will, be it Don Luis or the Pope himself.

He forces himself to concentrate on the problem in hand; they will wait another day to be sure that the Guardia have left for good and then they will leave. He takes one last look at what has been his home for more than half a century then heads back to the woods; he needs to let the others know to be ready to leave.

His sons are sitting by their makeshift tents waiting for him. 'Well, have they gone?' asks Tomás.

'Yes, it looks like it. What you need to do now is to make sure we have enough provisions for the journey. Can you organise that between you and Mateo, while Álvaro and I go and get us some transport?'

'Of course, Papa.'

He does not need to give them any more instructions; they have talked of nothing else for days. He leaves them arguing over who should do what and when, while he goes to retrieve his cache of gold. He would prefer to offer the *carboneros* pesetas, but he needs those for the journey; gold jewellery would look too conspicuous and draw unwanted attention to them.

'Wait there,' he tells his youngest son, and climbs up a rocky incline to the spot where he hides his treasure. He found this tiny cave years ago, when he was a child and often came here to play. As he grew older he decided it was an excellent place to hide his valuables away from the prying eyes of the rest of his family. He claws at the moss and weeds that have grown around the large stone blocking the entrance, then prises the stone away. The cave is too small for him to enter now, but he reaches in and pulls out a faded sack. It seems very light and for a moment he fears that someone has removed the gold, but then as he opens the sack, he sees the gold's warm sheen reflecting in the sun that is shining through the trees; it is all there and there is more than enough to pay for two wagons. He ties the sack tightly shut and is about to slither back down the slope when the glint of something small and shiny catches his eye. He stops and picks up a silver ring, the strands of which are twisted into a knot. He recognises it immediately; he had given it to Isabel when they first met. He had forgotten all about it; how strange that he should find it now. He rubs the dirt from it and slips it in his pocket. Is this an omen? Does it mean that what he has lost can be recovered? Or is it the opposite? Maybe it is telling him that the past should remain just that, the past.

'Have you got it, Papa?' asks Álvaro.

'I have indeed. Come on, time to do some bartering,' he tells his son.

Vano sees Clementina straight away, but to his surprise, instead of coming to greet him, she ducks down and goes into one of the *choza*. He waits, hoping she will reappear but when there is no sign of her, he goes to look for Jaime.

'Vano, are you all right? We have heard what the Guardia Civil have done. That's terrible news. I am really sorry.'

Vano nods his head. He is still thinking about his daughter; why is she avoiding him? 'Thank you for the warning; it would have been much worse if they had caught us unawares. As it was we were able to remove most of our belongings.'

'Thats something, I suppose. Have you come to see Clementina?'

'Yes we are leaving tomorrow and her mother wants her to come with us.' He taps his cane nervously on the ground; it hurts him that his daughter is ignoring him. He cannot understand it. Surely she realises that her place is with her family. They will protect her. That has always been their way, family first.

'I don't know if she will agree to that; she is still very upset about what happened to her.'

'But what did happen to her? Is she hurt? And why did Don Luis go and talk to the Marquess? It's only been a couple of months since he sent the son of one of his friends to buy a horse from me. And now he's labelling me a horse thief. I cannot understand what has happened to make him do that.'

'Come and sit by the fire and I will tell you what I know.' He offers a *bota* of wine to Vano, who refuses it so Jaime raises the *bota* above his head and lets a stream of the red wine flow into his mouth. 'Are you sure?' he asks.

'Yes. Thank you, but I want to keep a clear head.' Vano knows that if he starts drinking wine he will not be able to control his temper and he does not want to do something he will later regret.

The two men sit side by side while Jaime tries to explain what happened to Clementina. Vano becomes angrier and angrier as he listens to the *carbonero*. This cannot go unpunished. No, someone will pay for this.

'My wife tells me that your daughter is unhurt, except for some cuts and bruises but she is still very frightened. If Ramon had not been walking through the woods I dread to think what might have happened to her. As it was, Ramon hit him with a dead branch and knocked him unconscious. Then he brought her here to us.'

'Where is he, this Ramon? I would like to thank him for saving my daughter.'

'I told him to leave Doñana. He said that Clementina's attacker didn't see him—his attention was taken up by your daughter—but I thought it was safer for all of us if Ramon disappeared.'

'I understand.' Vano is finding it hard to concentrate on what Jaime is telling him; he wants to find the man who attacked Clementina and tear him limb from limb. 'This Ramon, is he one of your *carboneros*? Did he recognise the man who attacked her?'

'He has not worked here very long and no, he didn't recognise the man, but your daughter did; she says it was Don Luis's son. She was very definite about that.'

Vano stares at Jaime in astonishment. So it was Hugo who did this to his daughter. Surely not. That is hard to believe. He thought they were friends. Why would he do that to her? 'You are sure about that?'

'It's what your daughter told my wife. I have never met Don Luis or his sons. So what are you going to do now?' he asks, drinking a little more wine.

'I am going to take my family as far away from here as possible and when I know that they are safe, I am coming back to settle up with Don Luis and his son.'

'And Clementina?'

'We want her to come with us. That's why I must speak to her before we go.'

'I understand. I will ask my wife to talk to her. Wait here and I will go and find her. Was there something else you wanted?' Jaime asks, eying the bag in Vano's hand.

'Yes, I need two sturdy wagons. I have money to pay for them.' He pushes the bag towards Jaime, who looks inside and then says, 'You have indeed, more than enough. I'll see to it as soon as I've spoken to my wife.'

Vano watches as Jaime ducks and goes into the *choza*. He can hear his daughter's voice but cannot make out what she is saying. After a while, it goes quiet and Jaime reappears. 'She will speak to you,' he says. 'I'll go and sort out the wagons. You realise they will be full of carbon dust?'

Vano shrugs. Right now he cannot think of anything other than speaking to his daughter. At last she comes out of the *choza* and stands in front of him. 'Clementina, *Cariño*, I am so happy to see you. Your mother and I have been worried about you.' He steps forward to hug her, but she hurriedly steps aside. 'It's all right, *Cariño*, Jaime has told me what happened. Don't worry, we'll soon be away from here and you will be safe.'

'I'm not going with you, Papa. I'm sorry but I can't face anyone. Not now. Not yet.'

'But, dear child, you must stay with your family. We will protect you. How will you manage here alone? It's impossible.' Vano is struggling to know what to say. He is not used to his family refusing to do what he tells them; he knows Clementina has been through a traumatic experience but that is no excuse to defy her father.

'I can stay with Jaime and his wife. I will be safe with them,' she says, looking down at the ground.

Why won't she look at him? 'No, child. We are your family. You must come with us. We are leaving tonight and you will come with us.'

'I'm sorry, Papa, but I cannot. Tell Mama that I love her, and I'm sorry for what happened.'

Before he can stop her, she has turned round and gone back into the *choza*. There is nothing more he can do to persuade her; she is as stubborn as he is. Nevertheless he understands how she feels. That bastard did not manage to take away her virginity but he did take away her feeling of self worth; he knows that none of the *gitanos* will look at her in the same way now. Through no fault of her own her reputation is tainted. People will gossip and rumours will grow. No smoke without fire, he can hear some of the old biddies saying that already. He understands and it breaks his heart to think that his beautiful Clementina should have to suffer like this. He wipes a tear from his eye and goes to find Jaime and the wagons.

CHAPTER 19

As Ramon trudges through the fields his heart is heavy; he thinks about his poor brother locked up in prison for something he did not do and his guilt weighs heavily on him. He is to blame. As soon as the Guardia had identified him as the man who had struck their colleague, it was obvious they would come looking for him. It is no surprise; some unfortunate friend will have told them who he is. He does not blame them; whoever it was would have had no choice. Ramon should have known better; nobody is going to keep quiet about the culprit's identity if it means they will be thrown into prison too. He knows as well as the next man that you have to put yourself and your family first. He wonders what Pedro would have done if he had known where Ramon was hiding. He shakes his head; he does not want to think about it.

Ahead of him lies the group of flimsy huts which the bodega allocates to their workers; he prays that Ana and the children are still living there. He stops and looks around him; there is no sign of any police. In fact there is no sign of anyone; her neighbours are all inside their huts and probably asleep although the sun has barely set. He tries to orientate himself; he is sure that this is the spot where he sat and talked to Adolfo that night, but instead of the old man's makeshift hut there is just a pile of rubble. He kicks at it, scattering shards of broken pots and the remains of the burnt timber across the ground, then stops; there is a scorched and flattened wineskin lying amid the ashes. He picks it up and even in the growing darkness he knows it is the one he gave to Adolfo. So this is the remains of Adolfo's home and someone has destroyed it. In that case where is the ex-bandit? Have they caught up with him at last, after all these years? The noise of someone or something coming his way reminds him that he cannot delay any longer; he must find Ana and get her and the children away from here as soon as possible. He can ask about Adolfo's whereabouts later.

Moving as quietly as he can, he skirts the huts until he sees the one where his brother's family lives. He hesitates before going inside; what if she is no longer there and someone else is living in it now. It is impossible to see who is in there; the interior is pitch black but he knows that someone is in there because he can hear them breathing. The question racing through his head is, is it Ana and her children?

Suddenly there is a movement and a small voice asks, 'Is that you, Uncle Ramon?' It is his nephew, Pepe.

'Hush, Pepe. Yes, it's me.' As his eyes gradually become accustomed to the dark he sees the little boy curled up next to his mother, staring up at him.

'What's going on? Who's there?' Ana suddenly sits up and pulls her shawl over her shoulders.

'It's Uncle Ramon,' Pepe says in a loud whisper.

'What are you doing here? Do you want us all to get arrested now? Isn't it enough that your brother is in prison, if they haven't murdered him yet that is?'

'Hush, Ana. I've come to help you to get away.'

'Get away? What are you talking about? Where would we go? That bloody Enrique would soon know we'd left. He'd be after us in a flash. No, don't talk rubbish. It's impossible. We can't leave.' She starts sobbing. 'This is my life now. The only hope I have is that it won't be a long one.'

'Don't talk like that, Ana. You have Pepe and Amalia to think about. You have to be strong for them.'

'Be strong? You don't know what you are talking about. My life is a nightmare. Do you have any idea how difficult it is for a woman to live in this place with no man to protect her.'

'That's why I have come for you. As soon as I heard about Pedro I knew I had to help you.' He is whispering now, but Ana seems oblivious of the danger they are in and won't lower her voice. He needs to get them away quickly before any of her neighbours wake up and hear them. He puts his arm around her and says, 'Dress the children and then roll all your things into a bundle. We are leaving now and I don't want anyone to know, so please be quiet. You can shout at me all you want once we are out of here.'

At last Ana seems to understand. She looks at him and wipes her eyes on her shawl. 'Don't worry about them. Not one of them would put their heads outside to help me; they are all too scared of Enrique.'

'Please Ana, get your things together.' He is pleading with her now; why doesn't she understand the urgency?

'We don't have much stuff. I had to sell most of it,' she says opening her blanket and gathering her few bits and pieces into its folds. 'I was grateful for the money you gave me, Ramon, but it didn't last very long. We owed so much to the shop, you see.'

'That doesn't matter now. Come on. Is that everything?' She nods and picks up the roll of belongings. 'I am taking you to your parents in Cádiz,' he tells her but at this news she starts to cry again. 'Ana, we have to go quickly. Let me have the baby and you take Pepe's hand.'

He turns to his nephew and says, 'Pepe, we're going on an adventure and nobody must know, so no talking and walk as quietly as you can. Do you understand?' The boy solemnly nods his head. 'I will go first. You keep tight hold of your mother's hand.' Ramon pulls the curtain back and cautiously leans out of the hut but there is no sound and no movement from any of the other dwellings. Ana is right; even if her neighbours can hear them they are too frightened to come outside and see what is happening. 'All right, Ana, Pepe, let's go.'

It is not very far to Cádiz, possibly thirty or forty kilometres, but they have to take care that nobody sees them, which means keeping away from the main roads and any towns and villages. It is slow and difficult walking at night although they have been blessed with a clear sky and a bright moon. Ana now carries the baby strapped to her chest and her roll of belongings on her back, while Ramon has the sleeping Pepe clinging around his neck; the boy is so undernourished he scarcely notices that the child is there. If they are lucky they will not meet anyone who would care what they were doing walking at that time of night, and if they do then it will be someone who will wish them no good so he has taken the precaution of carrying a stout stick. He hopes he does not have to use it.

While it is still dark, they risk walking close to the main roads but once the sun comes up Ramon steers them off the road and into the woods. He knows that they will lose time doing this but it is safer than being stopped by the police. They walk most of the way in silence; he knows Ana blames him for what has happened and he finds it hard to talk to her. 'What has happened to Adolfo?' he asks at last. 'It looks as though somebody burned his hut down.'

'He's dead,' she replies and does not even look at him when she says it.

'Well, he was an old man,' Ramon replies. He is sorry to hear this; the old man had been kind to him.

'And that makes it all right for the Guardia Civil to shoot him?' she snaps. 'Good job your parents are no longer alive if that is your opinion of old people.'

'I didn't mean that,' he stutters. 'When you said he was dead I just assumed he'd died of old age or something.'

'Well he didn't. Somehow they found out that he was a wanted criminal and shot him as soon as he came out of his hut one morning. Didn't even give him time to say who he was.'

'But he's been living there for years and nobody told the police that he was a bandit, a wanted man, so why now?'

'Exactly my thought. And that is what everyone else is asking. Why now? Does it have anything to do with Pedro, they are saying? Is Pedro going to tell the Guardia everyone's secrets? They blame your brother, and because of that no-one speaks to me, and the man in the shop won't serve me any more. Do you see what you have done? You have turned everyone against us.'

He is horrified when he realises the ramifications of his actions. 'So how have you been managing to live?' he asks.

'I'm too ashamed to tell you.'

He remembers something she said earlier and asks, 'Who is this Enrique?'

'He is the foreman at the bodega.' She turns her head and won't look at him. 'He sometimes brings us food and occasionally he gets me to make some esparto mats for the hydraulic press.'

'The what?'

'It's a new press they have for pressing the grapes. They use mats made of esparto grass and lay the grapes on top of them. I don't know where they got them before, but lately he has been asking me to make them. He pays me, not much but it's something.'

'Is that all he asks you to do?' But she still won't look directly at him, so Ramon decides not to ask her any more questions; he knows the foreman would not bring her food if he did not expect something in return. He has met many men like him before, always ready to take advantage of someone's misfortune. If Ramon was feeling guilty before, he now feels even worse. 'Is it much further to your parents' house?' he asks, at last. 'I think we may have to stop and rest for a bit.'

'They live between Cádiz and Puerto de Santa María. Maybe another couple of hours.'

'All right. So we'll hide in these woods and sleep for a few hours; by then it will be getting dark again and we can carry on. I don't think it is safe to arrive at their house during daylight; we don't want any nosey neighbours to see us.'

They veer off the woodland path until they find an area of dense bushes alongside a narrow stream and settle down by its bank. Ramon bends down and drinks from the stream; Pepe watches him then does the same. The water is cold and refreshing. 'We should be safe here for a bit. Do you have any more food?' he asks.

'Just some bread,' she says, pulling a hunk of bread out of her bag and giving some to the children. 'Do you want any?'

Ramon shakes his head. 'No. I can wait. Give it to the little ones.' He can see that Pepe is starving by the way he almost chokes in his haste to eat the bread. 'Take it easy, Pepe. We will soon be at your grandmother's and then she will give you something lovely to eat.'

'*Puchero*?' he asks, his face lightening up at the thought of a plate of warm stew.

His mother looks at him and smiles, 'More likely *zarzuela*.'

'What's that Mama?'

'It's a sort of fish stew, like *puchero* but made with fish. Grandpa is a fisherman so we used to eat lots of fish when I was a child.'

'Fish?' Pepe does not look very excited at the idea of eating fish and puts the remains of his bread in his pocket for later.

'When did you last see your parents, Ana?' Ramon asks as they settle down in the undergrowth.

'The day Pedro and I got married,' she says and once again the tears run down her cheeks. 'You were there, don't you remember?'

'Of course I remember. It was a lovely day. Everyone was so happy and you looked beautiful in your wedding dress.'

'It had been my mother's,' she tells him. 'What a long time ago that seems now. We were so happy then.'

'I'm surprised that Pedro didn't join your father on the fishing boats?'

'He could have. My father would have loved him to go out on the boat with him, but he didn't want to; he doesn't like the sea,' she explained. 'A grown man who is frightened of the sea, I ask you.'

'So that's why you moved to Jerez?'

'Yes, he thought he would find plenty of work in the vineyards and there was, but not all the year. There were too many men and not enough jobs and each year it seemed to get worse. We talked of going back to live with my parents and maybe Pedro could have found work in one of the fish canneries, but there was Pedro's mother to think of; there was no way she would leave. She was born in Jerez and lived there all her life. She told us quite plainly that was where she wanted to die. Well she got her wish, poor woman. Now I don't know if I will ever see Pedro again.' She lies down between her children and closes her eyes. 'She was a good mother-in-law. I miss her,' she murmurs. Ramon can see her shoulders shaking as she silently cries herself to sleep.

The sky is studded with stars when he awakes. 'Ana we must go now,' he says, gently shaking the sleep from her.

'Is it time already?' She stands up and stretches. 'Oh, the children are still sleeping, can't we leave them a little while longer?'

'No, we need to travel while it is quiet. We must leave now. If we are lucky we will be at your parent's home by daybreak.' He leans down and splashes cold water on his face then drinks his fill from the stream.

Amalia begins to cry when her mother lifts her up, but she soon drifts back to sleep once Ana has tied her to her chest.

'Is she heavy?' he asks. 'Do you want me to carry her?'

'No, you look after Pepe. I can manage her.'

Pepe is wide awake now and pulls the remains of his bread out of his pocket and begins to chew it. 'Is it much further?' he asks. He is an observant child with big eyes which seem to see right through Ramon, who has never had much to do with children before; he finds the way his nephew stares at him disconcerting as though he too is accusing him.

'Why are there so many stars in the sky tonight?' the little boy asks, as they make their way back to the road.

'There are no more tonight than any other night,' says Ramon. 'It's just that we can see more of them because there are no clouds to hide them. Did you know that in olden times people could find their way by looking at the stars. They could cross continents and oceans by navigating from the stars.'

Pepe's eyes seem to grow even bigger and rounder as he hears this. 'So we can find our way to Grandma's house by the stars?' he says.

'Well yes, I suppose we can. Look up there. You see that very bright star?'

'Yes.'

'That's the North star, which tells me that if we walk towards it we are going north.'

'Is that where Grandma lives? In the north?'

'No, to get to her house we have to go south,' and he points the opposite way. 'So as long as the North star is behind us we will be heading in the right direction.'

'But when the stars disappear we won't know which way to go.' He looks worried at this realisation.

'Then we have to look at different things, like the names of the towns.'

'And we can ask people the way,' he says, his face brightening.

'If we have to, yes.'

Pepe nods his head wearily, and says, 'That's good.' He is struggling to keep awake, so Ramon picks him up and carries him on his back. The child's eyes shut and he too sleeps.

Ana's parents live in an old fisherman's cottage on the edge of a quiet cove; it is the last one in a row of identical stone built cottages and although it is small, with its chimney poking out from a red tiled roof and paned windows each side of the front door, it is a palace compared to Ana's previous home. Fishing nets are spread out to dry on the cobbled path in front of the cottages and two small rowing boats are beached on the sand but there is no sign of any fishermen.

Ramon feels a weight lifting from his shoulders as he stands and watches María's mother hugging and kissing her and then inspecting her grandchildren one by one. He knows they will be safe here although how they will live he has no idea; he has no more money to give her. He hopes that the fisherman can support three extra mouths to feed.

'I must leave now,' he tells Ana.

'No, you must wait until nightfall,' the grandmother interrupts. 'Come inside before anyone sees you and get some sleep.'

He stoops and follows her into the cottage; it is sparsely furnished but spotlessly clean. The smell of fish hangs in the air. 'Where is your husband?' he asks.

'Manuel is still out on the boat; he has to make an early start. They all do at the moment; the tuna season is almost over. He'll be back soon and he usually brings some fish for lunch.'

'Are you going to make *zarzuela*?' asks Pepe, who has been staring at his grandmother in wonder.

'I can do, little one. Do you like *zarzuela*?' she asks.

Ana bursts into tears. 'He has never had it,' she tells her. 'In fact he hasn't had a decent meal for months.'

'Oh, my poor child,' the grandmother says, hugging her daughter to her. 'Well, that's one thing about being a fisherman's wife, there's always plenty of fish in the sea.'

Ramon has already decided what his next move will be; he will return to Doñana to find Clementina. He won't be able to stay with the charcoal burners because Jaime has made it perfectly clear that his presence puts them all in danger and he does not want to be the cause of any more misfortune. Nevertheless he has to know how Clementina is and what has happened to her; is she still with the *carboneros* or is she with her family now?

CHAPTER 20

Ramon pulls out a piece of bread and a lump of dried tuna which Ana's mother had packed for him, eats half of it then puts the remains in his knapsack. It has not been a straightforward journey so far, and more than once he has considered abandoning his idea to return to Doñana. In the end, he has had to restrict his walking to the nighttime, much as he did with Ana and the children, and even now he finds himself hiding in the bushes while patrols of the Guardia Civil pass by. Something is happening; he can feel it in the air. He gets up and picks the crumbs from his shirt. He will try to get as far as the river bank before it gets light.

He moves along the edge of the vineyard as carefully as he can, hoping that he does not miss his footing in the darkness. There should be a full moon tonight, but at the moment it is shrouded in clouds. A slight sound alerts him; he stops and waits, holding his breath, frightened to move a muscle. There is someone or something ahead of him. Whatever it is, man or beast, it has stopped too. 'Who's there?' calls a voice. Ramon recognises it at once. 'Antonio? Is that you?' Antonio is also a member of the Republican Left; they were together in the demonstration.

'I don't believe it. Ramon. Is it really you?' The man comes up to him and throws his arms around him. 'My God, it's wonderful to see you, brother. I thought you would be dead by now. I'd heard you were going to be shot.'

When he hears those words, Ramon feels a pain in his chest; he knows why Antonio thinks this. They are going to shoot his poor brother who has done nothing wrong, who has worked hard all his life trying to feed his family.

'What are you doing here?' he asks.

'The same as you I expect, trying to avoid the Guardia Civil.'

'So where are you heading?'

'Back to Seville. I think it will have quietened down by now,' Antonio says.

'Are they after you too, then?'

'Yes and no. They don't know who we are, but we have been stirring things up, lately.'

'Be careful. You don't know who you can trust these days. Are you and your comrades the reason I've seen so many of the Guardia on the roads these last couple of days?'

'No, I don't think so. It could be, but it's more likely because there are rumours of another demonstration. I think the police are getting themselves prepared.'

'What's it about this time?'

'Land, as usual. What has been common land for as long as anyone can remember is now being stolen by the landlords; it is no wonder that the landless labourers are all anarchists. Not that they are organised enough to make their vote count.'

'Do you think there will be another election soon?'

'Who knows. But I hear that the Comintern has said that all anti-Fascist parties should align under the name of the Popular Front next year. Together we will be much stronger and then maybe we will win the next election.'

'So, is there going to be an election next year?' He feels Antonio is not telling him everything.

'Yes, it looks like it could be in February,' he eventually admits.

201

'Good. Then perhaps things will start to improve.'

'Well, they can't get much worse. An old family friend of my father's decided to grow some food on a piece of spare land he came across. It was good fertile ground and the owner had never even visited it and had no intention of ever using it, never mind cultivating it.'

'So, what happened?'

'When the old fellow tried to plough it up, he was beaten so badly by the owner's steward that he is unable to walk anymore; his family have to take care of him now. There is much talk of the hatred between the classes, but in my opinion it's really more a case that the rich landlords living in Madrid don't care about their estates in Andalusia, where they don't know anyone and don't particularly want to. They all rely on their unscrupulous stewards to manage the estates and of course, these men grow more powerful by the day.'

Ramon nods in agreement. 'I heard that when one of the dukes visited his estates in Andalusia last year he looked as though he was going on a safari in Africa, he had so much equipment with him, even tents. No wonder they don't understand what is happening here; the poor are like foreigners to them. Andalusia is a foreign country.' He feels bitter when he thinks of how his sister-in-law and her children have to live.

'Well, I could understand it if this was Africa and the land was infertile and dry, but to waste good productive land like ours is a sin. That's why we have to do something to change it.'

'Hush. I think there's someone up ahead, and I can see the lights of a police car.'

'Follow me. We can cut across the vineyard.'

'If the moon comes out we will be sitting targets,' Ramon says but he follows Antonio through the rows of stunted vines, keeping as low as possible; it is their only option.

Clementina feels sad as she remembers the look on her father's face when he saw her, how his joy at seeing his daughter changed to disappointment and bewilderment when she turned away from him. Her behaviour has hurt him but she cannot help it; she is too ashamed and she knows she can never face him and tell him what Felipe had tried to do to her. She cannot even bear to think about what happened; how close she has come to having her life ruined. It is a nightmare that haunts her day and night. When she lies in Jaime's *choza* listening to the gentle snoring of him and his wife, she still smells Felipe's damp breath on her neck and feels his rough hands on her body and if she manages to fall asleep, it is only to wake again, trembling with fear and covered in sweat. She shudders at the thought of what might have been. Papa would never be able to look her in the eyes if Felipe had succeeded; she would no longer be his little princess. She would be nothing. No-one would want to marry her and no-one would believe that she is not the one to blame. Her father will hold her responsible for bringing this trouble down on their clan; they all will. She knows that her brothers and sisters already resent her because she is Papa's favourite; now they will hate her. But what hurts her more than anything else is that they will be right. She has brought this down on her family and friends. It is her fault that they have been thrown out of Doñana; she knows she should not have spoken to Hugo when her father had forbidden it, but she did anyway. It had seemed a small thing, a little rebellion against the restrictions of being a girl. She meant no harm. She knows she can never marry anyone of Hugo's class and wealth, nor does she want to. She is happy with her life in Doñana, or she had been. Now she must face the consequences. Ramon has saved her but he was not able to save her family. Nobody can save them from the wrath of the Rodriguez family; they will have their revenge on whoever they can.

'Clementina, Mama wants to speak to you,' calls Kiko. The boy is dragging some branches of wood towards one of the *boliches*.

'Has my father left?' she asks him. This is the first time she has asked after her family since the day that Papa came to take her with them.

'Yes. They have all gone now. The place is very quiet without them.' For a moment he looks sad; his usual gappy smile is gone.

'All of them?' She is finding it hard to believe, even though Jaime has explained what has happened and that she should be with her family, even though her father had begged her to go with them. 'Do you think they will ever come back?' she asks the boy.

He shrugs his shoulders and continues on his way.

When Clementina arrives at Jaime's *choza*, his wife is sitting outside skinning a rabbit. 'Sit down, child,' she says. 'You can help me prepare the food.' She hands her a knife and some small and rather wrinkled potatoes. 'How are you feeling today? Did you sleep any better last night? I didn't hear you get up this morning.'

'Not really. I was awake long before dawn. I went and sat by one of the *boliches* until it got light; I didn't want to disturb you.' She dropped one of the potatoes into the pot beside her.

'Cut them a little smaller, my dear. We have a lot of people to feed.' She looks at Clementina and smiles, kindly. 'That's one of the reasons I want to speak to you.'

'Yes?' Her stomach begins to churn. Are they going to send her away?

'You can see how we live here; everyone has a job to do. It's not an easy life being a *carbonero*, but nobody starves and everybody pulls their weight. You are still very young, my dear, but the time has come for you to decide what you are going to do.'

'Are you sending me away?' Clementina asks. If she cannot stay with them then she has no idea what she can do or where she can go. It was a mistake to let her family go without her; alone she is helpless.

'No, child, of course not, but we have to find something for you to do. It's been almost a week now since you came here and, as I said, everyone has to work.'

'I can cook,' she says. 'Although Mama did most of the cooking.' She hesitates, 'Well all of it, I suppose. I can wash clothes and feed the horses.' She looks about her. The *carboneros* do not seem to care much about cleanliness and they only have two mules which are used to pull their delivery carts. There must be something she can do. For the first time she realises what an easy life she has had compared to the people around her; whenever her mother wanted to give her a task her father would always intervene and tell her to let the child be, that there was time enough for Clementina to learn all that.

'So what did you do to help your mother?' Jaime's wife asks.

'Collect the water from the stream, collect nuts and berries from the woods. Oh, and I can sew.' She smiles at her, trying to look confident.

'All right, that will do for now. You can start by seeing what you can forage in the woods, but do not stray too far; I am not convinced we have seen the last of the Rodriguez family. And this evening you can talk to Marta, and tell her that you will collect the water from now on; she will show you where to go.

205

She will be glad of a change and then she can give me a hand with the cooking.'

She nods happily. Jaime's wife seems to have everything well organised; she reminds her of her mother.

Clementina has found some flat mushrooms and she is sure that they are edible; one thing she is good at is foraging because she has been doing it since she was a little girl. She never thinks of it as work; for her it is just a pleasant way to explore the woods. This morning she has also located an active beehive so she will go back tomorrow with the right protection. She looks in her bag; she has done well, there are pine cones and almond nuts as well as the mushrooms.

'Clementina, is that you?'

She recognises the voice and turns around to see Ramon running down the path towards her. 'What are you doing out here in the woods, alone?' he asks.

She holds up her bag of provisions and says, 'Look what I've gathered. This is my job now. And tomorrow I'm going to collect some honey. And I have to bring up the water every morning and evening.' She beams at him, feeling like an excited child.

'But you shouldn't be wandering through the woods, on your own. It's not safe.'

She can see how concerned he is, but she says, 'Ramon, I have lived in these woods all my life; I am not frightened to be alone. There are lots of dangers in here: poisonous snakes, wild boar, the lynx, even mosquitoes, but they will not hurt me if I don't hurt them. Well, maybe the mosquitoes will but not all of them are dangerous. It's not the woods I am afraid of, it's the men.'

'I know. And that's what I was referring to. But why are you here? Why aren't you with one of your family? Surely they haven't just let you go foraging alone?'

Her eyes fill with tears when he mentions her family; she cannot explain to him how she feels. Not now. 'You still have the bandana,' she says instead.

'Yes, of course.' He removes it from his neck and ties it around his head. 'So, do I look like a real *gitano*?'

'Not really. To be honest it's not a very good disguise; you look more like a bandit. Tell me why you are here.'

'I came back to make sure you are all right,' he says.

'Are you coming to see Jaime?'

'No,' he says. 'I do not want to cause any trouble for him. I'll spend the night in the dunes.'

'But what will you do then? Where will you go?'

'I'm not sure yet. I might go to Seville.'

'But isn't it dangerous for you? Aren't the Guardia looking for you?'

'Yes, probably. So tell me what has been happening; has your father done anything about the man who attacked you?'

She looks away and says nothing.

'What is it Clementina? What has happened?'

She puts her bag down on the ground and sits at the foot of an old twisted oak tree. 'My family have left Doñana,' she says and tears stream down her face. 'The Guardia Civil have burnt all our homes.'

Ramon sits down beside her and puts his arm around her. 'Did they arrest anyone?' he asks.

'No, they all managed to get away. They have gone to Portugal.' She continues to explain the little she knows about their escape.

'But, I don't understand. Why didn't you go with them?'

'I just couldn't. I can't face them. I know they blame me and I cannot bear it. I am the cause of their misery. How can I go with them and be constantly reminded of what happened to me?'

'So you are staying with the *carboneros*?'

'I have nowhere else to go. I am alone.'

'Come with me, Clementina. I will look after you. You will never be alone, again.'

'To Seville?'

'Maybe. If that's where you want to go?' He holds her tightly against his body and for the first time since the attack she feels safe.

'I must go now, Ramon. They will wonder where I am. I'll bring you some food this evening when I go to collect the water from the stream,' she says and gently pulls away from his arms.

As she heads back to the *carboneros* she keeps thinking about Ramon and how brave he was to attack Felipe that morning. And now he has risked being recognised by the Guardia Civil just to find out if she is all right. Maybe the wise thing to do would be to leave with him, that or stay here forever. And what about Hugo? Where is he? And has he heard about what has happened to her?

Ramon watches until she is out of sight then heads for the dunes. He had formed a clear plan in his head before he arrived; he would check on Clementina to see if she was well and living back with her family then he would return to Seville and rejoin his comrades. However, now things have changed and the clarity that had existed before has been clouded by an emotion that he has been trying to deny; he is falling in love with Clementina and all the excuses that he has been giving himself for returning, were simply to deny what he really felt for her. Now his head is spinning. He cannot, will not, leave without her, but he is torn between his need to fight for democracy and his love for a beautiful young woman. He remembers the words he spouted so confidently to his brother that night when they sat together drinking sherry: '*This fight is important. Think of your children. Do you want them to have no future? Don't you think they are entitled to a better life than you and I have had? It's not right that children are under nourished and deprived of education. We have to fight these people.*' He had been so pompous, so full of himself but he had believed what he was saying. And he still does. Can he just give that up because he loves Clementina?

A familiar voice suddenly says, 'Ramon, where are you going?' It is Kiko. His face is covered in soot as usual and he gives Ramon a big grin.

'Hello there, young man. You gave me a fright jumping out of the bush like that. I thought you were a wild boar and I was about to spear you.' He holds up his staff and laughs.

'You won't kill any boars with that,' the boy says. 'You need a proper lance, and a horse or you'll be gored.'

'I don't think I'm much good at hunting, Kiko; I'm a city boy.'

'Are you staying?' the boy asks, his face lighting up in anticipation.

Ramon shakes his head. 'Not this time. I have business to see to in Seville.' As he says the words, he knows it is the truth; he must stay true to his beliefs. All he can do is try to persuade Clementina to go with him.

'I've got to go,' says Kiko. 'They are letting me watch over one of the *boliches* tonight.' He beams with pride.

'Well don't fall asleep then,' warns Ramon and grins at him. He knows this is like a promotion for the boy; he has been entrusted with more responsibility.

Once Kiko has gone, Ramon continues tramping through the sand until he finds a hollow and settles down out of sight; he should be able to get a couple of hours sleep before Clementina arrives.

CHAPTER 21

Vano cannot stop thinking about his daughter. Was he right to leave her there? They are good people but they are not *gitanos* and they are not her family. Lavinia has not spoken a single word to him since they left Doñana; she blames him but what else could he have done? The girl would not speak to him. Did his wife think he should have picked Clementina up and carried her off, screaming and kicking? He could have done that quite easily and he probably would have done so, once upon a time, but not now. Things are changing. He knows that and the sooth-sayer has confirmed his fears.

'Papa, I think we should stop soon before it gets dark,' says Tomás. 'We can't cross the river in the dark.'

'To be honest, son, I don't think we have any choice. I don't want to be on the Spanish side when the Guardia catch up with us.'

'Do you think they will?' asks his wife, acknowledging that her husband is there for the first time since they began this journey. 'Surely they got what they wanted when they drove us out of our homes. Why would they care where we go?'

'You are probably right Lavinia, as always, but I can't take risks with my family's lives.'

'And what of Clementina's life? Is she no longer family? You seem happy enough to leave her behind with strangers. As for the rest of us, you think it is all right for us to be swept out to sea in the dark?'

He feels his temper rising and looks across at Tomás, who is stroking the nose of the lead horse and pretending not to have heard his mother's words. Vano swallows his pride; it is a sign of how upset she is that his wife has spoken to him like that in public. He ignores her and instead he addresses Tomás, 'I know it's risky but we will find a ford and cross where it is safe. We want to draw as little attention to ourselves as possible.'

'Do you know Portugal, Papa?' asks his son. 'Have you been there before?'

'No, Tomás, but your uncle has spoken of it many times. He travelled there a lot when he was younger. I remember he often talked about a place which sounded not unlike where we have just come from; if I am not mistaken, once we cross the river we will be almost there.'

'And if you are mistaken?' mutters his wife.

He pretends not to hear her.

'Do you think we will find Uncle Geronimo?' asks Tomás.

'What do you think? That noisy bugger can't go anywhere without causing a commotion. He'll already have been selling his good luck charms and home-made beer to the locals. My worry is that he has upset them already and been made to move on.'

Tomás laughs. 'Why didn't you travel around the country like your brother?' he asks.

'Me? I don't know. I suppose it was because I loved the horses too much to leave them. We were living in a paradise there, you know. Once you've found paradise it's not easy to leave it.'

'Humph. It might have been a paradise for you,' snaps Lavinia. 'It wasn't much fun for me bringing up eight children in the middle of the woods.'

He stares at her. What does she mean? It has never once, in thirty years of marriage, crossed his mind that his wife might be unhappy. Why would she be? She has him to protect her and make sure that she and the children never go hungry. He is puzzled. Is this because she wants to hurt him, to punish him for abandoning Clementina? Doesn't she realise there is no need; it is punishment enough for him to know that with every minute that passes he is moving further and further away from his beloved daughter.

'I can see the river,' says Tomás.

'Yes, and there's a large copse of trees near its bank.' Vano looks around him. 'I don't see any houses, or roads; that's good.' For the last hour they have been travelling along dirt tracks and across the fields and they are well away from civilisation by now. The surrounding countryside is wild and covered with clumps of rock roses, olive trees and holm oak; to the north the land rises steeply and the setting sun casts its failing light across the lush green foothills. 'You lead the horses down there and find somewhere to camp until nightfall. I'll wait and tell the others what we are going to do. And keep an eye out for wild pigs. I noticed a few of them foraging among the holm oaks.' He turns to his wife and adds, 'As soon as we stop, get some food organised. Once we cross the river I don't plan on us stopping again until daybreak.'

She stares at him but says nothing. He knows it is a challenge for her; most of the food they brought with them has been eaten and he would not allow them to visit any of the towns to buy more. Well their journey is almost over and once they are in Portugal they can all relax; he will give her some money and she can stock up on provisions for the whole family.

He studies the evening sky; clouds are appearing on the dim horizon. This does not bode well; he has been praying for a clear night and moonlight to help with the crossing. He fingers the gold cross around his neck, lifts it to his lips and kisses it;

his wife gave it to him on his wedding day. If God helps him to get his family to safety then he will promise to return to Spain and find Clementina, no matter what the risk.

A stiff breeze scatters the clouds and by the time they are ready to cross the river, the moon is out and the sky is filled with stars. Perhaps there is a God after all, Vano thinks as he steps into the cold water. The lead horse bucks a little, but she is a good solid marsh horse and has soon settled into her new role as a draught mare. He talks to her all the time as he leads her deeper and deeper into the river. He prays he has not misjudged the depth and strength of the current.

'Papa, the water is nearly up to the wagon steps. Do you think we should turn back and look for somewhere shallower?' Mateo, his eldest son calls in a loud whisper.

Vano is just about to agree with him when he feels a slight change beneath his feet; the river bed is beginning to slope upwards. 'It's all right, son. We're going to make it.' He urges the mare forward with soft words and a firm hand on her bridle; she makes one final lunge forward onto dry land and the wagon rumbles out of the river and up the bank.

'Well done,' he says, patting the mare's neck. 'Tomás, you take over. Keep going until you are out of sight of the river and then wait for me. I'm going back to help the others.' All the women and children are in the two wagons but the rest are going to have to cross on foot. He knows that Álvaro is bringing up the rear but he wants to be sure everyone gets across the river safely; the crossing is not as easy as he had originally hoped.

The second wagon is making good progress, so he steps into the cold, black water once more and heads for the other bank. 'Everyone all right?' he calls.

'Yes, we're fine, Papa. Well, except for old Paco; he's struggling with his bad leg.'

'Why isn't he in one of the wagons with the women? He's got to be eighty, if he's a day.'

'He refuses to go with the women. Says he can manage perfectly well and he'll clip my ear if I don't leave him alone.'

Vano wants to laugh but instead he says, 'Well, that's as maybe. Once you get him to the other side, if you do that is, tell him that he is slowing us down and I want him to ride in one of the wagons, or we leave him behind.'

Álvaro stares at him. 'You wouldn't do that, Papa?'

'You never know what I might do, son. As for you, you just do as I tell you, or I'll leave you behind as well.' Of course, he doesn't mean it but he is cold, wet and hungry and not in the mood for discussion.

He waits until the last of the clan have waded into the river before following them. Now they need to find his brother.

Vano knows they have to be careful. They may be out of reach of the Guardia Civil in Portugal but he also knows that his people are not welcome anywhere they go; it has always been this way and here it will be no different. It may even be worse because even he has heard of the country's cruel dictator, Salazar; it is a name to be feared but he will not let that deter him. Yes the *gitanos* are viewed as thieves and beggars but at least no-one is looking for his family in Portugal. They will soon join up with Geronimo and then they will become invisible.

They stop on the outskirts of a small town, not much more than a village and dilapidated at that. They are waiting for Tomás and Lavinia, who have been sent to buy some food and to make enquiries about Geronimo. Vano looks at the sun; they have been gone a long time. Too long. He is just beginning to worry when he sees them coming along the lane; Tomás is leading an old donkey with a pannier hanging on each of its skinny flanks.

'So, at last. I was starting to think that you had met up with my brother,' he says to his wife.

'No, but we know where he is,' she replies.

'And this fellow?' he points to the donkey. It too looks as though it has seen better days.

'He was wandering along the road; he needs a home,' says Tomás. 'Mama bought the panniers.'

'Someone has just turned him out. Look, he can hardly walk,' she points to one of his hooves.

'I can see that.' Vano bends down and lifts the donkey's hoof and inspects it. He takes a knife from his belt and pokes at the hoof until he loosens whatever is bothering the animal. The donkey waits patiently, staring at the ground. 'Got it.' He extracts a sharp spike of wood from the hoof and holds it up. 'He'll be all right now, and with some food in his belly he'll soon be as good as new.' He takes the rope hanging from the animal's neck and hands it back to his son. 'Take the panniers off him and tie him to the back of the wagon.'

'All right, Papa.'

Vano turns to his wife. 'So, where is Geronimo? Tell me what you found out.'

'He was in the town, two days ago. You were right; he caused such a commotion that everyone noticed him.'

Vano groans. 'Oh, no. So the police threw him out?'

She smiles at him. 'No, just the opposite. Apparently they have so little here that the townspeople were delighted to see him; people wanted their fortunes told, some had their knives sharpened and others even bought some of Geronimo's herbal medicines. The woman we spoke to said that everyone was disappointed that the *gitanos* didn't stay longer. She calls us *ciganos*.'

'*Gitanos, ciganos*? Sounds the same to me. Did she tell you which way they went? Did Geronimo tell anyone where he was going?' His brother is so cocksure of himself that it would not surprise him if he has told them all about himself and his plans.

'Only that they are going towards the coast; she pointed in that direction, but it was pretty vague,' says Lavinia, indicating that they should go west.

'And that was two days ago?'

His wife nods at him, her attention is now focussed on the women who have gathered around her to sort out the food.

'Leave the food for now; just put it in the wagon. Let's get away from the town and see if we can follow Geronimo's trail.' And before anyone comes looking for their donkey, he thinks but this he does not say aloud. If Geronimo is heading for the sea, it is likely that he is going to the place he described to Vano, a place made up of sea marshes and woods, a place frequented by migratory birds, a place which sounds not unlike his own beloved Doñana.

CHAPTER 22

Hugo gets off the train at the station in Jerez and looks around him; it is so good to be back in Spain. The day is overcast and the smoke from the engine hangs in the air like a dark cloud, but it is not the permanent grey mantle of an English winter. Tomorrow the clouds will lift and the sun will be shining. The anticipation of seeing Clementina again makes his skin tingle. It would be untrue to say he has missed her; he has been too busy enjoying his trip to Bristol but he is looking forward to seeing her again.

'Señor Hugo,' a voice calls. It is his father's chauffeur, Diego.

Hugo picks up his portmanteau and walks towards him.

'Let me have that, *Señor*,' he says and takes the bag from Hugo. 'Welcome home.'

'Thank you. The trip took rather longer than I had planned,' he says, getting into the back of the car. He has been away almost a month, although most of the delay was of his own making; he has quite a few young friends in Bristol and decided to make his trip more enjoyable by looking them up and spending most of his time hunting and fishing with them. He is not going to mention this to his father; all Papa needs to know is that the business meetings went smoothly and now they have not one new distributor but two. He feels very pleased with himself. 'So, has anything happened while I have been away?' he asks the chauffeur. If there has been any scandal Diego is sure to know about it.

'Yes, *Señor*, quite a lot has happened. For a start the gypsies have left.'

'What do you mean, left? Left Doñana? All of them?'

'Yes, they've moved on, lock, stock and barrel.'

Hugo cannot believe what he is hearing. For the last twenty-four hours he has thought of nothing else but seeing Clementina again. 'That doesn't make sense. They have always lived in Doñana. Are you sure about that, Diego?'

'I am, *Señor*. The Guardia Civil drove them out and burned down their homes. They won't be coming back.'

'But why? Who would want rid of them?'

'I don't know, *Señor*.'

Something about the way the chauffeur answers him makes him press for more information. 'What is it, Diego? Tell me exactly what happened.'

'It's not my place to say, Don Hugo, but I do know that your brother was involved somehow, and your father was mighty angry. He went to visit the Marquess and the next thing I heard was that the Guardia Civil were moving the gypsies on.'

'Thank you, Diego. I will probably hear all about it when I get home.' For propriety's sake he keeps his voice calm but inside he is raging. Is this their way of keeping him and Clementina apart? Well it is not going to work. He is no longer a child; he will be friends with whomever he wants. Even as he is thinking it, he cannot really believe that his father would go to such lengths to keep him away from Clementina. There is something very odd about his father's attitude towards the girl, and why does his mother become so upset every time someone mentions Hugo's interest in her? Even he realises that Clementina will never be accepted into their family; his parents' friends are all far too snobbish to welcome a gypsy into their society, no matter how beautiful she is. So what are they frightened about?

He can remember that when his brother Felipe was younger he fell in love with one of their maids. His father had spoken to him and told him that it was inappropriate, but nobody had made a fuss about it. They called it a schoolboy crush and it was soon over and never mentioned again, although now that he thinks about it, his mother had dismissed the girl the next day. He remembers seeing her leave with tears streaming down her face and carrying a small canvas bag containing all that she owned. At the time he had never given her another thought, but now it dawns on him how hard it must have been for her to be dismissed like that and the disgrace that went with it. For a moment he wonders what has become of her.

They turn off the main road and head up the lane to the *cortijo*. 'Diego, how long have you worked for us?' he asks.

'Sixteen years, *Señor*.'

'So, I was just a young boy when you came to the bodega?' As far as he is concerned Diego has always been a member of the household; he can hardly remember a time when he was not driving his father's car.

'Indeed, *Señor*.'

Maybe Diego knows what is behind all this subterfuge, but now is not the time to ask him; first he needs to know exactly what has gone on while he was away. He will make a point of speaking to him later, when no-one is around.

'Anything else happen of interest?' he asks casually.

'You know your father is standing for mayor?'

'Yes, he told me before I left. I suppose the elections will be next year?'

'Normally yes, but the current mayor was taken ill and died. So the election is next month.'

'I bet Papa is pleased about that.' The chauffeur does not answer, so Hugo continues, 'When did they announce that, about the election? Before the gypsies left or after?'

'I am not sure, *Señor*. Before, I think.'

So his father is behind all this. Were the gypsies kicked out because his father is worried about any scandal that might affect the election? Is he worried that Hugo's friendship for Clementina will spoil his chances of becoming the mayor? When he considers some of his father's rich friends, it is a plausible assumption. As he sits in the back of his father's plush Daimler, watching the familiar fields of chalky white soil and truncated vines flash past, his anger grows steadily stronger when he thinks of the plight of the gypsies. And Vano? What about him? His father always spoke so highly of him; that's what he cannot understand. Whatever his father's personal reasons are, there is no need to punish the whole clan of gypsies.

'Almost here, *Señor,*' says Diego. 'I expect you are glad to be home. I hear that England is a cold, gloomy place.'

'It can be.' They are approaching the bodega and he can see his mother loitering on the veranda. She spots the car and waves. If anyone can explain to him what this is all about, it is her. But will she betray her husband? Once he would have had an answer to that question, but now he is not so sure. He has seen a change in his mother's attitude; she is being more forceful and his father does not seem to have the authority over her that he once displayed.

Don Luis is not at home; Hugo's mother explains that he is with his campaign manager, discussing the election. Hugo is relieved; he needs some time to process all that he has learned from Diego before he speaks to his father. First of all he is going to ride over to Doñana and see for himself what has actually happened. He places the signed contracts on his father's desk and then puts on his riding clothes.

'Hugo. Are you going out already?' asks his mother. 'Your father won't be long, you know. He said he would join us for lunch. He's anxious to hear how your trip went.'

'It went well, Mama. I'll tell you and Papa all about it over dinner. Now I just need to get out and blow the cobwebs out of my head. I hear a lot has happened while I have been away.'

'Very well. I'll tell him, but he will be disappointed not to see you for lunch.' She looks away and he cannot tell if she too is disappointed or too ashamed to look at him. Surely she realises that Diego will have already told him about the gypsies. He cannot stay there a moment longer or he will say something that he will regret, so he strides across to the stables, cracking his whip against his thigh; he has to get away, right now. Never has he felt such loathing for his father and all that he stands for.

Hugo rides for an hour, across the fields and through the lanes. He stops in Rocio and heads for a small bar next to the church. Today is Monday and the sandy roads of the village are deserted but the air still has a strong smell of manure left by the horses that thronged the square the day before. He ties his own horse to the railing and goes into the bar. The small space is dark and smoky and crowded with customers. The stone floor is covered in a fine coating of sand, blown in from the streets and littered with small paper serviettes.

'*Buenos días, Señor,*' says the barman. 'Haven't seen you in a long time.'

'*Buenos días,* Mario. No, I've been away.'

'The usual?' he asks, already pouring some beer from a large jug into a glass tankard.

'Thank you,' says Hugo, taking the beer and drinking it down in one go.

'Thirsty, I see.'

'Yes, fill it up again, please. And give me some of that *tortilla*.' Now that his thirst is quenched, Hugo sits down on the stool at the bar. 'I hear that there have been some changes in my absence,' he says. Mario is very typical of the barmen in the area; he knows everyone and everything that is going on. If anyone is going to know what happened to the gypsies, it is him. The village of Rocio lies by the lagoon, on the very edge of Doñana and Mario's customers are both the people who work there and those, like Hugo, who come to hunt and fish.

'Yes, indeed. I take it you're talking about the *gitanos*?

Hugo takes a mouthful of the *tortilla* and nods.

'Well that was a shock to everyone. We're all worried now in case the Marquess takes a dislike to any of the village people.'

'I wouldn't think that is very likely. He must have had a particular reason for contacting the Guardia Civil about the gypsies.'

'Maybe he did. He and his wife are new here, of course. The previous owner had no problems with them. They kept to themselves and, as I see it, their leader Vano was very popular with the landed gentry.' He looks at Hugo as if to say, so why didn't you do anything about it.

'Have you any idea why it was? Did something unusual happen?'

'No, nothing. Someone must have put the Marquess up to it, because they are hardly ever here. I doubt if they even knew about the *gitanos* being on their land.'

'So where did they go? The gypsies?'

'As I hear it, they've gone to Portugal. Been gone nearly a month now.'

So this happened almost as soon as Hugo left for England. His chances of finding Clementina are looking more and more remote.

'Did you have much to do with them?' he asks.

'One or two used to come in for a beer, and occasionally Vano would buy a full goatskin of wine. There were a couple of women who made baskets and things like that out of esparto grass, but except for when the fair was on, we never saw much of any of them.'

'So you don't know a girl called Clementina, one of Vano's daughters?' He might as well come straight out with it.

'Her that was violated?' the barman says, pouring out some beer for another customer.

'What?' Hugo feels himself grow cold. 'What did you say?'

'The young girl who was attacked, Vano's girl. Attacked in the woods, she was. Luckily one of her brothers, or maybe someone else, probably one of the *gitanos* anyway, heard her screams and pulled him off her.'

'Was she hurt? Is she all right now?' Hugo manages to ask. Keeping his voice steady is taking all his concentration. 'That's a terrible thing to happen to a young girl.'

'Yes. I think she's all right now. Her father was pretty angry as you can imagine, what with that and then having to leave Doñana.'

'Do they know who attacked her? Is that why the Guardia Civil were called?' He cannot bring himself to use the word violate.

'No. But he wasn't a local. Odd though, that he should be wandering through the woods like that. Like he was lying in wait for her.'

'Tragic business,' says Hugo, trying to appear only slightly interested. He finishes the *tortilla* and drinks down the last of his beer. 'Well, I'll be off.' He places a coin on the counter.

'Not made any the easier for Vano when she refused to leave with them,' one of the customers adds.

Hugo looks at the old man sitting near him. 'Sorry, what did you say?'

'Well she wouldn't go. Told her father. Refused point blank to go to Portugal. He tried to persuade her but nothing would move her.'

'So where is she? Is she still in Doñana?' For a moment he lets his guard drop and instantly he can feel everyone looking at him. 'I mean it's a bit strange for a young girl to stay here on her own.'

'It is indeed.'

The old man turns away and begins to talk to his neighbour. Mario has moved to the other end of the bar. *Mierda*, now they will think it was him who attacked her. Hugo knows that now he will get no more information from either of them, but still he has plenty to think about. He remembers that Diego said that Felipe was involved somehow; surely he didn't mean that it was his brother who attacked Clementina. No, that is impossible. But he cannot leave it alone now; the thought is burying its way into his head like an earthworm. He knows his brother can be a hard man at times but he has always shown respect for women. Why would he do this? It does not make sense. Hugo steps out of the bar and for a moment is blinded by the sun glinting on the surface of the lagoon. Something disturbs a flock of flamingoes nearby and instantly they take to the air, honking and cawing in protest, only to land again at the far side and resume feeding. He stands there watching them and wondering what he should do next. His head is spinning. His father is not going to admit to anything and he cannot bring himself to believe that his brother would try to rape Clementina. It just is not possible. His mind in turmoil, he climbs back on his horse and heads for the bodega. He has to find out exactly what his family are hiding from him.

His mother is having her usual afternoon nap and there is no sign of his father when he returns home, so he goes into the kitchen to look for Conchita; she has worked for them since she was a girl and given the most menial of jobs. Now she is approaching fifty and has graduated to being their cook and housekeeper; as his mother often says, the house would grind to a halt without her. Another thing his mother is fond of saying is that Conchita holds the keys not just to the house but to all its memories and even its secrets. She is referring to practical things such as how to stop the chimney from smoking, recipes for their favourite dishes and where the keys to the cellar are kept, but it has occurred to him now that there may be more to what his mother says than that. Surely Conchita must know all the family secrets. How could she not. Almost forty years of living in a house which has become as much her home as theirs, if anyone knows what is the mystery behind his parents antipathy to Clementina then it is her.

'*Buenas tardes*, Conchita. Is there anything to eat?' he asks, putting his head round the kitchen door.

The housekeeper's plump body is reclining in a wooden armchair by the kitchen range. A pile of cotton napkins are on the table next to her and the one she is embroidering lies in her lap, momentarily forgotten. Her chin rests on her ample bosom as she drifts in a half sleep.

'Conchita?'

'Oh.' She jerks awake. 'Don Hugo, is that you? I heard you were back.' Now she is up and bustling around the kitchen, the napkin and sewing things dropped onto the chair to be redeemed later. 'You must be starving. I noticed you didn't come in for lunch. What can I get you? Some nice fresh bread and a couple of eggs? Or a few slices of ham?'

'The ham will do nicely,' he says and sits himself at the kitchen table. He pours himself a glass of sherry from the flagon on the table.

'So how did you like Bristol?' Conchita asks. 'Was the weather kind to you?'

'If you mean did it rain, then no it wasn't kind. It rained most days, but that didn't stop me from getting out and doing a bit of hunting.' He smiles at her and adds, 'Best not to mention that to Papa.'

'As if I would tell your father anything, my boy.' She slices the cured ham and puts it on a plate with some homemade bread. 'Some olives?'

'Please.' He always feels at home in this kitchen; since he was a boy he has been able to escape from the strictures of his father and the taunts of his brother into this warm, friendly space.

Conchita chatters away about what has been happening at the bodega since he left then suddenly she stops and asks, 'What is it, my boy? Something is worrying you. I can tell.'

'I want to ask you something, Conchita and I feel it is wrong of me to do so because you might get into trouble.'

'What is it? Speak up. If I can answer your question I will, if not then I will tell you so. You know you can always speak your mind to me.'

Now he feels worse than ever. If she tells him something that is a family secret and his father finds out he will dismiss her without a second thought, regardless of how long she has worked for them. What would become of her at her age, if she were suddenly homeless? 'No, don't worry, Conchita. It's not important.'

'If it's not important why do you look as though someone has stolen your favourite horse?'

'Talking of which, I ought to go and check that Beauty is all right after her long ride.'

'You mean you just handed her over to Pablo?' says the housekeeper with a smile. 'Something must really be worrying you when you forget to rub down your Beauty.'

Hugo stops. They are alone. It is the perfect opportunity to ask her about what happened. 'Do you know why my father is so angry about me talking to Clementina? I feel there is something going on that I don't know about, and now it seems that she has disappeared. No-one knows where she is, and I feel it's all my fault.'

'The gypsy's daughter?'

'Yes, you know the one I mean; I used to play with her when I was a boy. She lives, sorry lived, in Doñana.'

'I know who you mean although I have not seen her since she was a baby. So they christened her Clementina, did they?'

'Who are you talking about, Conchita? Tell me what you know. I swear I will never tell anyone who told me.' He grabs her hand and looks up at her beseechingly.

'Very well. I will tell you what I can.' The housekeeper sits down opposite him. 'It's time you knew anyway. I could see this was going to end in tears. I told your mother so at the time.' She pauses, then takes a deep breath. 'You may have already guessed, but I will tell you anyway. Clementina is your half-sister.'

He stares at her in bewilderment. He has imagined many scenarios but not this. 'So that is why Papa is so angry that I went to see her. He doesn't want me falling in love with my sister. What a two-faced bastard he is. He tries to tell me that it is beneath me to have anything to do with a gypsy girl and will bring disgrace on the family, when all the time he is having an affair with Vano's wife. What a hypocrite he is.' He pours himself a second glass of the amontillado. 'I cannot believe he would do that to Mama, humiliate her in that way. With a gypsy. What was he thinking of?'

'Before you say any more and regret it, I have something else to tell you,' Conchita says, but Hugo is already on his feet.

'I have heard enough. I don't want to hear any more.'

'Hugo, wait.'

'I suppose I am the last to know, as always. Does my brother know about this?'

'I don't think so; he was away at school at the time. Please sit down, Hugo and let me explain.'

'There's nothing to explain,' he says and marches out of the kitchen. He has to find Clementina and tell her. 'How could he do that to his own daughter?' he mutters. 'His own daughter.'

'Ah there you are, Hugo. I saw the contracts you left on my desk. Well done, lad. I knew you would get us some new business. Come into the lounge and we'll celebrate.'

Hugo stares at his father and says nothing. He is speechless with rage.

'What's wrong, son?'

'So family is everything to you, is it Father?' And without explaining himself further, Hugo strides out and slams the door behind him. All he can think about is finding Clementina and telling her the devastating news.

He knows the gypsies have left Doñana, but he decides to go there anyway. It is dusk by the time he arrives and even in the failing light he can see the devastation left by the Guardia Civil. Not a house is left standing. There are no horses in the corral. A few scattered belongings lie among the ashes of what was once their homes. He gazes around him in horror. Where is she now? His sister, where is she? Part of him cannot believe that he is really Clementina's brother, and yet another part of him says that he knew all along. Those feelings he had for her were not the feelings of physical attraction that he usually gets when he sees a pretty girl, they were deeper and now he knows why.

A shadowy figure moves among the trees. 'Who's there?' Hugo calls. 'Who are you? Come out where I can see you.'

A man steps out into the clearing. His face is grimy and he has a red bandana around his neck.

'What's your name? You are not one of the gypsies?'

'Ramon. No, I'm not *gitano*. They've all left.' He waves his hand over the desolation. 'You would hardly know they had ever been here.' He stares at Hugo. 'Who are you? Have I seen you before?'

'I'm Hugo Rodriguez Gil de la Cruz. My father owns the bodega Butler & Rodriguez.' He tries to sound imposing but the man's penetrating stare is unsettling.

'So, Don Hugo Rodriquez Gil de la Cruz, what are you doing here?'

'I'm looking for someone.'

'Well, as you can see, there is no-one here. They have all gone.'

'Do you know a girl called Clementina? She used to live here. Do you know where she is?'

'I expect she is with her family. Why do you want to see her?'

'I have some important news for her. Devastating news, actually. I must see her. I have to speak to her. She is my sister,' he finally blurts out. The words sound strange in his mouth. The woman he has been fantasising about for months turns out to be his sister. How cruel is that.

'Your sister? What are you talking about? The only Clementina I know is the daughter of a gypsy called Vano.'

'That's the one. Where is she? I must see her.'

'I'm sorry, she has disappeared. I think she left with her family.'

Hugo looks at him carefully. 'How do you know her if you're not a gypsy?' he asks then pauses. 'Were you the one who saved her?'

The man nods. 'You have heard about the attack, then?'

'Yes. It was lucky that you were there. I hate to think what could have happened to my sister if you had not come by. Did you recognise the man who attacked her?'

'No, I didn't know him, but Clementina did. He has the same name as you, Rodriguez.'

'Felipe?'

'That's right.'

Hugo stares at him. Why would Felipe attack a young woman? For all his faults, Felipe is not a rapist. 'I find that hard to believe.'

'Why would she lie? He attacked her and if I hadn't come along I think he would have violated her as well. She saw him clearly. There is no mistake.'

'So where did you take her?'

'I can't tell you that. All I can tell you is that I do not know where she is now.'

'If you see her again, please tell her Hugo is looking for her and that he has found out that he is her brother.'

'So that makes Felipe her brother, too? What a fine family you are.' The man looks at him in disgust.

On any other occasion Hugo would not have tolerated that comment, but now all he can do is hang his head in shame. 'If you see her, please tell her I love her and want to protect her. She is my sister. Promise me.'

'If I see her I will promise to tell her what you have said. Now I must go.' He turns and almost instantly has vanished into the dark shadows of the woods. The call of a lynx breaks the silence and for once in his life, Hugo has no interest in it. He pulls at the bridle of his mare and turns her back, away from the setting sun and the place that once meant so much to him.

CHAPTER 23

Ramon does not sleep well despite the comfortable hollow he has dug for himself in the dunes. There is a full moon tonight and it pours all its brilliance over the estuary which for once is gently lapping against the shore. He closes his eyes tightly and turns his back on the beach, but the moon has made him restless. He cannot stop thinking about Clementina and how much he wants her. His desire for her and his duty—as he sees it—are in constant conflict. He cannot abandon her yet neither can he abandon the fight for what is right. He is not a man who has travelled widely, nor is he well educated but he knows inequality and injustice when he sees it. It is not enough to complain about it, only action will make things change. He cannot waste any more time hiding like a frightened sheep; it is time to return to the fight. He will tell Clementina everything he has done and everything he wants to do; he will tell her how he feels about her and ask her to go with him. He stands up and stares out across the estuary; he has made up his mind and now he feels easier. In the distance he can make out the faint light of some fishing boats bobbing on the water and he thinks of Ana and the children; things have to change, if not for his generation then for their children's, for his niece and nephew. He owes that at least to his brother.

He must have slept at last, for he is suddenly awakened by a gentle hand on his shoulder; it is Clementina. Even before he

233

opens his eyes he knows it is her; the scent of lavender lingers on her skin.

'I've brought you something to eat,' she says, sitting down beside him and unwrapping a cloth containing a slice of *tortilla*, half an apple and a handful of berries. 'Not much, I'm afraid. I didn't want to tell anyone that you were here. I'm sure Jaime's wife would have sent you some food if she knew.' She hands him a flagon of water.

'That's plenty,' he says, picking up the *tortilla* and cramming it into his mouth. He cannot take his eyes off her, her long hair is still damp from where she has bathed in the river and her skin glows like that of a newborn baby; he longs to stroke it but instead he picks a watercress leaf from her hair.

She laughs and gives her head a shake, the wet strands of hair fanning out from her head and brushing his face. 'Why so serious?' she asks him.

'I have a lot to tell you, Clementina and I'm not sure where to start.' He hesitates, and to cover his embarrassment he picks up a couple of the berries. 'Did you pick these this morning?' he asks.

'Start at the beginning,' she says. 'I love a good story.'

'I'm not sure you will like this one,' he says, 'Nor me when I have finished.'

Clementina does not reply but curls up on the ground beside him and waits for him to begin. He longs to reach out and hold her but instead he takes a deep breath and says, 'I was born not far from here. There were five of us and I am the youngest in my family. I was fortunate that my mother was determined that I would not grow up illiterate like her and my father. Although they were poor they managed to find the money to pay an elderly neighbour of ours—who used to be a schoolteacher back in the days when we had a local school—to teach me to read and write. My brothers worked in the fields with my father, and as soon as I was ten-years-old I had to work alongside them. One of my sisters died when she was only five, and another married an *obrero* and is living in Huelva. I have no idea where my brother, Severiano is now; nobody has heard from him since he was fourteen and left, saying he was going to South America to make his fortune. I don't think he even knew where South America was, never mind how to get there.'

'And the other brother?'

'Pedro? Well at the moment Pedro is in prison and it is all my fault.' He starts to tell her what has happened to his brother and finds the words choking him. He stops and sips some of the water. 'So you see, it's me they want and because they can't find me they have taken my brother instead. I think of turning myself in, but I know it will do no good. They will only say we were colluding and arrest both of us.'

'What about his family? You say he has a wife and children?'

'They are with her parents. I think they will be safe now, but Pedro is still shut up in that awful prison. I dread to think what is happening to him. Every day I wonder if I'm going to receive news of his execution.'

'But you didn't intend to hurt the policeman; it was an accident. Wasn't it?'

'Of course it was, but that's not how they see it. Besides which they know I took his gun.'

'What?'

Ramon opens his canvas bag and removes a Berreta pistol wrapped in a bloodstained rag. 'It was lying on the ground beside him. I don't know why I did it, but I just picked it up and stuffed it into my bag. I forgot I had it until I got to my brother's house and then I didn't know what to do with it.'

'Is it loaded?'

'Yes, but I don't have any more ammunition, so it's useless really. I ought to throw it away.'

'No, don't do that. You might need it one day.' Clementina is no longer smiling; he knows she is remembering what has happened these last few days.

He takes her hand and smiles at her. 'Don't worry, Clementina. I won't let anyone hurt you ever again.'

'So, what are you going to do?' she asks. 'Your parents are dead, and there is only your brother and he is in prison.'

'I'm not quite sure, but one thing I know is that I'm not going to keep hiding. I can't stay here in Doñana. Spain is in a dreadful state, I can't just sit back and watch people starving. This is supposed to be a democracy so everyone should have a voice, not just the rich and powerful.'

'How are you going to change that? That's always been the way of the world. Look at my family. They did nothing wrong but they have been thrown off the land where they have lived for generations. Now they are in Portugal and I am homeless.' A tear trickles down her face and she brushes it away angrily.

'You could join them,' he says, hoping against hope that she will refuse. 'I can take you there.'

Clementina shakes her head. 'No. I will not be exiled from my country. I have done nothing wrong.'

Ramon is about to suggest that she goes with him to Seville but then he remembers what Hugo has told him. 'I saw Hugo yesterday,' he says. 'I went to look at your old home and saw him arrive on that big horse of his. He was very upset with what he found. Or rather what he didn't find, because there is virtually nothing left of your old homes. I didn't intend to speak to him, but he saw me hiding in the woods and I had no option but to go out and talk to him.'

She is staring at him in astonishment.

'He has been away in England and only arrived back yesterday. He came straight here when he heard what had happened,' he explains. 'He was hoping to find you.'

'Does he know what Felipe did to me?'

'He does now. And he knows that it could have been worse if I had not been passing.' He realises she wants him to continue. 'Hugo has some news for you; that is why he was looking for you. It seems that he has found out that you and he are related. I expect that was why his father was so against you being friends.' He does not know what else to say. If he tells her that Hugo is her brother he will be condemning her mother as an adulteress. He does not want to be the one to do that.

'Related? How so? Is that all he said? Did he explain any further?'

'He wanted to speak to you in person but I said I didn't know where you were.'

For a while Clementina says nothing; she sits staring at the estuary in silence. The tide continues to ebb regardless of the drama taking place in the dunes and the sun is slowly rising above the horizon just as it always does. Suddenly a flock of screeching gulls land on the shore and startle her into life again. She looks up at Ramon and says, 'That is probably for the best.'

'You don't seem surprised,' he ventures.

'Oh, I am surprised. Very surprised. Hugo and I have been friends since childhood; I don't understand why he has never mentioned it before. And he didn't give you any more details? How exactly are we related for example?'

'Hugo has only just found out for himself. I don't know how. I don't even know if it's true. But he was really upset about his brother and what he did to you; that much was very clear. I don't think he believed that his brother was capable of such a thing.'

'Dear Hugo. He's always been so fond of me, and I of him.' She turns her face to Ramon, 'It's interesting news but really it's of no consequence now. So what are your plans? How do you think you will be able to make any changes to our country? After all, you are one man, a poor one at that with no powerful contacts, and to make it more difficult you are wanted by the Guardia Civil. What on earth do you think you can do?'

Recent events have hardened Clementina; she is no longer the frightened, vulnerable girl he rescued from Felipe's brutal attack. For the first time he can see beyond the physical desire he has for her to the woman beneath that lovely exterior. There is no doubt in his mind now. This is the woman he wants to spend his life with. He takes her face in his hands and says, 'I won't be alone. I will have you, Clementina. I want you by my side, forever. We will leave Doñana, beautiful though it is, and go to Seville. I have friends there who will help us to find somewhere to live. Once we are there I am going to become a member of the socialist party and together we will work to win the election, restore the policies that our previous government introduced and build a regime of political liberty. Everyone will have the right to vote however they want.'

'We will help to change the world,' Clementina says, staring into his eyes as though everything is possible.

If only that was true. Ramon is in love, but that does not cloud his judgement; he knows that it will be hard in Seville. His photo will be in every police station; he is a wanted man. He is going to have to tread very carefully and trust no-one. And what of his comrades? Will they feel it is too risky to have him there? And then there is his brother; he has to find a way to help him.

'I will go and get my things,' says Clementina. 'Then we can leave as soon as it gets dark.'

'What will Jaime and his wife say?'

'Nothing. They know I will be leaving sometime. They will not be surprised.' She stretches up and kisses him lightly on the cheek. 'I will be back soon.'

He sits and watches as she disappears amongst the trees. Why didn't he tell her that Hugo was her brother? She has a right to know who her parents are, that Vano is not her real father.

CHAPTER 24

Vano drives his people hard, making them journey through the night. Only when a pale dawn brightens the sky does he let them stop and rest, and then he is only thinking of the horses' welfare. He would have them all out of the wagons and walking if he thought he could get away with it. However, now that old Paco is driving one of the wagons they are making faster progress. Some of the children are becoming irritable but he leaves that to his wife to sort out; he has enough to do supervising his sons. He has instructed Álvaro to go ahead of them and make enquiries about Geronimo in every town and village that they come to; it seems that he is right in his assumption and his brother is headed for a village called Tavira. He has never heard of it but that is hardly surprising since he has never been away from the area around Doñana before. The land here is flat and they are close to the sea; a steady breeze is blowing in from the west and there is the smell of rain in the air. It is different to Doñana but it seems a pleasant enough place, if a bit remote.

A small village lies ahead of them and he can see Álvaro waiting by the roadside. His son waves and ambles back towards him.

'Well?'

'Uncle Geronimo came through here yesterday evening. It seems he is heading for the islands.'

'Islands? What bloody islands? I thought he was going to Tavira.'

'The islands lie along the coast, close to Tavira. Nobody lives there except a few tuna fishermen and a handful of crofters. It's mostly marshland. No forests. Plenty of birds.'

Vano feels his heart sink; this is not what he expected. 'What about horses? Any wild horses?'

'No, I don't think so. It sounds as though it's nothing but tuna and birds.'

'What the hell is Geronimo thinking about?'

'Maybe he doesn't intend to stay there. Maybe he plans to move on; it's not far to a big town called Faro and according to the locals there is plenty of work there for those willing to do it.' He nods towards two old men who are sitting outside a bar, playing dominoes; they have suspended their game to watch Vano and the wagons roll up. 'They say that most of the young folk have moved there. Hardly anyone lives on the islands. That's good, isn't it?'

'No, it isn't good. How are we going to live? We are *gitanos*, not bloody fishermen. I should have known better than to even consider following my idiot brother to Portugal. Still we are here now and the best thing we can do is find him and see what bright scheme he is cooking up now.'

'We just keep following this road until we come to the coast,' adds Álvaro. 'We can't be far from the sea now; you can smell it in the air.'

'Right, well we'll keep moving until we catch up with them. Let your brothers know. I don't plan to spend the next few weeks wandering all over Portugal looking for my damned brother.'

That evening they find the road takes them along the edge of a sandy beach; beyond the beach lie the salt marshes and beyond that the sea is crashing along the shore in huge white-topped breakers. The sky seems to be full of screaming gulls and a variety of waders are feeding in the shallow marshes; for a brief moment he feels as though he is back in Doñana. Then he sees the islands; they lie close to the horizon, small, uninhabited and treeless. This has to be the place the old men spoke about. But where is Geronimo?

'Papa, I've found him,' yells Álvaro, running back along the road towards them. 'They are camped on the beach, about two kilometres from here. Do you want me to go ahead and tell Uncle Geronimo we are coming?'

'Yes. Tell him to stay there until we get there; I don't think the horses can make it much further without a good rest and we're almost out of hay for them.'

'All right. I'll wait for you there.'

For once in his life Vano is pleased to see his brother and the two men embrace warmly.

'Well this is a surprise, Vano. What has dragged you away from Doñana? Something drastic must have happened to get your wagons on the move.' His tone is jovial but his expression is serious.

'It has, brother. The Guardia Civil have burnt our homes and most of our possessions. They drove us out of Doñana.' Vano goes on to explain what happened.

'But everyone is all right? They didn't shoot anyone?'

'No, we are all fine, well except Clementina.' He explains how she was attacked by Hugo and only narrowly escaped being raped. 'Now she refuses to come with us. I tried to force her, but she wouldn't listen. And Lavinia wasn't a lot of help.'

'Well she wouldn't be, would she. So that's what it's all about, then. The old man is getting his revenge at last.'

'Yes, it looks like it. I had hoped he'd forgotten all about her; I do my best to keep her out of his way. Then that son of his, Hugo, turns up unexpectedly one day and sees her. I don't think he knew who she was but he started hanging around the place, wanting to talk to her. I don't know what he was hoping to achieve, but I knew it wasn't going to end well.'

'Does he know she is his sister?'

'I don't know. Probably not. I haven't spoken to Isabel in fifteen years and haven't seen Don Luis for almost as long. He has continued to buy horses from me but he always sends someone else to do the deal; he never comes in person. I think he is frightened he will see Clementina.'

'She is very like her mother,' says Geronimo. 'An identical likeness. It's just as well he never saw her.'

Vano nods sadly. His brother is right. It is a relief to speak to someone about her; for years he has kept his love a secret, not able to speak to anyone about it, denying its existence even to himself. He pulls the silver ring out of his pocket. 'I found this the other day; I gave it to Isabel as a token of my love just before Clementina was born.'

'Where was it?'

'In my hiding place with the rest of my savings. I'd forgotten I had it. She gave it back to me, you know. She wanted Clementina to have it.'

'I felt sorry for you at the time,' admits Geronimo. 'But it was never going to end any other way.' His voice is kind. 'You could never have given Isabel the sort of life she was used to. Even if she had left Don Luis and run away with you, she would soon have regretted it. As for you, you would have felt guilty about all the things you could never give her and she would soon grow to resent her new life. If you had chosen her, you would have been forced to leave the clan and never see your family again; I knew you could never do that. In the end it was the best solution for everyone; you had your child and Isabel kept her dignity.'

His brother is right. It was him who had helped Vano through those awful weeks when Clementina was born. Geronimo had not been the patriarch then, their elder brother held that role and they had kept her birth a secret from him and the rest of the clan. Vano had brought Clementina home one day, a small bundle of pink skin with a shock of black hair, no more than two days old, and told everyone that he had found her abandoned outside the church. It was obvious she had *gitano* blood in her veins so he suggested that they adopt her. His wife had taken her to the church and had her christened and never once asked him about the child. It is obvious that she knows the baby is his but she has never said anything and he is sure that even now she has no idea who the mother is. Why would she. Nobody would ever imagine that the beautiful, elegant, rich wife of Don Luis could fall in love with a *gitano* horse trainer, but she had.

'I remember the first time you saw her,' says Geronimo. 'She came to the stables looking for help with her horse. I think it was lame, or something.'

'He had a stone in his hoof.'

'Yes. The look on your face. It was as though the Holy Mother had just come down from heaven. Your eyes were popping out of your head and you could hardly speak.' Geronimo laughs. 'I'll never know what she saw in you that day.'

'I made her laugh.' He can see it all as though it were yesterday. She was like a goddess. She had walked into his life, leading a lame mare and captured his heart. Her face was flushed from the ride and her hair had come loose; a single curl hung down, resting on her cheek. When he had removed the stone from her horse's hoof, she rewarded him with a smile that lit up his world and he immediately knew things were never going to be the same. That summer she had found many excuses to come to Doñana and gradually their love grew and grew. He knew it was wrong. Adultery is not tolerated in the *gitano* community; if anyone found out he would be instantly expelled but this did not deter him. He was young and in love and nothing else mattered. He had given no thought to his own wife and the six healthy children she had borne him, no thought to Don Luis who with a single word could destroy their lives. Now he can see clearly how reckless he was, how reckless they both were but he still cannot bring himself to regret his actions. How could he. She gave him the most precious thing in the world, his beautiful Clementina.

'What is it, brother? Regrets?'

'What use is it having regrets? What is done is done. We can't change the past.'

'But you can change the future.'

'Yes, you're right, brother.' He knows what he has to do. He must find Clementina. It was stupid of him to let her stay alone in Doñana. 'And that's what I plan to do. It's time that we joined forces. I am going to entrust my family and the rest of our clan to you. You are the patriarch; I know you will look after them.'

'And you?'

'I will go and find Clementina and bring her back to her family. I was wrong to leave her. I am her father and until she is married, she is and always will be my responsibility.'

Geronimo smiles at him and holds out his hand. 'Very well, brother. They will be safe with me. When do you leave?'

'At first light.' He has decided. First he will seek out Hugo and punish him, then he will find Clementina and take her back to her family, where she belongs.

CHAPTER 25

Hugo's head is spinning as he rides back to the bodega; he cannot believe that this is happening. His world has been turned sideways. He and his brother have always been at odds; since they were boys they have fought and argued over many things but in his own way he has always respected Felipe and, although he does not like to admit it, he has tried to win his brother's approval. Now he is struggling to believe that he could behave in such a vile way. Just thinking of what his brother has done makes him feel sick.

He rides up to the stables and hands his horse over to Pablo.

'*Buenos dias, Señor*. You went out early this morning. I didn't see you,' the groom replies, taking the reins from him.

'No. I was in a hurry so I saddled Beauty myself. Have you seen my brother?'

'Señor Felipe? He is in his office, *Señor*. I saw him go in there about half an hour ago.'

Hugo does not bother to reply and heads towards the back of the house where the offices of Butler & Rodriguez are located. As he approaches, the foreman steps out.

'*Buenos dias*, Señor Hugo. How was your journey to Bristol?' he asks, stopping in the doorway.

'Is my brother in there?' asks Hugo, brushing Enrique out of his way. He has no time for the foreman today; he has never liked his brutish ways anyway, and now he is in no mood to make conversation with him.

'*Si, Señor.*'

Hugo slams the door behind him and goes straight up to Felipe and hauls him out of his chair. 'How could you do it? How could you? I know you can be a bastard sometimes but I never thought you would stoop so low as to try to rape a defenceless girl.'

'Hang on there. Why do you say it was rape? She wanted it. It was her who led me on. I...'

Hugo hears no more, his fist catches Felipe straight on the nose and sends him flying back against the wall. His legs crumple under him and he slides to the floor.

'What the hell did you do that for?' Felipe mumbles, blood streaming down his face. 'Damn you. You've broken my nose.'

'I'd like to break a lot more.' Hugo sits down and holds his head in his hands. There is no way that Clementina would have encouraged Felipe. He cannot believe that. His brother is lying to save himself. 'Why did you do it?' he asks again.

'I told you.'

'I do not believe you. Did you know that Clementina is our sister? Yours and mine. Our sister.'

'Well no, not at first. I thought this was just to do with encouraging you to get married to Mari Carmen. Papa just told me to get rid of her.'

'What do you mean, not at first?' Hugo is itching to hit him again.

'I knew about the baby, of course, but I didn't know that it was Clementina. So what?'

Hugo stares at him in amazement. 'You knew? How? Who told you?' This is worse than he thought; his brother has known all this time and never thought to tell him. 'Did you know the baby was a *gitano*?'

'Not really. Though I guessed it was because I overheard something Conchita said at the time. But I didn't know it was Clementina.'

'And you didn't connect the two things? You didn't think Papa might want rid of Clementina because she is our illegitimate sister?'

'No, why should I? It all happened years ago. You forget that I am older than you, Hugo. I was there when the scandal unfolded and I was old enough to understand what was going on. You were barely five years old and much too involved in your own little world to take any notice of the arguments of the grown-ups. Anyway neither you nor I ever saw her; when the baby was due to be born we were both packed off to our grandparents and when we came home again everything was back to normal. Nobody ever spoke of it again.'

Hugo does not believe his brother. Surely he isn't that stupid? 'So when did you realise who she was?'

'It was when Papa kept going on about his reputation being at stake. I remembering hearing him saying the exact same thing when he found out about the baby.

'How could he do that to Mama? I know Papa can be a selfish bastard at times, but to humiliate Mama like that, it's unforgivable. Why have the mother give birth in the house at all?' He pauses. Something does not make sense.

'You stupid son of a bitch, Hugo. Even you cannot be so naive. Papa is not to blame. It's that scoundrel Vano. He and Mama had an affair. She was even talking about leaving Papa and running away with him. Can you imagine that? Mama living with a gypsy.' Felipe spits some blood on the floor and then wipes his nose with his sleeve.

Hugo cannot speak. He wants to pinch himself to see if he is awake. This has to be a dream. No, not a dream, a nightmare.

His mother was in love with Vano. She bore his child and that child is Clementina. No, he cannot believe it. It is a lie that Papa has made up to cover his own weakness. 'If that is true, and I can't believe for one minute that it is, why didn't Clementina stay here with her mother? Why did Vano take her to live with him?'

'Think about it for a minute. The scandal. The humiliation. Papa's reputation. He was not going to let that happen. He could not let his wife leave with Vano. All he wanted to do was to hush it up, and all they wanted to do was to tell the world how much they were in love. And of course, under the law, Clementina was by rights Papa's child; he was the husband of the mother. The biological father had no rights to the baby and neither did the mother. And divorce was both unthinkable and illegal. Even Mama knew that; she was torn between her lover and her love of the Church. Even so, she refused point blank to let the Church take the baby and put it in an orphanage. So, in the end they came to a private agreement, the child's father would take her and bring her up and in return he would tell no-one that Mama was its mother. Also, he would promise never to see Mama again.'

'And you didn't know it was Vano?'

'Not then. As far as I was concerned it was just a gypsy.'

'And what about his own wife? Did she have to take care of the baby?'

'I suppose so. As I said, I never realised that the baby that was born in our house was Vano's until one day I heard Papa arguing with him. The gypsy had come to the bodega to see Papa; he had brought him a new horse, which was unusual in itself as he never visited the bodega in person, only ever sent his sons. It seems that Mama had asked our father if she could pay for her daughter to go away to a boarding school for girls, so she that could get an education. She said she would pretend that she was an orphan that she wanted to help.'

'What did Papa say to that?'

'He refused pointblank. Even though it was Mama's own money he wouldn't let her spend it on the girl. He said it would be like throwing pearls before swine. She must have told Vano what he had said because I heard the gypsy threaten him. He said if he didn't let Isabel provide for her own daughter's future then he would tell everyone what had happened.'

'But that would have ruined Mama's reputation. She would have been labelled a whore and excluded from society. Surely, if he loved her, he would not have done that to her?'

'I don't think Mama cared about her reputation, but Papa certainly did. Vano knew what he was doing. He made Papa promise to set up an inheritance for the girl, so that when she was twenty-one she would have some money to do what she wanted, and in return he would maintain their secret. And it would have remained a secret if you had not become smitten by Clementina.'

'And Adriana?'

'No, Adriana knew nothing. She was away at school most of the time, or else staying with grandma.

'So that is why Vano has had a free rein with the horses all these years. Papa wanted him to stay here where he could keep an eye on him.'

'Yes, and he wanted to keep Mama happy. But then you started sniffing around Clementina and he couldn't risk everything coming out, so he told me to get rid of her.'

'Papa said that?' Hugo stares at his brother. 'And you agreed?'

'You know Papa; one doesn't disagree with him. I had no choice.'

'But he didn't tell you to rape her, your own sister? Surely not.'

'Hugo, that was never my intention. I've explained already that I did not realise that Clementina was our sister. Believe me, I would never rape anyone. I am happily married. I was just trying to frighten her so that she would stay away from you.'

'Well you succeeded in that.'

'Look I'm really sorry; it just got out of hand and then that bloke turned up and attacked me. Papa had no choice but to get rid of them all.'

Hugo wanders over to the window and looks outside. He can see the rows and rows of cropped grape vines. Come the spring, green shoots will grow and a new crop will flourish; it will all look so pure and fresh yet what intrigue, what selfishness, what cruelty has lain behind that rural scene. He turns back to his brother. 'So what do we do now?'

'What can you do? They've gone. Who knows where they are by now. And they are unlikely to come back. So Papa has his wish.'

'Revenge, more like.' He almost adds that Clementina is still here but stops himself in time. It will be safer for her if his family believe she has left with the other gypsies. 'What does Mama have to say about all this? Does she even know what has happened?'

Felipe shrugs his shoulders. 'Probably not. I doubt if she cares anymore. She seems happy enough with her new role setting up the local branch of the *Sección Femenina*; I doubt if she would want her past to come out now. It wouldn't look good, would it?'

'I suppose not.' He cannot help wondering what his mother really feels about this. Powerless to do anything else, she let her husband dictate what should happen to her and her child. Forbidden to see her daughter ever again, did she wonder what her life was like, if the child was happy, if Vano's wife looked after her. Did she long for Vano in the same way Hugo has longed for Clementina? He will never know the answers to these questions because he will never ask them of her. She has suffered enough. Her decision was made fifteen years ago. He loves his mother and he does not want to blame her.

'What the hell is going on here?' Don Luis stands in the doorway, his face red with anger. 'Enrique told me you were here, Hugo and said you were arguing with your brother. I didn't realise you had resorted to a fist fight.'

'It's nothing, Papa,' says Felipe. 'Nothing to concern you.' The blood is still dripping from his nose and he tries to wipe it away.

'Here, take this, boy, and try to clean yourself up.' He turns to Hugo. 'Well, what have you got to say for yourself, young man?'

Hugo laughs. 'I think the question is, what do you have to say for yourself, Papa. It's *you* who has some explaining to do.'

'What the devil are you talking about?'

'Let's start with Clementina. When were you going to tell me that she was our illegitimate sister?'

Don Luis stares first at him then at Felipe. 'You were supposed to keep that information to yourself, Felipe. Can't I trust you with anything.'

'Felipe didn't tell me, Papa. Although I was surprised that he knew all about it and I didn't. I would have thought that all the family should have been told.'

'And what good would that have done? You couldn't keep a secret if you tried. At least your brother hasn't blabbed about it.'

Hugo can feel his anger growing, but he is determined not to rise to his father's taunts. 'What I don't understand is why you had the Guardia Civil run them out of their homes and then burn everything they owned so that they can't return. What does that achieve? Or is it the revenge that has been smouldering inside you all these years? It must have hurt your pride when your wife preferred a common gypsy to you, a leading figure of the community. You couldn't stand for anyone to know, could you. So Mama had to abandon her child and live a lie.'

'She got what she wanted. I set up the inheritance for her bastard. But I could see it wasn't going to be enough. That girl is the spitting image of your mother when she was young. I couldn't have you hanging around her, but you wouldn't listen, would you. If you had just kept away then none of this would have happened.'

'So, it's my fault? Is that what you are saying? If I had known she was my half-sister then I would have behaved differently. Can't you see that?'

Don Luis snorted with derision. 'Really, Hugo? I don't think so. Yes, you would have realised that you couldn't marry her, but you would have wanted to get to know her better, to introduce your beautiful sister to your friends, you would have had no qualms about people knowing who she is. I couldn't have that, especially now when I am standing for mayor.'

'And there we have it. It has nothing to do with Mama's reputation or Clementina's well being; it is all to do with your image. A cuckolded husband would not be a good example as mayor, especially nowadays. The Falange party would want nothing to do with you, would they. All this emphasis on happy families and there you are, a man whose wife cheated on him with a gypsy horse trader.'

'How dare you speak to me like that.' Don Luis's face is even redder by now. He looks as though he will explode with rage. 'The sooner you get married and settle down the better. Then you might understand how the real world works and drop this sentimental posturing that you have adopted.'

Hugo knows he will get nothing more from his father and nor does he need it. He has a clear picture of his family now, and it is not pleasant. 'I think I understand now, Felipe,' he says. 'Sorry about the nose.'

CHAPTER 26

Don Luis turns his back on Hugo and waits until he hears the door slam shut. What a mess. After all these years their secret is about to come out, right at the moment when his opponents will be looking for any little bit of scandal with which to discredit him. What a gift this is going to be for them. A cuckold, Hugo called him. A cuckold. The disgrace of it all. He will have to back out of the election now. What other option does he have; if he remains a candidate the opposition will be raking through his past looking for anything they can use to smear his name. He is surprised that they have not found out about Clementina already.

'This is all your fault,' he shouts at Felipe who has returned to his desk and is staring blankly at the papers in front of him. 'Why did you have to attack the girl?'

Felipe looks at his father and sighs. 'Can nothing please you, Papa? You told me to get rid of her and that's what I was trying to do. Wouldn't it have been easier if you had explained to Hugo why you didn't want him hanging around her. And then, to make it worse, you sent in the Guardia Civil and now everyone is wondering why the gypsies were kicked out of Doñana. Lots of your political supporters used to buy their horses from Vano; they are not going to be very happy when they find out that you got rid of him.'

'I don't care what they think. It's none of their damned business.'

'When you are in politics everything is everyone's business, Papa.'

'And when did you become so knowledgeable about politics?' Don Luis sneers. He knows it has all gone wrong and that his son is right; it is his own fault. He could have handled Hugo better. After all his son would never want to hurt his mother, no matter what she has done; her secret is safe with him.

'Get me the secretary of the Falange party on the phone,' he snaps.

'Very well. Why do you want to speak to him?' asks Felipe.

'To tell him it's over. I'm dropping out.'

'Isn't it a bit late in the day for that? The election is next week. How will they get another candidate in time?'

'I don't care about that. Just get him on the bloody phone.'

'And Mama? Do you want her to resign from the *Sección Femenina* as well?'

'*Mierda*. Why the hell did I agree to let her join it. I must have been mad.'

'Well?'

'Just leave it for the moment. I need to think this through more carefully or I might make the situation even worse.'

'Exactly. How about a heart attack?'

'What? Who has had a heart attack? What are you talking about?'

'You. Nobody can condemn you if you resign from the campaign because of your health. You can say that the strain of campaigning has brought on heart problems. I'm sure Doctor Cabello will back you up; you have been friends for a long time.'

'Yes, and also he knows about Clementina, so he will understand.' He smiles at his son; he is not so stupid after all. 'Ask him to come round to see me this evening, at the house.'

'All right, Papa. Then you can ring the Secretary of the Party tomorrow. Tell him that you are prepared to take on a lighter role within the Party but your doctor has advised that you drop out of the campaign.'

'You should think about going into politics, my boy. You have the right sort of devious mind. Just like your old man.' He laughs. 'Yes. I will do as you say.' Don Luis takes a cigar from his pocket and twirls it in his fingers, savouring the smell of the tobacco. 'I'm going for a walk in the gardens, if you need me,' he tells Felipe.

It looks as though it will rain today, and right on time. Most of the winter work in the vineyard is complete, all they need now is the February rains and they can sit back for a while and wait for the new growth. Then, when the rains finish, Felipe can get the men to level the ridges of the *asperpia* so that the rain-water remains trapped in the soil. He nips the end off the cigar, puts it in his mouth and lights it. It is one of a box of Cuban ci-gars that Benito gave him as a Christmas present on the day of the Three Kings; he gives him cigars every year. Thinking of Benito reminds him that he ought to speak to him about Cle-mentina; it was he who set up the inheritance for her, so maybe now the lawyer can find a way for Don Luis to revoke it. He does not see the point in putting aside money for the girl now that she has disappeared. It was a stupid idea, anyway; her fat-her would most certainly have got his hands on it and she would have received nothing.

He wanders through his wife's flower garden, thinking about when he discovered that his wife was pregnant again. At first he had been delighted, if a little surprised because Isabel had not expressed an interest in having any more children; she always maintained that two boys and a girl were sufficient for anyone. If the baby was a daughter Don Luis had the perfect husband in mind for her, the young son of one of his hunting friends, a man with very good business connections, and if it was a son, then even better, another man to take over the business. Three sons, he had liked the sound of that. But then, after a few months, he noticed that his wife was becoming more and more depressed and one evening, after the children had gone to bed and they were sitting on the terrace drinking a glass of brandy before going to bed, she had turned to him and told him that she was leaving him. Then it had all tumbled out, Vano, the bastard she was carrying in her belly, the new life she wanted; she talked of love and feeling stifled in the bodega, while he sat there, sipping his brandy and unable to understand what was happening to his marriage.

'Papa, there's a phone call for you,' calls Felipe. 'It's Don Manuel.'

Mierda, he is probably ringing to talk about finalising the alliance between Hugo and Mari Carmen. Well, he cannot speak to him right now and he does not want him talking to his son; in Hugo's frame of mind, who knows what he will say. 'Tell him I will call him back,' he shouts.

His cigar has gone out, so he strikes another match and attempts to relight it. His hand is shaking, but the familiar routine calms him a little and he soon begins to puff contentedly, blowing the smoke into the air and watching it curl into rings.

In the end, he and Isabel had come to an agreement. Her words had wounded him, but if he was honest it was mostly his pride that was hurt. Theirs had never been a marriage of love and certainly not passion; she was a beautiful woman and came from a very wealthy family. He smiles as he thinks back to when his father had announced the betrothal. He was the envy of all his friends when he told them that he was to be married to a wealthy heiress; he remembers the celebrations and banter, and the lavish wedding that his father-in-law had paid for. No, he had had no intention of allowing Isabel to leave him and bring disgrace on the family. To be fair to his wife, she had agreed to most of his stipulations, even letting the child go to live with her gypsy father—although that had been a compromise; he would have preferred to have left the child at a convent, anonymously. If he had done that they would not be in this mess now. However, that was when Isabel had turned on him, saying if the baby could not have its mother, at least it would have its father and she would pay to support it. Well he has paid out enough money to those bloody gypsies. Now it is going to stop.

The next morning, at breakfast, he tells Isabel that he is going to Seville.

'Again? Something to do with the election?' she asks, pouring some olive oil on her bread.

'Sort of, yes. And I may pop in to see Benito while I'm there. I haven't thanked him for those excellent cigars he sent me for the Three Kings.'

'Wonderful idea. I'll come with you. I need to buy some things and I want to withdraw some money from the bank; you can arrange that for me, can't you my dear?' His wife smiles at him.

Although she does not know anything about the scandal that is simmering beneath the tranquility of her present life, she seems to be different. For a moment he wonders why he didn't just let her leave with her lover when she told him about the baby. Why he didn't face the consequences then and there. After all, he was not the one to blame; she was the adulteress and it was her bastard child. He should have braved the storm; once she had left him, it would soon have been forgotten. He could have employed a nanny to look after the youngest child and the others were at boarding school anyway. It was a huge mistake to cover it up and if it comes out now it will be more of a scandal for having been a secret all these years; he will no longer be able to adopt the role of a betrayed husband.

'Well?' she asks. 'I can be ready in half an hour if you are in a hurry.'

'Of course you can come. We will have lunch if you would like to, when you have finished your shopping of course.' He pulls out his cheque book and removes a cheque from it which he then signs with a flourish. 'Here, take that to the bank. It should cover what you need.'

He knows the real reason why he would not allow her to leave that day, money. Her father, God rest his soul, had given him the money to set up the business; Don Luis had already had his eye on a rundown bodega owned by Harold Butler, an elderly Englishman with poor health and no-one to inherit his business. Isabel's father had been more than happy to invest in his son-in-law's new venture and Don Luis had been delighted to accept. Since then he has had control of his wife's money and does not intend to relinquish it any time soon.

'Hugo, I didn't see you at dinner last night,' Isabel says, raising her face so that her son can kiss her. 'Is everything all right?'

'Everything is fine, Mama. I went over to the Almudanza residence last night to see Mari Carmen. They kindly invited me to stay for dinner. You were in bed when I got back.' He sits down opposite Don Luis. 'We have decided to have the wedding this summer,' he says, ignoring his father and looking straight at his mother.

'Oh, *Cariño*, that is wonderful. Isn't that good news, Felipe.' She beams at her husband. 'This summer. My goodness we are going to have a lot to organise between now and then. Thank goodness I am going to Seville with you today, my dear. I will have to start looking for a suitable dress.'

'What about the one you wore to Felipe's wedding? You looked lovely in that,' says her husband.

'That was five years ago. Fashions have changed. No, I want to wear something smart for Hugo's wedding.' She leans across and grabs Hugo's hand. 'I am so happy for you, *Cariño*.'

'Yes, congratulations, my boy. It's a good match.'

'For whom? Me and Mari Carmen or the businesses?'

'Both.'

'So you're going to Seville, Papa?' Hugo asks. 'To see Benito?'

'Not really. I may pop in as I will be there anyway. Mostly election business. Anything you want me to take for Cristóbal?' he adds.

'Ah, the election.'

Don Luis is tempted to tell him that the doctor has advised him to withdraw from the election, but decides that it can wait. 'Isabel, if you want to come with me, you should be getting ready.'

'Of course. I will be right down.' His wife almost bounces out of the room, she is so happy about the wedding. He is pleased too that Hugo has at last agreed to marry Mari Carmen, but until the ring is on her finger he will not believe it. He knows that there is still a great deal of anger simmering inside his youngest son.

Diego brings the car around to the front door at exactly ten o'clock. Don Luis has arranged to see Benito at twelve, which should be ample time to get there.

'I hope there are no more demonstrations, this time,' says Isabel. 'It was quite disconcerting last time; I felt very frightened at one point.'

'No, I think you will find the city much quieter today,' says Diego.

Don Luis thinks about how he will approach Benito; although they have been friends for some years he knows that Benito takes his duty to the law very seriously. If he thinks it is illegal to close the account set up for Clementina, he will not be persuaded by friendship. Perhaps when he tells him that the doctor wants him to step down from the election campaign he will be more sympathetic.

He climbs the stairs to the lawyer's office and rings the bell. He can feel his heart pounding in his chest; perhaps the doctor was not lying after all. Perhaps there is something wrong with his heart. Maybe he should think about cutting back on his nightly glass of brandy.

'Don Luis, come in. It's a pleasure to see you. You look a bit weary; let me get you something to revive you.'

Don Luis is about to refuse, but changes his mind. Another glass is not going to make any difference to his health and it might just make him feel better. 'Thank you, Benito. A small brandy would be nice.'

The two men sit in the armchairs by the window, drinking their brandy in silence for a while. Then Benito says, 'You didn't say why you were coming today, Don Luis. Is there a problem or is this just a social visit?'

'A bit of both, my friend. Isabel wanted to come to Seville to buy a new outfit for Hugo's wedding and I have a couple of things I want your advice on.'

'Hugo's getting married? That's sudden isn't it?'

'Yes, he's at last seen sense and agreed to marry Don Manuel's daughter.'

'Ah, the lovely Mari Carmen. That's good news. An alliance of two excellent bodegas. You must be pleased.'

'I am.' Don Luis sips the brandy; he does not know how to begin. 'My doctor came to see me last night.'

'Your doctor? Goodness me. Are you unwell?'

'Just a bit of a heart problem. Nothing really to worry about but he says if I continue with the campaign I may have another heart attack.'

'Another heart attack? You have had one already? You never said anything.'

'Well, I didn't want everyone to know. You know how people react if they find out you have a slight problem with your heart, they start treating you as though you are about to collapse and die. I didn't want that. But now it seems that I must withdraw from the election, so everyone will have to know.'

'Oh, my dear fellow, it's far better for you to retire gracefully than to continue and damage your health. Everyone will understand.'

'Or drop dead outside the polling booth. I don't think the Party would appreciate that. Especially if I had just won.' He laughs bitterly.

Well, I must say, you seem remarkably calm about it all. So have you told the election committee that you cannot continue?'

'That's what I wanted to talk to you about. Is that what you think I should do, withdraw?'

'If your doctor says it's a risk, then most definitely.' The lawyer pauses for a moment. 'Isn't the election next week?'

'Yes. I should resign today then at least that will give them a few days to find someone else.'

'Arrange to see the secretary today, while you're here. Let me make an appointment for you. I have their number.'

'Thank you, Don Benito.'

'Just stay there; I'll be back in a minute. Oh, and I don't think that brandy is any good for you.' The lawyer removes the glass from Don Luis's hand. 'I'll be right back.'

So, this is it. The die has been cast. No more chances to become mayor but at least he will retain his dignity. He sits looking out of the window; the rain has stopped and the clouds are clearing. A short sharp pain stabs at his chest; he winces and his hand automatically goes to relieve it.

'Are you all right?' asks Benito, who has just returned. 'Are you in pain? Do you want me to call my doctor? His surgery is just around the corner.'

'No, I'm fine.' Goodness, is this what he has to look forward to, people watching his every move in case he is going to have a heart attack. He knows Benito is just being a considerate friend, but it is irritating. 'Please don't fuss.'

'Well, if you are sure. I rang the Secretary and you have an appointment for three o'clock. I didn't mention what it was about, but I think he was surprised that I was ringing him.'

'Thank you. I'll explain that I just happened to be visiting you on other business, which in fact is true.'

'I see. What is it?'

'Do you remember that about fifteen years ago I asked you to set up an inheritance for a young girl?'

'Yes, a Clementina Rodriguez, mother unknown. What do you want to know about it?'

'I want to close it, eradicate it. I want it never to have existed. Is that possible?'

'In theory I suppose it is. I will have to look at the papers carefully. May I ask why? Has something happened to the young woman in question?'

'No, you may not ask why. I just want you to do it.' His tone hardens. 'It is no longer applicable.'

'Very well. If you don't mind waiting, Señor Rodriguez, I will find the documents and look through them. It may take a few minutes. In the meantime, can I offer you anything? A glass of water?'

'No, thank you.' He can see he has offended him but so what. He may be his lawyer but he does not need to know everything about his life.

In fact Don Luis does not have to wait very long before Benito returns carrying a slim manilla folder. 'This is all the information I have. I do remember that I had to go to your bank to set it up. And your wife had to countersign it.'

'Let me see.' Now he remembers. Isabel's father had left a stipulation in his will that her inheritance could not be spent by her husband without her agreement. This was contrary to normal practice but his father-in-law knew that the laws were in a state of flux. In 1931 the Second Republic had given new freedoms to women in terms of what they were allowed to do, divorce was allowed and women could have control of their own money, but after only two years the new government began to rescind some of these new laws. Isabel's father realised that in such an uncertain economic state, his daughter could be in danger of losing her inheritance, money that his family had worked hard for and he definitely did not want it to go to anyone other than his daughter. He wanted to make sure that Isabel, who was his only child, would never be left penniless and so he had made a stipulation in his will that although her husband, Don Luis would have access to her inheritance, all withdrawals over a certain sum had to be counter-signed by Isabel. It had never been a problem until Clementina was born; then Don Luis saw another side to his acquiescent wife. Illegitimate or not, her daughter was not going to be penniless; her father would not have wanted it.

'So you see, we need your wife to accompany us to the bank to sign it,' adds Benito, who is looking very uncomfortable.

'Oh, I'm sure that's not necessary. My wife's head is full of thoughts of the wedding; she won't want to be bothered by this little matter.'

'Mmn. This little matter amounts to over ten thousand pesetas.'

'What?'

'The bank have been investing it wisely. The young lady will have a very comfortable inheritance when she reaches twenty-one.'

'Even so, do we really need to bother my wife about his? Surely you and I can go along to the bank and sort this out together.'

Benito looks even more uncomfortable. 'I'm sorry, Don Luis. I would lose my licence if I did that, and the bank would never agree anyway. Why don't you speak to your wife when she is less busy and then come back to me and the three of us can go to the bank together.'

Don Luis realises he is getting nowhere with the lawyer, so he gets up, retrieves his hat and umbrella, and says. 'I am disappointed in you Don Benito. Very disappointed. Maybe it is time for me to look around for another lawyer.'

'I am sorry you feel like that, *Señor*, but any other lawyer will tell you the same thing; to close that account, your wife's written permission is required.'

If Don Benito is saying anything else, Don Luis does not hear it; he is already halfway down the stairs and he is fuming.

CHAPTER 27

Hugo is toying with the idea of going to Seville to see Cristóbal, but now that he knows his parents are there, he decides to telephone him instead. He waits until his father's Daimler leaves for Seville and goes into the lounge and rings the number of his friend's house.

'Buenos días,' he says when their maid answers. 'Is Don Cristóbal at home?'

'Si, Señor. Who would like to speak to him?'

'Don Hugo Rodriguez.'

'One moment, please.'

He hears a scurrying in the background and a whispered conversation and then his friend comes on the line and says, 'Hugo? You're back in Spain then. How did you know I'd be at home?'

'Where else would you be?'

'I'm supposed to be at the university. I have my exams next week. Papa says I'm more likely to study here than at the university.'

Hugo smiles. It will be a miracle if Cristóbal passes his exams; he never seems to attend any classes.

'What is it? Is something wrong? Don't tell me you've got yourself involved with some other little filly?'

'I'll have you know that you are talking to a betrothed man. Mari Carmen and I have set the date and we want you to be there to witness it.'

'What, you're getting married? Well, that's good news, if a bit surprising.'

'It was always a possibility.'

'So I suppose I will need to get a new tie? I take it you will want me to sell bits of my tie to raise money for your wedding celebrations?' He laughs.

'You have hundreds of ties; you won't miss one. And yes, Mari Carmen wants us to have all the traditions. You are my best friend, after all. It can't go ahead without you.'

'I will be delighted to sacrifice a tie for you, my friend. So when will this great event take place?'

'Some time in the summer. Her parents will be sending out the invitations next month.'

'And what of the beautiful Clementina? I thought she was the one you wanted to marry, unlikely as it was.'

'Well I discovered something that made that even more impossible than we thought. Turns out she's my sister.'

'What do you mean? How can she be your sister, she's a *gitano*?'

Hugo begins to tell him all that has happened since he got back from England. As he listens to himself recounting how Clementina had been attacked and the gypsy encampment burnt to the ground, he still cannot believe it is all true; it is more like a Hollywood film. When he finishes, he says, 'You mustn't tell anyone about this, Cristóbal. We have to keep it a secret. It won't do anybody any good if it comes out and it could do a lot of harm to the people I love.'

'But, Felipe. How could he do that? I know he likes to play the hard man, but it sounds as though he went too far that time.'

'I know. My father told him to get rid of her and Felipe always does what Papa says; you know that.'

'Still, that's taking filial duty a bit far, isn't it?'

'Look, I want to see her. I need to know she doesn't hate me. What should I do, Cristóbal?'

'Look Hugo, my advice would be to keep well clear of her and her family, but I know you won't do that. Do you even know where she is?'

'I think she's still in Doñana; I met the man who saved her and he told me that she refused to leave with the rest of her family, so I think I will start there.'

'Do you want me to come and help you?'

'No, you should be studying. I don't want your father blaming me when you fail your exams.'

'Can I tell him about the wedding?'

'Of course. That at least is not a secret.'

'Take care of yourself, my friend and give my congratulations to your bride-to-be.'

Hugo replaces the telephone and stands looking at the sparrows pecking at the bread that Conchita has strewn on the grass for them. If only life could be that simple. He is still very angry with his father and disappointed with his mother; she has done the unforgivable, betrayed her husband and broken her vows. Does she regret her actions now? He would like to speak to her about it, but how can he. No, he must put that idea out of his head. He has a half-sister he can never acknowledge and a brother who tried to rape her. His mother is an adulteress and his father is more concerned about his reputation than his family. He knows he cannot change the past but at least he can build a different life for himself with Mari Carmen.

Well, if he is going to look for Clementina, he might as well start now. He puts on his jacket and heads for the stables.

'Pablo, saddle up Beauty for me. I'm going over to Doñana.'

'It's a bit late in the day to go hunting,' the groom comments as he lifts the heavy saddle onto the mare's back.

'I just need some exercise,' Hugo replies. 'There's been too much work and no play lately. What I need is a good long ride.'

'The gypsies have gone now, *Señor*.'

Hugo looks at him in surprise. Does everyone know what is on his mind? Has he been that transparent?'

Vano leads his horse back towards the clearing which once was his home. Already the grass is growing over the ashes of their old house; soon there will be no sign that they were ever there. It pains him to see their lives obliterated in this way, their history rubbed out as though they have never existed. At least the rest of his family is safely out of harm's way; the long arm of the Guardia Civil does not reach into neighbouring Portugal. He sits down on a pine log and tries to decide what to do next. Rage and the need for revenge have driven him here but now that he has arrived he is not sure how to proceed. If he goes to the bodega they will send for the Guardia Civil and have him arrested before he can even get to see Hugo. Perhaps he could try to lure him to the marshes by sending a message to say that Clementina is waiting for him. In normal circumstances he would have sent Álvaro, but his son is far away. Patience is what he needs. There is no hurry. He knows Hugo will come looking for Clementina one day and when he does Vano will be waiting. He moves deeper into the woods and chooses a spot to lie down; he is tired from the long journey. He tethers the mare to a tree and makes himself comfortable on a bed of pine needles. Later he will build himself a shelter from some dead branches and go and ask the *carboneros* if they know where Clementina went. With luck she will still be with them.

He is woken by the mare nuzzling his back; something has disturbed her. He gets up and strokes her nose, whispering in her ear until she calms down and becomes still, then he crawls through the undergrowth until he can see into the clearing. Someone is there. He recognises the horse at once, it is the Retuerta that he sold to Hugo; that is what the mare was trying to tell him, she has caught the scent of the Retuerta. He picks up a dead branch and silently gets to his feet. As quiet and as deadly as a lynx, he creeps up behind Hugo. The Retuerta begins to paw the ground anxiously and as Hugo moves forward to pacify her, Vano strikes him across the head. He falls to the ground like a stone. For a moment Vano thinks he has killed him, which would not be good because he is Isabel's son and he would never want to hurt any child of hers, but he does want to punish him. He walks back to the mare and unhooks a length of rope from the saddle. He will frighten him just as he frighted Clementina. There is a groan from the body stretched out on the floor; it sounds as though Hugo is waking up. Quickly Vano winds the rope around his wrists, tying them behind his back then pulls him into a sitting position.

'*Mierda*, what was that?' Hugo mumbles. He opens his eyes and stares at the gypsy. 'Vano? What's happened?' He pulls at his wrists but they are securely tied and do not move. 'Untie me, man. How on earth did this happen? Come on, untie me.'

'Not yet, *Señor*. Not until you tell me why you attacked my daughter. Although I think I know the reason—she spurned your advances and you thought you would force her—but I want to hear you say it.'

'Vano, what's going on? It's me, Hugo. I haven't done anything to Clementina. Why would I? She's my friend.'

'Yes, but you wanted more, didn't you.' Vano hauls at the rope which he has slung over the branch of a tree, until Hugo's feet are clear of the ground. The young man hangs there, wriggling like a worm on a hook.

'Let me down; it bloody well hurts. Do you hear me, Vano. Let me down. You won't get away with this you know. My father will make sure you get punished.'

'Oh, I'm sure he will. What father wouldn't want to punish someone who attacked their child. And that's what I am doing right now.'

'Vano, I swear I did not touch her. On my mother's life, I did not hurt your daughter.'

At the mention of Isabel, Vano pauses. Maybe it was not Hugo. Admittedly he was surprised when Ramon said it was him who had attacked her; he would never have thought him capable of hurting anyone. No, he is lying. It was him. Clementina had seen her attacker clearly. She said it was Hugo and he believes her.

'Help! Someone help me,' shouts Hugo. His voice echoes through the trees and his cries bounce back as though they are mocking him.

'Oh, the poor boy is calling for help. Is that what my lovely Clementina did? Did she call for help? Did she ask you to stop? Did she beg you to let her go?' Vano takes the scarf from around his neck and ties a knot in it. 'You heartless bastard, you would have raped my daughter if that *payo* hadn't come along.' He lowers Hugo to the ground then goes behind him and stuffs the knotted scarf into his mouth.

'No, please Vano...' Vano pulls the scarf tight and silences Hugo, then hauls him up once again so that his feet are dangling free. 'No more talking. You need time to think about your actions and now you have it. You may be rich and well educated but that does not give you the right to treat my daughter like scum.

CHAPTER 28

Ramon has not slept; he has been thinking about it all night. Even though it is always there at the back of his mind he really cannot believe it will actually happen. In two days time his brother is to be shot; the Guardia Civil have posted notices about it everywhere. Jaime has sent Kiko to look for him and warn him; Ramon's name is everywhere. But this is not just a warning for Ramon; it is a warning to everyone. The message is plain: aiding and abetting in the murder of a police officer is as bad as actually committing the murder. There can be no plea for clemency for either of them; the Guardia Civil have made that very clear. Now he has no option; he must go and hand himself in before the sentence is executed. He cannot desert his brother even if it means losing Clementina and betraying his principles. If only he could be sure that they would release Pedro in exchange for him; the old man's chilling words still linger in his mind. *'One brother is as good as another.'*

He gathers together his few possessions and puts them into a bag. There is no point in Clementina going with him; it will only undermine his resolve and who knows what might happen to her in Seville. He plans to leave as early as possible but he has to tell her first; he wants her to know that it is not easy for him to abandon her. He wants her to understand and to promise to go back to her family.

Cautiously he approaches the clearing where the *carboneros* live. He can see Kiko stretched out on the ground beside a smouldering *boliche*. The boy is awake and when he sees Ramon he immediately gets up and comes over to him.

'You shouldn't be here,' he whispers and looks around to make sure no-one is watching. 'You will put us all in danger.' Ramon knows he is repeating his father's words.

'Don't worry; I'm not staying. I just want you to know that I am going to hand myself in to the police. I cannot stand by and watch them murder my brother for something he did not do. I want you to tell your father.' He grabs Kiko's hand and adds, 'Clementina? Is she still here?'

'Yes. Somewhere. I saw her heading into the woods earlier.'

'Thank your father for all he has done for me,' Ramon adds, and turns away and disappears amongst the trees before anyone else notices him.

Now he must tell Clementina what he plans to do; she will not like it but he cannot take her with him. She must find her family and go back to them.

As he makes his way through the trees he can hear the sound of voices; they are coming from the old gypsy encampment. A woman is shouting and he immediately recognises her voice; it is Clementina and she sounds frightened. Has that bastard come looking for her again? His heart pounding, he starts to run towards the clearing.

Vano cannot believe his eyes. There she is, his lovely daughter running out of the woods towards him, her eyes blazing, screaming at him, trying to defend this monster who attacked her. For years he has tried to ignore it but recent events have reminded him of how much she resembles her mother; she is bold and brave and capable of defending those she loves from the whole world. For a moment he is transported back fifteen years to when Clementina was a baby.

'Papa. What are you doing?' His daughter runs up to him and grabs the rope. 'Let him down. Papa. Let him down. You're hurting him. Why are you doing this? What's the matter with you? It wasn't Hugo's fault the Guardia Civil burnt down your homes. Not all *payos* are bad, you know. Untie his hands, right now.' She continues to scream at him as she tugs at his arm.

At last Vano lets go of the rope and lowers Hugo to the ground.

'Untie him,' she says, trying to pull the gag out of his mouth.

Slowly Vano takes out a knife and saws through the rope binding Hugo's wrists together. 'But you said Hugo attacked you, child. I was just trying to get him to admit it.'

'No, Papa. He didn't attack me; it was his brother, Felipe. Hugo would never hurt me. He loves me.' She goes across to Hugo and hugs him. 'Are you all right?'

'I'll survive.' He rubs his wrists. 'What about you?'

Vano is staring at them. Although Hugo has brown hair and his skin is fairer than Clementina, he can see how alike they are. They both have Isabel's eyes, the colour of the sky on a cloudless day. His heart begins to ache when he remembers those days, both wonderful and agonising, and how much he had loved her. Then later, when he had taken the baby home, how everyone had remarked on the unusual colour of the baby's eyes but then said no more. If anyone thought the child had *payo* blood they never spoke of it and certainly not his wife. 'My apologies, Señor Hugo,' he reluctantly says.

'Think nothing of it,' Hugo mutters, still rubbing his wrists but unable to take his eyes from his half-sister. 'Do you mind if I speak to Clementina for a few minutes, Vano? Alone.'

Vano grunts his assent and moves out of earshot but still remains where he can see them. So he was wrong about Hugo

276

after all, but that does not mean that now he trusts him; he is still Don Luis's son.

Ramon approaches the clearing stealthily; the shouting has stopped but he can still hear voices. He hesitates, scanning the area beyond the trees. He can see Vano holding the bridle of a horse and watching his daughter who is deep in conversation with Hugo. All seems to be calm. Whatever has been happening is now over. He steps from behind the tree and calls out, 'Clementina. Are you all right?'

The girl spins round and a smile spreads across her face. 'Ramon, come here. Come and greet my brother.' She is so excited she cannot stop smiling.

So Hugo has told her at last. 'So you know?' he says. Well, it is for the best. If he is to leave her, at least she will have Hugo to look out for her.

'Yes, Hugo has explained everything.'

'And you are not upset?'

'I don't know. I am still trying to get used to the idea of having two mothers.'

'Two mothers? What are you talking about?'

Clementina looks at Hugo. 'Can you tell him? I know he will keep our secret.'

Ramon looks from one to the other; what secret is she talking about?

'I told you that Clementina is my sister, but I didn't tell you everything and that was because at the time I didn't know the whole story.' Hugo begins to explain about his mother and Vano and how she refused to give the baby away for adoption, so Vano's wife had brought up Clementina as her own.

'And she will always be my mother,' interrupts Clementina. 'That will never change.' She walks over to her father and puts her arms around him. 'I am so sorry, Papa. It must have been very hard for you.'

'I had you, my child. What more could I want,' says Vano, fighting to hold back the tears.

'I am very sorry about what has happened, Vano. My father was just trying to protect his family.'

'People will do anything to defend their families,' the gypsy replies but his face is stern. It is obvious that he still considers Don Luis's actions to be completely unjustifiable.

'Why are you carrying a bag, Ramon?' Clementina asks. 'Are we leaving right now? My things are still at the *carboneros*.'

'I am leaving, *Cariño,* and I am going alone. You must go with your father. They are going to execute my brother in two days; if I do not hand myself in to the Guardia Civil as soon as possible, it will be too late. I am going there now but I could not leave without seeing you first.'

'What's that?' asks Hugo. 'Why have they arrested your brother?'

Ramon explains what had happened and how Pedro has been in prison now for months.

'Hang on. I remember hearing about that arrest; it was before I went to Bristol. The man was one of the *braceros* working for us at the time. The Guardia Civil came here looking for a man who had killed one of their officers. The *bracero* was the man's brother and they wanted him to tell them where he was.'

'It was an accident. I was part of a demonstration against the underuse of agricultural land; it was supposed to be peaceful but the Guardia charged in, beating people with their truncheons and even firing into the crowd. I just tried to get away and shoved one of them out of the way, but he stumbled and fell; he hit his head on the ground. I knew they would blame me, which is why I ran away. To be honest I didn't even know he was dead until they arrested Pedro. My poor brother is completely inno-cent of any crime. He has never been to a demonstration in his life. He doesn't even belong to any political party. I can't let him die for something that is my fault.'

'But you can't turn yourself in,' says Clementina. 'Please don't do that, Ramon. They will shoot you. You know they will. Please don't go.' She turns to Hugo. 'Can't you help him? Please. You know influential people.'

'Me? I don't think there is anything I can do. I don't know anything about the law.'

'But surely you know someone who can help Ramon's brot-her? A lawyer perhaps? What about that friend of yours, Cristó-bal?' She is pleading with him and tears are running down her face. 'They will kill him if he hands himself in.'

'They will shoot them both,' adds Vano who is following every word. His eyes have not left his daughter's face for a mo-ment.

'But Cristóbal's training to be a doctor, and he's not even qua-lified in that,' says Hugo.

'It won't do any good, anyway.' says Ramon. 'I just hope that I can get there in time to stop his execution.'

'Wait, maybe I'm wrong. Maybe Cristóbal can help us. We'll get him to speak to his father; he's a lawyer but more than that he has some very good contacts in the judiciary in Seville,' says Hugo at last.

'Do you think he will help us?' Clementina asks. She wipes her eyes with her scarf and tries to look composed.

'I don't know, but we will soon find out,' says Hugo. He turns to Ramon, 'You stay here. It is highly unlikely we can do any-thing to help you my friend; you were involved in the death of a policeman—even if it was an accident—and then you fled the scene of the crime. There's no way you can wriggle out of that.

But I don't see why we can't make a case for getting them to release your brother. And as he was one of our employees we can give him a good character reference. What is his full name?'

'Pedro Molina Moreno.'

'All right. Come on, Clementina, you come with me to the bodega. We will telephone Cristóbal and see what he can do to persuade his father to help us.' Hugo turns to Vano. 'You keep an eye on him; don't let him do anything foolish. I do not intend to spend time chasing about the countryside looking for him.'

'What will your parents say when you take Clementina to the bodega?' asks Vano. He is looking anxious.

'My parents are in Seville. They will not be back until this evening.'

'Good luck, and thank you,' says Ramon, shaking Hugo by the hand. He smiles at Clementina and adds, 'I will be waiting here, *Cariño.*'

He watches as she goes over to Vano and hugs him. She whispers something in his ear and he is surprised to see Vano surreptitiously wipe a tear from his eye.

'Do you think they will be able to do anything?' he asks Vano, as they stand in the clearing watching Hugo and Clementina ride away.

'I know nothing about the law except that it always favours the rich. If Don Hugo's rich friends decide to help your brother—although I cannot see why they would want to do so—then yes, maybe they will get him freed. All we can do is wait. And there is no point standing here where everyone can see us; follow me and we'll see if we can catch ourselves a rabbit or two. I'm feeling pretty hungry after all that excitement.'

CHAPTER 29

Clementina sits behind Hugo, her arms around his waist. She would have preferred to ride her own horse. The last time she rode like this was when she was very young; she would go out to look for her father and he would lift her onto his horse and they would ride home together. She is nervous; she worries that they might meet someone who knows Hugo and they will think it is odd that a gypsy girl is riding on the back of his horse, but she does not mention it and they ride in silence for over an hour until finally Hugo says, 'We are almost there.'

She has never been this far from home before; in fact she has never left Doñana before. On the occasions when her father would allow her to ride one of the horses, she was given strict instructions not to go far. Her favourite place to ride was along the beach; she would walk the horse through the woods until they came to the dunes and as soon as they had crossed them she would let the horse have its head and gallop along the shore. But she never admitted that to her father.

Hugo has slowed the horse to a leisurely trot and they are making their way along a long driveway between rows and rows of truncated vines. Ahead of them, in the distance is an impressive white *cortijo*. 'Is that your home?' she asks.

'Yes. We are almost there.'

'What will your father say when he sees me?' She feels even more nervous than ever and would like to ask Hugo to turn around and take her home, but she knows she cannot do that.

She must do all she can to help Ramon's brother before it is too late.

Bumping into Hugo's father is not all that is going through her mind; she is feeling more and more confused. Even before she knew that Hugo was her brother she had no illusions about their relationship; they were friends before and she hopes they will always be friends but she was not in love with him. Finding out now that he is her brother is even better because that link between them will never be broken. Nobody in her family has ever spoken about being in love, not even Zita. When her sister knew she was getting married she was happy, excited, giddy even but she never said she loved her betrothed. She remembers the day she asked her mother if she had ever been in love and she had stared at her as if she had said something awful. Is love so bad that no-one will speak of it? Is it because her father had fallen in love with Hugo's mother—her mother—that nobody will say its name? At the moment there is a strange cocktail of emotions are running through her body and clouding her mind. What she feels for Hugo she can now identify as brotherly love, but what is it she feels for Ramon? He is her saviour. He saved her from disgrace and much more, but it is not because of that. She could feel herself being attracted to him before the attack had happened. Ramon makes her smile and he makes her feel safe; is that all that love is?

'You will not have to see him. He is in Seville. Mama is shopping and that will take her hours. We will have left by the time they get home.'

Hugo's words bring her back to earth. Now she tries to imagine what his mother, their mother, looks like and what it would be like to go shopping with her, but she cannot conjure up any image of her at all. The news that Isabel Gil de la Cruz is actually her mother has not really sunk in yet. Clementina wonders if it was difficult for her to give up her daughter. Had she cried when the baby was taken away? Or was it simply the most convenient thing to do at the time? She thinks about Zita's new baby, how tiny and fragile he was when he was born. Zita would never have parted with him, no matter what anyone said; she would have defended him with her life. Maybe that is what love is.

She feels Hugo move his weight backwards to stop the horse; they have arrived. A man runs out from the stables and takes the reins of the horse from Hugo.

'*Señor*, can I help you?' he asks, trying not to stare at Clementina.

'Yes, Pablo. Help the young lady get down then take Beauty to the stables; she needs a good rub down and some water. It has been a long ride for her.' He dismounts and waits while Pablo holds out his hand to Clementina.

'It's all right; I can manage,' she says then swings her legs over the horse's rump and lands beside him.

Hugo smiles at her and says, 'I had forgotten you were such a good horsewoman.'

'Tomboy, is what you used to call me.'

'That too. Come on; let's telephone Cristóbal.'

She lets him lead her into the house, trying not to gape at everything around her. The house is very large and much grander than she has imagined. An elderly woman comes bustling into the hall. 'Don Hugo, what are you doing? You shouldn't have brought her here. Your father will be furious,' she says, staring at Clementina.

Who is this woman? Is she her mother? Why is she looking at her like that? Hugo hasn't even told her Clementina's name and yet she seems to know her. Does everyone know who she is?

'Don't worry, Conchita,' Hugo tells her. 'We are not staying for long; I just need to use the telephone. Perhaps you could give Clementina a glass of water.'

He turns to her and says, 'Conchita will look after you; she's our housekeeper. Go into the kitchen with her for now. I will ring Cristóbal then come and tell you what is happening. Don't worry,' he adds. 'My father will not be back for ages.'

Fortunately when Hugo telephones, his friend is at home; for once, according to their maid, he is ensconced in his room studying. 'I will get him for you, Señor Hugo,' she says. It is Lourdes, the pretty one with plump cheeks and a sweet smile.

'Thank you, Lourdes. Tell him it's urgent. A matter of life or death, in fact. Otherwise I would not disturb him while he is studying.'

'Very well, *Señor*.'

He can imagine her smiling at that, and almost certainly she does not believe him.

'All right, Hugo, what is this matter of such importance? Life and death, you say? Could it be that you want me to go hunting with you?'

'No, for once Cristóbal I am deadly serious. I need your help and I, we, need it right now.' His friend has gone quiet. 'I want you to do your best to persuade your father to help save an innocent man's life.'

'All right. You had better tell me all about it.'

Hugo explains as much as he knows about Pedro's situation. 'His name is Pedro Molina Moreno and he is being held in a prison in Seville. I'm afraid that's all I can tell you. Oh yes, his brother's name is Ramon and he is wanted for killing an officer of the Guardia Civil.'

'Does he know where his brother is hiding?'

'No, but he thinks he might have fled to France. Apparently some time ago his brother was talking about joining the French Popular Front, some socialist type of organisation. That's all he knows.' It's not a very convincing lie but it might help.

There is a long pause while Cristóbal makes some notes then he asks, 'When was he arrested?'

'Just a minute. Let me work it out. I remember, you were staying with us at the time. We went over to Doñana the next day to see if your horse was ready to be collected. Do you remember?'

'Yes, I do. The gypsies were celebrating a christening or something.'

'That's it.'

'Bloody hell, that was months ago. He's been in prison all this time and not had a trial?'

'I don't think so. I think they just arrested him at first in an attempt to flush out his brother, but that didn't happen. He's been there ever since, waiting for his brother to hand himself in, I suppose.'

'No, well if he's in France his brother probably doesn't know what's happened to him,' says Cristóbal. 'I'll talk to my father right away.'

'Please. He's to be executed the day after tomorrow. There is not much time.'

'I'll do it now.'

'Ring me when you know anything. I owe you a big favour, Cristóbal. Thank you.'

'Don't thank me yet, my friend.' He hangs up.

Hugo knows he will do his best, but will his father agree to help them, and if he does, will he be able to convince one of the judges to stop the execution? He replaces the receiver and goes to the kitchen to find Clementina. As he opens the door he hears

Conchita saying, 'You were the prettiest little baby I had ever seen and so placid. You hardly ever cried and spent all your time gurgling and smiling. I was heart-broken when they took you away.'

'Conchita,' he snaps. She is someone who loves to gossip; it is a miracle that she managed to keep this secret from him all these years.

'Señor Hugo.' The housekeeper leaps to her feet; her cheeks are scarlet with embarrassment.

'It's all right, Hugo. It is my fault. I asked her how long she has been working here,' says Clementina, getting up and coming over to him. 'What did Cristóbal say?'

Hugo glowers at Conchita and leads Clementina into the garden, out of earshot. 'He will ring me when he has spoken to his father.'

'So what do we do now?'

'We will sit in the garden and wait.'

'But what if your parents come home while I am still here?'

He shakes his head. 'They won't. My mother will go shopping while my father talks to his old friend, Benito, then he will go to the bank and then he will meet my mother for lunch in some expensive restaurant. When they have done all that, then they will come home. It never varies. Trust me.'

'Can I get you anything, Don Hugo?' asks Conchita. She is looking very contrite. 'A little bit of ham, maybe some cheese?'

Hugo turns to Clementina, 'Are you hungry?' She nods. 'Very well, something to eat and a couple of glasses of sherry. We'll eat out here, on the terrace.' He reaches across and squeezes his sister's hand. 'Don't worry. Relax. We will be far away by the time my parents get home.' He knows it is not a good idea but he would like them to see what a beautiful woman Clementina has grown into. Especially his mother, what will go through her mind if she sees her now? He suddenly remembers what has been bothering him. 'Just a minute, Tina. I'll be right back.' Hugo hurries into the drawing room and picks up his parents' wedding photograph, a photograph in a silver frame which he has walked past almost every day of his life. Now he knows why Clementina seems so familiar; he can see it in the image of his mother when she was younger; mother and daughter are identical.

They do not have to wait long before Conchita comes hurrying out onto the terrace saying, 'Señor Hugo, the telephone. It's your friend Don Cristóbal. He says he would like to speak to you, urgently.'

Hugo leaps to his feet and brushes the crumbs from his lunch onto the floor. 'Come with me, Clementina. Let's see what he's managed to do.' His heart is racing. Despite the fact that he does not know this man Pedro, he feels a great debt towards his brother, Ramon. After all it was Ramon who saved Clementina from Felipe. Although his brother has sworn that it was never his intention to rape her, Hugo is not sure that he can believe him. He glances across at her; he can see the expectancy in her eyes. She truly believes that he is able to help her save Ramon's brother. How can he let her down? And what will become of her if Ramon decides to hand himself into the Guardia Civil? He feels more responsibility for her now that he knows she is his sister than he ever did before.

'Why are you hesitating?' she asks, watching him carefully. 'Answer it.'

His hand is trembling when he picks up the telephone. 'Cristóbal? Well?'

'It's good news. My father is looking into it; he thinks they can make a case for his release. He is a good friend of Judge

Cañuelo and has arranged to discuss it with him this afternoon. I know you may be angry with me, but I told my father about Clementina.'

'What? I told you it was a secret. Cristóbal, how could you?'

'Don't worry; my father knew already. Your mother insisted that some money be put into a bank account for her, but now Don Luis has asked my father to help him block it.'

'What a wretch he is. But what has that to do with helping Pedro to get released?' Hugo is annoyed with his friend. Why is he complicating things.

'Nothing directly; I just want you to know what your father is trying to do. Anyway, Judge Cañuelo is also a friend of your father's. If he does anything to help get Pedro released it will be to cover up for his friends, not because he believes he is innocent. Did you know the judge was one of your father's supporters in the election for a mayor? My father is just putting more pressure on him.

'I didn't. That's good.'

'Yes, he won't want any scandal to come out about your father and the men he employs, not at the moment.'

'The judge does know that he has to make a decision by tomorrow?'

'Yes, he knows that. So all we can do now is wait. If Judge Cañuelo is not able to get him released then there is no more we can do. So it's time to get down on your knees and do some praying, my friend.'

'Thank you, Cristóbal. When will we know?'

'Either this evening, or tomorrow morning.'

'So not much sleep tonight then.'

'Do you want me to ring you when I know?'

'No. We won't be here. I will ring you. You'll be at home?'

'Yes, unfortunately. Papa has threatened to lock me in until the exams are over.'

'Thank you again. You are a true friend.'

'So it's good news?' Clementina asks, watching him carefully.

'So far, so good,' he replies. 'But we may not know until tomorrow if they have succeeded in getting him released.' Her face drops in disappointment. 'Don't lose heart, *Cariño*. We are doing all we can.'

'We should go,' she says. 'I do not want to be here when your father gets back. It must be getting late now.' She points at the sun, which is moving towards the horizon.

Hugo pulls out his pocket watch. 'You're right; it's almost four o'clock. I'll go and get Pablo to saddle up the horse.' He pauses. 'You can still ride?' he asks her.

'Of course. Better than you, probably.'

'Good, you can ride your own horse then. It will be quicker. I'll get Pablo to choose you a gentle one.' He grins at her. He's enjoying having Clementina as a sister.

Hugo sets off towards the stables but as he turns towards the main drive, he sees his father's Daimler coming towards him. He is too late; he and Clementina will have to face them together.

The car grinds to a stop on the gravelly driveway and Don Luis winds down the window. 'Hugo, you're not off out again, are you? I need to talk to you.'

'All right, Papa. I just have to speak to Pablo.'

'Right now.' His father steps out of the car and stops, staring at something in the distance; he looks as though he has seen a ghost. 'What the devil?' he splutters. 'Hugo, is that who I think it is? What on earth is she doing here? Are you out of your bloody mind?' He looks around him as though he expects to see hordes of people gathering to watch his humiliation.

'Relax, Papa. No-one knows she is here. We just came to use the telephone. I will take her home now and then you will never see her again.'

The other door opens and his mother steps out of the car. 'Clementina,' she calls, ignoring Hugo and her husband and hurries towards the figure standing in the doorway of her house. 'Clementina, is that you?'

'Isabel, stop right now. Isabel, I forbid you to speak to her.' Don Luis is purple with rage. 'Isabel.'

'It's all right, Papa. Let them meet. Nothing is going to happen. Tina is leaving soon; you will never see her again. That's what you want, isn't it?' He watches as his mother hurries towards her daughter; she has gathered her skirts into her hands and is almost running now. Neither he nor his father move. They just watch as Isabel enfolds Clementina into her arms and the two women embrace.

'This is all your doing, Hugo. You just won't leave well alone. Now the whole world will know about your mother's shame and my humiliation.'

'Some people already know, Papa, but they are not people who are worried about humiliating you, nor have any intention of exposing Mama. They are people who love Tina and want her to be happy.'

'Where do they think they are going now?' Don Luis asks. He looks lost. His wife pays him no heed and neither does his son. 'Take the car to the garage,' he tells Diego. 'And not a word of this to anyone, or you will be looking for a new job.'

'What shall I do with the *señora's* shopping, *Señor*?'

'What the hell do I care what you do with it,' Don Luis barks and marches up to the house, leaving Hugo standing there trying not to look pleased with himself.

'Señor Hugo?'

'Give it to Conchita; she will know what to do with it. Thank you, Diego.' He hopes his father does not say anything he will regret. For a moment he is worried for his mother, but then he remembers the look on her face when she saw Clementina; she has never forgotten her daughter and she is not going to let her husband spoil this moment for her. He turns back to Diego. 'Just a minute. I am going to need you to take the young lady back to Doñana; it will be evening soon and I don't want her riding in the dark.'

'Very well, *Señor*.'

CHAPTER 30

Ramon watches Vano pacing up and down; he is like a caged wildcat, wary and ready to pounce. It has been dark for almost an hour now and still there is no sign of Clementina and Hugo. What on earth has happened to them?

'What's that?' says Vano, stopping in mid-stride and looking in the general direction of the small town of Rocio.

'Sounds like a car. A big one, but not a truck.'

'It's stopped.' Vano moves to the edge of the trees and peers across the lagoon to where the car has parked. The driver gets out and opens one of the passenger doors at the back of the car and waits as a young girl scrambles out.

Ramon can see her looking around nervously, but the headlights of the car are shining across the surface of the water, making it impossible to identify her. 'Who is it?' he asks. 'Is it them?'

'Who else could it be?' says Vano. 'But why are they in a car? And where is Hugo's horse?'

The man speaks briefly to the girl, gets back in the car and drives away, leaving her standing there. She looks around her as though expecting to see someone, and then begins to walk towards the woods on her own. Now that the car has turned away the headlights no longer impede their vision; they can see the girl more clearly but she is still too far away for them to be certain that it is Clementina.

'Come on,' says Vano. 'I'm sure that's my daughter.' He begins to run towards the lagoon.

'Wait, you don't know for certain,' says Ramon, hoping against hope that it is her but hanging back, dreading that it is someone else. 'Why would Hugo leave her alone, like that? Where is he? I don't think he would leave without making sure she was safe? Wait, Vano. Wait. It might be a trap.'

'It's her I tell you. I would know my Clementina anywhere,' the *gitano* replies. 'Even if I were blindfolded.'

'Then where is Hugo?'

But Vano is not listening; he skirts the edge of the wood and runs straight towards her. Ramon races after him; his heart is pounding, partly from fear and partly in the anticipation of seeing her again. As they draw closer he can see that it is Clementina after all; Vano is right. It is her. Will she have any news of Pedro? He stops for a moment and watches as father and daughter embrace. Dear God, please let her have good news about Pedro. Please God. He walks towards them slowly; he does not know what he will do if she tells him that their plea arrived too late and his brother has already been shot. He will never forgive himself. Never.

'Clementina, thank God you are all right. We have been so worried about you,' he says, still hanging back.

Vano releases his daughter from his arms and says, 'Yes, thank the Lord you are safe. I thought I was never going to see you again.' There are tears in his eyes.

Ramon would never have thought that a hard man like Vano would have such a soft heart. He smiles at Clementina and takes her hand. 'Come, let us get away from here before anyone sees us. And you can tell us what has happened.'

Clementina nods and lets him lead her into the woods and back towards her old home. Her father walks behind them.

'I think it will all be fine,' she says. 'Hugo's friend has agreed to help Pedro. We should know by tomorrow if he has been released. Hugo will come and tell us himself.' She looks back at her father. 'I saw Isabel,' she says. 'She is a lovely lady. She told me that they wanted to take me away and put me in an orphanage, but she wouldn't let them. She said that if I couldn't have my mother at least I would have my father. She swore she never wanted to give me away. She loves me.' The words were tumbling out of her so fast, he could barely follow them.

'Of course, child. We both love you and always will,' says Vano. 'Here, I have something for you.' He takes the silver ring from his pocket and hands it to her. 'I understand how difficult this is for you, Clementina. I do understand. I gave this to your mother fifteen years ago but when you were born she wanted you to have it. I think you should have it now.'

Clementina takes the ring and slips it on her finger. She smiles at him sadly. 'She says she has missed me.'

At first Vano does not speak—he seems too overcome with emotion—then he says, 'She was forbidden to come anywhere near you. It was that or you would have been given to the nuns. That was the agreement. We had no choice but to do what Don Luis told us. It must have been so hard for her to know you were so close by and yet she could never visit you. At least I had the pleasure of watching you grow up.'

'And Mama? What did she think when you brought me home? Does she know you are my father?'

'Your mother is a kind, generous-hearted woman. She accepted you as her own and she never asked any questions. I told her what I was instructed to say, that I had found you outside the church, and that was it. You became part of our family and nobody spoke of it again.'

'I love Mama,' she says. 'This news doesn't change anything. She is still my mother. You will tell her that, won't you, Papa.'

'Of course, but soon you can tell her yourself. We will leave right away and within a few days we can join her in Portugal. You can be with all your family again: Zita, Álvaro, all the people who love you.'

She stops and looks at Ramon. 'No, Papa, I am not coming with you. Ramon is going to Seville and I am going with him.'

'No, you cannot do that; you are still a child and you will come home with me.'

'I am not a child, Papa. I love Ramon and he loves me. I will go where he goes.'

Vano turns to Ramon and says, 'You are welcome to come with us. You can live with us in Portugal. I will happily give my blessing if you want to marry my daughter, although I don't know what my wife is going to say about it.' Ramon is still looking at Clementina; he barely hears Vano's words. 'It will not be safe for you in Seville, Ramon. Even if Hugo's friends have been successful in getting the release of your brother that will not make your situation any better; you will still be a wanted man. You will be spotted the moment you arrive in the city and you will be arrested. Then what will happen to my daughter, alone in a strange place? She has never been anywhere but here. She knows nothing of towns and cities; all she knows are the woods and marshes. How will she survive on her own? You see how beautiful she is; someone will take advantage of this beauty and destroy her. I may not have travelled much in my life but I know men and I know there are men who will covet her and exploit her. If you love her, you cannot want this for her?'

Vano is right; it is too risky to take Clementina with him. He has known this all along but his heart chooses to ignore it. 'Of course I do not want any harm to come to Clementina. You are right, Vano, she must leave with you.'

'No. I am not going to Portugal without you,' says Clementina. 'If you force me, then I will run away as soon as I have a chance.'

'She may look like her mother, Vano but she is as stubborn as her father,' says Ramon. 'Very well, I will go with you to Portugal, but I cannot promise to stay for long. I have responsibilities here in Spain.'

'We will dress you as a *gitano*,' says Clementina, a smile lighting up her face. 'Then no-one will recognise you. You should grow a beard, that will help and let your hair grow long.'

'That's not hard to do; I already look like a vagrant.' He pulls at his hair; it is already almost down to his shoulders and living with the *carboneros* did not require him to be clean and close shaven.

'Or a *carbonero*,' she says pointing to his soot streaked face. She smiles at him and does not appear concerned that he says he intends to return to Spain at some point. Maybe she does not believe him or, and this is more likely, she intends to return with him.

'We cannot go yet,' says Ramon. 'We should wait to hear what Hugo has to tell us. If he does not come by midday tomorrow then we know it is too late and Pedro has been shot.' Saying it out loud pains him more than he can endure.

'Very well,' says Vano. 'I suggest we get some sleep now. We will have a long journey tomorrow.'

They head back to the hollow where the two men had been sleeping before and settle down on their bed of rushes and straw. Once Clementina has fallen asleep, Vano says to Ramon, 'Well?'

'I will leave now,' he says. 'Before she wakes up. I need to find out what is happening in Seville and make sure my brother is still alive.'

'You must be careful. Do as Clementina suggests and dress like a *gitano*.' He unties his red scarf and gives it to Ramon, showing him how to tie it around his head. Then he places his wide brimmed hat on top of the scarf. 'That's better. Now you look like a real *gitano*. Can you ride?'

'Yes, sort of.' Ramon tugs at the brim of his hat.

'Well then, you can take the horse. Don't worry about us; I will find another one to get us back to Portugal. When you get to the ferry just let her go free; she will soon find the rest of the herd. If you ride into Seville on a lovely mare like her, everyone will notice you and the first chance they get someone will steal her from you.'

'Thank you, I will do that. Please tell Clementina that I do love her and that is why I can't take her with me, but I will be back for her. Here, in Doñana you are cut off from the world; you have no radio and no newspapers. I need to know what is happening out there; I want to help. It is my fight as much as anyone else's. She understands that. Once I have spoken to my comrades I will come and find you and tell you what I have decided to do.'

'Be careful. Keep away from the main roads and remember, you are a *gitano* now. Nobody is interested in *gitanos*.'

The next morning Vano wakes before the sun has risen; he sits up and looks at the sleeping figure of his daughter. How will she react when she finds that Ramon has gone. 'Clementina,' he whispers. 'Time to wake up.'

His daughter turns over and stretches out her hand to where Ramon has been lying but finds nothing but straw and reeds.

'Ramon?' She sits up, instantly wide awake. 'Where is he? Papa, where's Ramon?'

'He left early. Don't worry, he says he will catch up with us in Portugal.'

'No, I am not going without him. Why did you let him leave, Papa?' She gets up and brushes the straw from her skirt.

'Where are you going, child?'

'To find him.'

'But you don't know where he has gone.'

'Yes, I do. He's gone to Seville. I will go there and persuade him to come to Portugal with us now.' Tears are streaming down her face. 'Why has he done this? Last night he promised to go with us. He promised.'

'He still intends to keep that promise but first he must see someone. Don't ask me who, or what about, but he says he will come and look for us as soon as he has done it.' Vano pauses then adds, 'He asked me to tell you that he loves you and he will be back for you.'

Clementina collapses back on the bed of straw. 'Yes, but when will that be?'

'I don't know. A week, maybe two. In the meantime you and I will head back to Tavira.'

'I am waiting here. He will come back for me.'

'No. There's no point in you waiting for him here; he will not come back to this place. He knows you cannot stay here alone. He will expect to find you in Tavira. Be sensible, Clementina; he has not left you but he has something he must do first.' She does not look at him, but sits there silently weeping. 'I know it's disappointing for you, but he doesn't want to put you in danger. And anyway, I expect you would slow him down. This way he can see to his business quickly then catch us up; I have told him exactly how to find us.' She still does not answer. 'We need to leave soon, before it gets light. Come on, I must find a horse for us to ride.' He kicks at the straw beds, pulling the bushes back to cover their traces. 'Check to see that we have left no trace of being here, then when you are ready we will leave.' He expects her to make a fuss and refuse to go with him, but she is quiet now. He watches her dry her eyes and rake over her part of the bed.

'I will never forgive you, Papa, if he does not come back.'

He looks at her stubborn, tear-stained face and is reminded of when she was a little girl; well that is something he will have to live with. 'Come on child, let's find us a nice strong mare to carry the both of us.'

Ramon cannot shake off the feeling of emptiness that is overwhelming him; he knows he has to do this but leaving Clementina behind is pulling at his heart. He is not very comfortable riding Vano's mare; he has little experience of horses but it will certainly be quicker than walking all the way. He heads back through Doñana towards the ferry crossing, He hopes the ferryman does not recognise him; he knows his photograph is on display in every police station and he does not want to be connected to any of the people living in Doñana; they do not deserve to be associated with him. He knows only too well that the Guardia Civil will not treat them kindly if they think they have helped him.

The ferryman is on the other side of the river; he is collecting a traveller, a man on a horse. It is Hugo. A flood of emotions run through Ramon; now he will know for sure about the fate of his brother. Part of him is eager for news and the other part dreads to hear that his fate has been sealed. He waits on the banks of the river, staring at Hugo as if he can determine from his demeanour what has happened to Pedro but Hugo has not even realised it is him. Maybe his disguise, flimsy though it is, is working.

The ferryman pulls the boat alongside the bank and helps Hugo alight, then leads his horse onto dry land; his behaviour is quite different from the night Ramon crossed. Ramon waits until Hugo has paid the man then he dismounts and removes the rope bridle from Vano's mare. He gives it a slap on its rump and watches as it canters off into the woods. Then he walks casually towards the river. 'Hugo,' he whispers, when he reaches him. 'How is my brother?'

'Ramon, what are you doing here?' He looks around him to see who else might be watching, but apart from the ferryman who is oblivious of Ramon's presence and is more intent on catching some fish from the fast flowing Guadalquivir, there is no-one else around.

'I'm going to Seville.'

'And Clementina?'

'She is going with her father to Tavira. I will join them later. Well, what news of my brother?' He holds his breath.

'Your brother will be released. He should be on his way home by now.'

Ramon lets out a gasp of relief; a weight has been lifted from his heart. 'Do you know where he is, or where he is going?'

'No, no-one does and if you have any ideas, then keep them to yourself. This is not over. Remember, you are still a wanted man and there is nothing I nor my friends can do to change that. Let your brother enjoy his freedom; he never deserved to be there in the first place.'

'I know. Thank you for what you have done for him. I will always be grateful to you and your friends.'

'Just make sure that no harm comes to Clementina, and be careful when you arrive in the city. Trust no-one.' He bends forwards and strokes the mare, who is getting restless. 'When you see Clementina, tell her I am so sorry about all the awful things my father did, and that I love her. I will always think of her as my dear sister.'

'I will tell her.' Ramon watches as Hugo rides away then calls across to the ferryman, who does not appear to recognise him. So his brother is a free man at last. He feels as though he has been living inside a black cloud and now the sun has come out. He knows exactly where Pedro will go, to see his family in Cádiz. There is such a longing inside him to change his plans and go there to be with him—Cádiz is so close—but he knows he can never do that. He cannot put them in danger a second time.

Nobody seems to notice Ramon as he wanders through the back streets of Seville, head down, for all the world like any other *gitano*. He crosses the Triana bridge and heads for a bar where he knows some of his friends hang out; they will be able to tell him what has been happening in his absence. He is nervous about being in the city again after the peace and tranquility of Doñana, and already he can feel the tension in the air, the expectation that something momentous is about to happen. He notices that election posters have been ripped from the walls and thrown in the gutter, a sure sign that the election is over, but there is no clue as to who has won. He looks around for anything that could tell him the result, but there is nothing although the streets are littered with signs of celebration. He is tempted to stop someone and ask but prudence prevents him from doing so; he must not draw attention to himself. Surely he is the only person in Seville who does not know which party is in power and that alone makes him stand out. He tries to contain his impatience and hurries towards the bar. It is in the heart of Triana, an area of the city known for its gypsy inhabitants and its large working population. A group of *gitanos* stand on the corner chatting; the women are dressed in bright colours and their long dresses, layered with frills and flounces trailing in the road, are muddy from the recent rain. One of the women gives him a sly smile as though she knows he is not really *gitano*. The men stare at him, their thumbs stuck in their belts. Some have their waistcoats undone revealing a knife tucked in their belts. There is no hostility from them, but nevertheless he does not feel welcome. A drunk workman staggers in front of him, stops and shouts to nobody in particular, 'Watch out you bastard landowners, things are about to change.' He falls against Ramon, and for one dreadful moment he thinks he will be sick all over him, but one of the gypsies grabs him by the collar and pulls him away. The man collapses against the wall and slides to the ground. The gypsy turns away and ignores him. Then Ramon notices that the drunk is wearing an armband with the initials PF embroidered on it; so the Popular Front must have won the election. He is elated. If the fight is almost over he will be able to leave and go to find Clementina. He is glad she is not with him in Seville; he knows she has never been in a city before and Seville is a city in turmoil, even if they have won the election. What would she make of it, this bustling conurbation, crowded, dirty and noisy. It would seem like a different world to her.

Ramon recognises the tavern ahead of him and quickens his step; it is quieter than he expects. There is no-one standing in the street, smoking and drinking and the doors are shut. Cautiously he goes in and looks around; he can identify one or two people inside but nobody appears to recognise him.

'Ramon. Over here,' someone calls out. Thank goodness, it is José; he will know what's happening. 'It's good to see you.

We've been worried about you. We saw the police posters. And the news about your brother's release has spread throughout the area; I'm so glad they decided to release him, although I have to admit I was amazed when they did. He must have a guardian angel watching over him.' José lowers his voice and continues, 'You shouldn't be here you know. The Guardia are still looking for you.'

'I know, but I felt I was deserting you. I had to come back, especially once I knew that Pedro was all right. So we won the election?'

'Yes. Isn't that great news.'

'It's amazing but I must admit that I'm surprised that you're not out celebrating in the streets instead of hiding in here as though you had lost.'

'It wasn't exactly a landslide. In fact the result was very close. I'm worried that the opposition are not going to accept it.'

'They may not like it, but what can they do? There won't be another election for four years and by then people will have accepted the changes that are going to be implemented.'

'Maybe. I just have a strong feeling that the landowners and other right-wing nationalists are not going to take it lying down. They are much more united in their aims than we are. We have too many opposing opinions in the Popular Front; I know it's a coalition of many factions: communists, socialists, anarchist trade unions and republicans, and there are constant disagreements between them, but we need to be a cohesive group if we are to retain power. So I think you are being very optimistic.'

'You are worrying too much, José. The Popular Front may be made up of different parties, but whatever their individual aims, we are all united against fascism. This is a democracy and the Left have won; the opposition might not like it, but they will have to accept it.'

'I hope you are right. So what are you going to do now, Ramon?'

'Now that we have won the election, I feel that I am not needed here, so I won't stay in Seville. It would be foolish; I would be looking over my shoulder all the time in case the Guardia Civil recognised me.'

'That's a wise decision. Your disguise is not very convincing; I knew it was you straight away.' He reaches up and pulls Ramon's hat further down over his eyes. 'There is a reward for your capture, you know. Not a big one but enough to tempt someone to turn you in. So take care. Where will you go?'

'It's best that you don't know. I have some friends; I will go to them. And José, never admit that you have seen me or spoken to me, or ever knew me. You saw what happened to Pedro; I don't want you ending up in jail as well. They would love an excuse to lock you up after all the trouble you've caused them over the years.'

José smiled at him. 'Well, wherever you go, take care,' he repeats.

'Thanks.'

'Are you hungry? Have something before you go.' He gets up and goes to the bar.

Ramon looks around him but nobody is looking his way; maybe José is wrong and his disguise is working. Suddenly he feels a chill go through him; a police officer is standing outside the window of the tavern. Ramon gets up slowly and joins José at the bar. 'I have to go,' he whispers, nodding towards the window.

'Yes, you should leave right away. There's a back exit. Here, take this with you.' He shoves a roll filled with fatty ham into Ramon's hand and a bottle of beer. 'Take care, my friend.'

'Thanks.' Ramon squeezes his arm, sticks the food and beer in the pocket of his coat and heads for the back door.

Once outside, he can see a second policeman waiting at the corner of the street. He stops, unsure of what to do; right now the officer is looking the other way but at any moment he could turn round and see him. He has no choice; Ramon turns and walks briskly in the opposite direction, away from the bar and the policemen, all the time battling with the urge to break into a run. Keep calm, he tells himself but with every step he takes he fears that he will hear his name called out, or worse, a shot fired. If there is a reward for his capture, as José has said, then it is clear that he cannot stay in Andalusia; it would not take long for someone to turn him in to the Guardia Civil. It has been decided for him; he will go to Portugal and look for Clementina. He will keep his promise to her. His heart quickens when he thinks of her. Now despite José's gloom, the balmy air of Andalusia feels full of hope; one day things will be better and then they can both return to Spain. Let it be sometime soon.

CHAPTER 31

Pedro squats on the stone floor of his cell; although it is cold and not very clean it is more comfortable than the iron bedstead with its filthy mattress covered in stains of vomit and blood and its broken springs that have a knack of finding the most tender part of his anatomy. There is nowhere else to sit; the only chair is broken as though someone has smashed it against the wall in frustration or anger. If only he was capable of summoning the energy to do that; he no longer has the will nor the strength to live.

They moved him here two days ago. This is the condemned cell they tell him and there is only one way out of here and that is through a long corridor that leads to the firing squad. They enjoy watching his face while they give him this information. He looks around the room; it is spacious compared to what he is used to, larger than his own home and not as crowded as his previous cell. When they had first brought him here to the infamous Seville prison he had been thrown into a room with ten other people, dirtier and even more ragged than himself. Nobody wanted to talk about themselves but gradually he found out that most of them had been arrested at one demonstration or another. Like him they had been repeatedly beaten in the police station in attempts to get them to give the names of other demonstrators. Some had capitulated hoping to be released, but instead they had been thrown into prison. None of them has had a trial, all of them have the scars of their harsh treatment at the hands of the Guardia Civil and none of them expect to see their families again. Maybe he is the lucky one; they may be looking at a lifetime in this hellhole whereas he has only two more days to wait. He tries to be positive but inside he is a quivering mess. Fear tears at his belly. Pedro is not an aggressive man. He is not a brave man; his wife always says that he is too soft for this world. He knows she means weak and she is right; he is a weak man. He loves his family and he loves to work with the land; that is his life. He does not long for riches and fame, all he wants is to be able to feed his children and sleep well at night. It does not seem a lot to ask for, but now he realises it is out of the reach of many Spaniards. He recalls the words of his brother; it is not about now, it is about the future. Our duty is not to just think of today and how we are going to feed our children but also to think of tomorrow and what will become of our grandchildren and great grandchildren. Now he has the time to think about what Ramon was trying to tell him and now he understands.

Pedro stands and stretches up to grab the bars of the window. He tries to haul himself up to see where the noise is coming from, but he barely gets a glimpse of the prisoners running around the yard before his strength gives way and he slithers to the ground again. Nevertheless he has a moment of pleasure where he thinks he can smell the scent of the fields beyond the prison compound, that damp, sweet smell that the land gives out in the evening. Soon it will be dark and if he is lucky the moon will shine for a brief time through his window. Now it is there again, taking control of his mind; the thought that will not go away. With the night comes another day and with that the moment of his execution grows closer. It nestles in his brain like a close friend who will not be parted from him.

The guard is a cheery man whom he has not seen before. He comes into the cell and places a tin plate on the floor; it is Pedro's breakfast, bread and olive oil and a cup of lukewarm coffee. It does not vary. 'Only one more day,' he says with a big smile, as though he is talking about Pedro's release. 'One more day.' He almost sings it.

For the first time in his life Pedro feels real anger. Isn't it enough to beat him, torture him, leave him for days without food and then lock him up under sentence of death for something he did not do, now this goon has to make a joke of it. Well he won't let him humiliate him. He lifts his foot and kicks the plate so hard it spins towards the door and the food splashes onto the guard's trousers.

'That was a mistake, my friend,' the guard says, his smile now gone. 'You will regret that action.'

'So what will they do, shoot me twice?' Pedro says, but he knows it was a mistake because there are plenty of things they can do to make his death more unpleasant and nobody will be any the wiser.

The guard leaves the plate where it is and slams the iron door shut. The noise reverberates along the corridor; it is a sound which haunts him. At night when they take prisoners out to be shot, it is the noise of the cell doors slamming shut which wakes the other prisoners. Then they hear the shots. Sometimes a single shot, sometimes more. Those in the condemned cells know that one night it will be their door that will slam shut on their life for good.

The night of the execution arrives. Surprisingly Pedro is not as frightened as he expects to be; maybe he has become used to the idea that his life is over. He has not seen his wife and children since the day when the Guardia arrested him, and he has had no news of them. They have already become ghosts to him. He loves them dearly, but he finds it hard to bring their images to mind; he cannot see the details of their familiar faces. No matter how much he tries he cannot conjure them up, he cannot bring them into this dreadful place; they remain shadowy memories. He sighs. It is just as well. Pedro kneels by his bed and prays to God to look after them. He reminds Him that his wife is a good woman and should not be punished for any of the sins that he may have committed. He tries to believe in the deity to which he is talking because he knows Ana believes, but it is hard. If there truly is a god, then why does he let people suffer so much, and why do evil people prosper. He hears the door of a neighbouring cell slam shut and the sound of someone moaning and being dragged along the corridor. Soon it will be his turn.

He must have fallen asleep while kneeling by the bed because when he awakes the sun is streaming in through the tiny window and his head is pressed against the mattress. He leaps up. What is happening? No, he shouldn't still be here. Is this because he upset the guard by kicking his breakfast over him? Have they got something else in mind for him? His stomach turns over and he wants to retch. Not more torture. Please God, just let them shoot him and make it quick.

The door to his cell opens, but it is not one of the prison guards who comes in, but a tall man in an immaculate black suit. His hair is slicked back from his face which is expressionless. The man is accompanied by the prison commander. Pedro recognises him from the day when they announced that he was to be shot; to be fair, the commander had not looked very happy at having to give him the news. So why is he here now? Standing in the corridor behind the men, are two guards whom he has never seen before. A shaft of sunlight glints on the gold buttons of one of them.

'Pedro Molina Moreno?' the commander asks.

'Yes, *Señor,*' he replies. His throat is dry and he can barely speak. 'That's me.' Then, before he has time to be worried about what is going to happen, the prison guards come in and stand either side of him. So this is it. The moment has come; they are going to take him out and shoot him.

'You are being released immediately, on the orders of Judge Cañuelo, the presiding judge at ...' the commander continues to talk but Pedro is no longer listening. His legs buckle under him and he slides to the floor. What? Released? Can that be possible? They are not going to shoot him? Is this a dream? He does not have the chance to say anything because the two guards haul him up from the floor and march him out of the cell, along the corridor, through the prison gates and into the sunshine. It all happens in a flash. Pedro stands there blinking in the bright light. He hears the clang of the prison gates as they shut behind him.

'Let me introduce myself,' says the man in the black suit. 'I am your lawyer. For now, my name is not important. Please get into the car and I will take you back to Jerez.' He smiles at him. 'Don't worry. You're free now.'

'But, I don't understand,' Pedro stutters. He is totally bewildered.

'Although you may not realise it, you are a man with influential friends. Come on, I will explain everything on the way. The most important thing right now is to get you away from this place as soon as possible.'

Pedro watches the countryside flash past as if he is in a dream. He has never been in a motor car before. This is all too strange; he still cannot believe what is happening. He can hear the lawyer talking to him, explaining how this miracle has occurred, but he cannot take it in. Then he hears his brother's name and interrupts the lawyer's story. 'Ramon sent you?'

'Not exactly. Your brother saw the police handbill about your imminent execution and contacted some of his friends—I hope you don't mind but I am not at liberty to disclose their names. All you need to know is that you are free now and you will not be arrested again.'

'And my brother?'

'Your brother is a wanted man. I do not know where he is, nor do I want to.'

'So, I won't see him again?'

'No. And do not try to contact him. A lot of people, including your brother, have put their lives at risk to get you your freedom. I have been instructed to tell you that you must never talk about this to anyone, not even your wife.'

'My wife, do you know where she is?'

'Yes, I am taking you to her. My advice to you is that you never return to your old home. Change your name and make a new life for yourself with your wife and children. And keep out of trouble.'

Pedro nods. There is no need to reply; he is beginning to understand now. He is innocent of the crime for which he was charged but nobody would listen to him because he is poor and uneducated. It required someone else to speak for him, someone with influence and money. He has always known this and accepted it for what it is, until now. Now the unfairness, no, the injustice of it is something not to be tolerated. Ramon is right to be demonstrating for a better life. For him nothing has changed; his brother is still running from the Guardia Civil. There is a lump in Pedro's throat; he wishes he could speak to him, just once, just for a moment. He wants to thank him, not just for saving his life but for opening his eyes to what could be. Now he understands why it is important to fight for a better future. Unless they fight, nothing will ever change; those with the power will always be in control.

He stares out of the window. 'Where are we?' he asks. 'Is that the sea?' The car is driving across a narrow spit of land; there are salt flats on either side of them. This is where his wife is from; this is Cádiz. 'I thought you said we were going to Jerez?'

'I did, but we are not. Do you recognise where you are now?' the lawyer asks.

'Yes.'

'Good.' The lawyer leans forward and says to the chauffeur, 'Here will do, Diego. Stop here.' The chauffeur does as he is told and pulls off the road and stops the car. 'This is as far as we go, Pedro. I am sure you will be able to find your father-in-law's house easy enough from here. You realise, I expect, that it wouldn't do for us to drive up to their house. It would set too many tongues wagging. As I have told you, no-one needs to know what has happened to you—that is why I said we were going to Jerez, in case anyone should overhear us. I am sure you can make up a story about mistaken identity and false arrest, enough to keep your neighbours from becoming curious. I wish you luck.' He holds out his hand for Pedro to shake.

Pedro is so overwhelmed that he wants to hug this serious, well-dressed man. Instead he takes the outstretched hand and shakes it. 'I am so grateful to you, *Señor*. I do not have the words to express my gratitude, but I assure you it is from the heart.'

'Off you go then and God be with you,' the lawyer says. He waits until Pedro has scrambled out of the back seat and begins to walk towards the beach then instructs Diego to turn around and take him home.

When Pedro hears the car start up, he turns back to watch the Daimler drive away. What a shame he cannot tell his son that he has been in a motor car; he would love to do that. Maybe, if the world changes, one day he will. It is a long time since he has been in Cádiz but he remembers clearly where his father-in-law's cottage is, right by the beach. He imagines how excited they will all be to see him; and now he can see their faces clearly.

The Winds of Change

EPILOGUE

Here are a few facts about the start of the Spanish Civil War, which centred on the city of Seville.

FEBRUARY 1936

Election between the two main political parties, the Popular Front and the National Front. The Popular Front (Frente Popular) was formed by a coalition of various left-wing political parties including PSOE the Spanish Socialist Workers' Party, PCE the Communist Party of Spain, the IR Republican Left and the UR Republican Union. A number of smaller left-wing parties were also included and the main thing they all had in common was that they were anti-fascist. The opposing political party was the National Front, a conservative right-wing party, with fascist ideas and anti-communist beliefs. They were supported by the Falange Party and the Catholic Church.

The election took place in February and was won by the Popular Front with a narrow majority of 150,000. They formed a government with representatives from all sections of the party, including many professional people and people from wealthy backgrounds. However during the following months there was a distinct lack of unity within the various factions in the government and acts of violence were perpetrated by extreme left-wing radicals against the Catholic Church, Falangists and other right-wing parties.

JULY 1936

Due to the continuing ideological conflict within the government they were unable to stay in power for long. Dissatisfied with the result of the elections and the growing violence, a group of right-wing generals attempted a political coup.

On 17th July the army garrison in Melilla, under the command of General Francisco Franco, rebelled against the government and the Spanish Civil War had begun. The main aim was to take over control of the major cities in Spain, especially Seville, the capital of Andalusia. The generals involved were General Sanjurjo, General Francisco Franco, General Mora, General Goded and General Quiepo de Llano. The attempted coup took place just five months after the election and led to three years of civil war.

SEVILLE

Quiepo de Llano was the head of the frontier police force known as the *carabineros*. He marched into Seville on 17th July 1936, arrested General Villa Abrille, bombed the civil government offices and threatened to arrest the governor, José María Varela. When he was promised that nobody would be hurt, the governor surrendered. Instead of keeping his word, Quiepo de Llano had the chief of police and all the assault guards shot and the governor imprisoned. The Civil Guard then decided to join the uprising. When the colonel of the 6th regiment Manuel Allanegi, refused to join the rebels, he was also arrested. In retaliation the unions called a general strike and the workers barricaded themselves in the working class districts of Triana and Macarena, but they were completely unprepared for the attack that came. On 20th July the 4,000 Nationalist rebels now occupying Seville, bombed the workers and gained control of radio stations, the telephone exchange and all routes in and out of the city. Moroccan troops and the Spanish Foreign Legion entered the city and began slaughtering all the men they could find, and throwing grenades into homes, killing women and children and leaving their dead bodies in the streets. In the first few weeks of the onslaught three thousand Republican supporters were shot. During the same period the Republicans, the majority of whom were unarmed, only killed thirteen of the Nationalist rebel troops; they were completely unprepared to defend themselves against the battle-hardened troops from North Africa.

Once he had Seville under his control Quiepo de Llano sent troops out to subdue other towns in the province. Then in August he started the advance on Madrid.

GLOSSARY OF SPANISH WORDS

Asperpia	System of digging channels to collect the rainwater
Bandido	Bandit
Bichos	Midges, insects
Boliches	Conical shaped fires for making charcoal
Bota	Wine skin for drinking, usually made of goatskin.
Braceros	Casual workers with no guarantee of regular work
Buenas tardes	Good afternoon or evening
Buenos noches	Good night
Buenos días	Good morning
Cacique	A despotic form of economic control whose four main features are authoritarianism, nepotism, fetishism and totalitarianism
Canto Jonda	Flamenco songs, dark and sad.
Carboneros	Charcoal burners
Cariño	Darling, dear
Chozas	Charcoal burner's huts
Cortijo	Spanish farmhouse
Coto	Hunting area
Duro	Five peseta coin
Dios Mio	My God
Gitano	Gypsy
Gracias a Dios	Thank God
Mierda	Shit
Mujer	Woman or wife

Payo	Non gypsy
Puchero	A stew of potatoes and chickpeas.
Pueblo	Village or town
Señor	Sir
Señora	Madam
Si Dios quiere	God willing
Tortilla	omelette
Zarzuela	Fish stew

BIBLIOGRAPHY

Spanish Testament by Arthur Koestler   1937

The Spanish Holocaust by Paul Preston   2012

Doñana y su Entorno   2020

The Spanish Labyrinth by Gerald Brennan   1943

The Face of Spain by Gerald Brennan   1950

Andalusia, Between Dream and Reality by T Bryant   2017

The Story of Spain by Mark Williams   1990

YouTube video 'Julio de 1936, la toma de Triana'

Thank you for taking the time to read THE WINDS OF CHANGE. If you enjoyed it, please consider telling your friends or posting a short review. Word of mouth is an author's best friend and much appreciated. Thank you, Joan Fallon.

CONNECT WITH JOAN FALLON ONLINE AT:

https://joanfallon.co.uk/

https://www.facebook.com/joanfallonbooks

https://www.instagram.com/joanfallonbooks